"C'mon, lady. Do you really think after what you saw and heard that you can just waltz out of here and no harm will come to you?" Special Agent Sam Rawlins asked.

"But...if he's locked up—"

"Look, Carlo Giovessi knows that without your testimony we won't have much of a case. Killing you is going to be his number one priority."

Lauren felt the blood drain from her face. "But...if that's true...won't his goons still be after me, even after he's sent to prison?"

"Yes. After the trial you'll go into the witness protection program."

"What!" He said it so matter-of-factly, as though it were no big deal. It was to her. "What if I refuse to testify?"

"He'll kill you anyway. Look, you can walk out of here, but if you do you won't last an hour. Or you can testify and we'll do all we can to protect you. So what's it going to be?"

Lauren had sworn that she would never again allow herself to be dependent on someone else. Now she had to put herself totally in someone else's hands. Again. "Put that way, what choice do I have? I don't want to die...."

GINNA GRAY

THE
WITNESS

ISBN 1-55166-832-7

THE WITNESS

Copyright © 2001 by Ginna Gray.

Visit us at www.mirabooks.com

Printed in U.S.A.

THE
WITNESS

One

The shots came from just beyond the door—two sharp pops in rapid succession.

Lauren Brownley's head jerked up. She stared at her reflection in the mirror above the sink. Her eyes were so wide they seemed to fill her ashen face. The only gunfire she had ever heard before had been on television or in the movies, but she recognized the sound instantly, and it sent a chill down her spine.

Her first instinct was to run. She shut off the faucet and darted a frantic look around the ladies' rest room for an escape route, but other than the high window that opened onto the alley, there was none.

Out in the lounge someone cried out in agony. Lauren's scalp crawled. She stared at the door, gripping the edge of the counter behind her with wet hands. It was after hours. Except for her boss, Carlo Giovessi, who had retreated to his office when they had parted company ten minutes ago, the Club Classico was supposed to be empty.

Dear God, had he encountered a burglar? If so, which one of them had been shot?

After casting another desperate look around, Lauren swallowed hard and crept across the tile floor to the entrance. She reached out to push the door open but at the last instant jerked her hand back. Her heart beat double-time when she realized the mistake she had almost made. If there was a burglar out there with a gun the last thing she wanted to do was reveal her presence.

The moaning on the other side of the door hit another crescendo that made Lauren jump and flick the light switch off. In the darkness, she pressed her lips together and eased the door open a crack.

Lauren caught her breath. Three men stood on the dance floor near the piano. Two of them she had seen around the nightclub, but she had no idea who they were. The third man—the one with the gun in his hand—was Carlo.

At his feet a man writhed on the floor clutching his bloodied legs with both hands. Lauren nearly gagged when she realized that he had been shot in both kneecaps.

Groaning and gasping, the man rolled onto his side, facing her. Surprise shot through Lauren. It was Frank Pappano!

Two months ago, when she had first started playing the piano in the lounge, Carlo had introduced Frank as a business associate. Since then she had seen him around the club frequently, but she didn't know him. Nor did she want to.

Frank was considerably younger than Carlo, somewhere in his mid-thirties, and handsome enough, if you liked the swarthy type. On several occasions he had tried to flirt with her, but she had pretended not to notice. There was something cold and soulless about Frank that made her skin crawl.

Even so, he didn't deserve to be shot. She couldn't believe Carlo had done such a thing.

Lauren leaned her forehead against the door frame and closed her eyes. Dear God, what a fool she'd been. She had read the allegations in the newspaper and heard the talk, and since coming to work at the Club Classico she'd noticed the rough characters going in and out of Carlo's office, but she had blocked it all out. Like an ostrich with its head in the sand, she thought with disgust.

Granted, deep down she had felt uneasy, but she'd refused to examine the matter. After all Carlo had done for her, merely having suspicions had made her feel disloyal.

And now just look at what your blindness has done for you.

Oh God, she couldn't believe this!

"You shot me! Jesus Christ, Carlo! Why? *Ahhhh,* shit, my knees! My knees!"

Carlo Giovessi's shock of white hair and distinguished face gave him the look of a stern patriarch even when he was enjoying himself, which made his slow smile even more chilling. "Don't play games with me, Frank. You know why. You stole from me. I can't allow that."

Without taking his gaze from Frank, Carlo snapped

his fingers, and one of the other men handed him a square, plastic-wrapped bundle. He opened the package, picked up some of the contents and trickled white powder down on Frank. "This last load of coke you picked up for me is mostly sugar." He hefted the package experimentally and pursed his lips. "Too bad you got greedy. It might've worked if you hadn't skimmed off so much. That was stupid, Frank."

His demeanor changed in a blink, and he delivered a vicious kick to Frank's leg. Frank's scream made the hairs on Lauren's neck stand on end.

"You little prick," Carlo snarled. "Did you really think you could steal almost half my coke and get away with it?"

"No, Carlo. I didn't skim. Swear to God, man! It…it must've been those damned suppliers! They're the ones ch-cheating you. Not me. You know I wouldn't do that! *Ahhh*, Christ, my knees!"

"I'm running out of patience, Frank. And you're running out of time."

Even in the dim light, Lauren saw Frank's face pale.

"I'm doing you a favor. You know I don't soil my hands with this sort of thing anymore. But this…this is personal. Because it's you, I decided to handle this myself. I owe you that much."

Frank's groans turned to blubbery weeping. "Jesus, Carlo, I'm sorry. I'm sorry, man. Please. Please, don't kill me."

"You've worked for me a lotta years, Frank. I took

you off the streets when you were just a kid. I trained you. Christ, I treated you like a son, you fucking scumbag.''

"Please, Carlo, don't kill me. Don't kill me. Please! *Please, man!* I'm beggin' you! It'll never happen again! Swear to God! I'll do anything! *Anything!* Just don't kill me!" He rolled on the floor, clutching his knees, his contorted face streaming sweat. "Oh God, oh God, oh God.''

"Save your breath, Frank. You were a dead man the first time you stole from me. Now it's just a question of when and how you die, and that's up to you. You tell me where you stashed my goods and I'll kill you quick. Stall, and you'll soon be begging me to kill you.''

"Christ, man, if you'll just listen—''

"Those are your only choices, Franco," Carlo said with deadly calm. "And I warn you, lie to me, and I'll kill your family, too.

"I don't want to do that. You know how fond I am of Maria and little Frank and Mario. It always distresses me to kill women and children, but you know I don't make idle threats.

"So, unless you want that pretty little wife and those boys of yours to suffer, too, then you'd better not lie." Carlo leaned forward and smiled. "Now then, Frank, you got three seconds. Either you tell me where I can find my goods or the next shot is going into your balls.''

Lauren watched the scene unfold with disbelief and

horror, her fist pressed against her chest. She saw Frank shudder and squeeze his eyes shut. He muttered something under his breath and crossed himself, then drew a deep breath. "It's...it's in a warehouse on...on Patton and East Third."

The words had barely left his lips when another loud pop exploded and an obscene hole appeared in the center of Frank's forehead.

Though Lauren had known the shot was coming, she jumped. Her hand flew to her mouth but she was not quick enough to stifle the gasp that burst from her.

Frank jerked, then slumped on the floor. Frozen in place, Lauren stared at the dead man, and felt bile rise in her throat. The hideous black hole in his forehead seemed to blossom as blood began to ooze from it.

"What was that?" Carlo's gaze shot around the lounge and came to rest on the rest rooms, zeroing in first on the men's then the ladies'.

Lauren flinched and stepped farther back into the darkness as terror overtook shock. Dear God, she had just witnessed a cold-blooded murder! She had to get out of there! Now, before they discovered her.

She glanced toward the window, where a faint glow seeped in from the streetlight at the end of the alley. Even if she could hoist herself up that high, she would never make it out before they got there. Panic welled, but she fought it back. There had to be a way. There had to be! Think! *Think!*

"What was what? I didn't hear nothing, boss."

"Were there any cars in the parking lot when you came in?"

"I dunno. Me'n Tony, we brought Frank in through the back like you told us."

"Go outside and check. Tony, you check out the rest rooms. I'll search the rest of the place."

Oh God. Oh God. Oh God. Wringing her hands, Lauren cast a frantic look at the toilet stalls, but she dismissed the idea of hiding in there. That would be the first place Carlo's thug would look.

A crash from the other side of the wall made her jump. Seconds later the noise sounded again, then again. Lauren realized that she had been right; at that very moment that Tony person was in the men's room kicking open the stall doors.

Lauren hesitated only a second before running to the window. She unlocked it, shoved it open as far as she could reach and raced back to the sink. Grabbing her purse off the counter, she opened the door to the tiny cabinet beneath, hiked up her long evening gown and scrambled inside. Extra rolls of toilet tissue and plumbing almost filled the interior, but she scrunched up into a ball and wedged herself in, grateful, for the first time in her life, for her small stature.

She barely managed to pull the door shut behind her before the rest room door opened a few inches.

Carlo's henchman reached inside and flipped the switch. Light flooded the bathroom, glaring off the black-and-white tiles. A thin line of light at the edge of the cabinet door sliced into Lauren's hiding spot.

She caught her breath and pressed back as far as she could. Through the crack, she watched the man Carlo had called Tony peer around the edge of the door, then ease into the room, gun drawn.

He reminded her of a snake, moving with sinister smoothness, his cold eyes darting constantly.

Lauren's heart began to thud so hard she was certain he would hear it, but he moved past the cabinet and out of her line of sight. An instant later the first stall door banged open, then the second and the third. She pressed her lips together to keep from crying out and flinched with each crash.

''Find anything, Tony?''

''No, nothing, Mr. Giovessi.'' The evil-looking man reappeared in her field of vision. ''If there was anyone in here, looks like they climbed out the window. It's wide-open.''

''Shit!''

Lauren's heart almost stopped when Carlo appeared in the bathroom doorway. He looked at the open window, then motioned with the barrel of his gun. ''Go outside and see what's keeping Leo.''

''I'm here, boss. There's one car in the parking lot. A red Lexus.''

''Damn. That's Lauren's.''

''That classy little auburn-haired chick that plays the piano?''

''Yeah. I thought she'd left fifteen minutes ago. She must have come back inside to use the rest room." Carlo sighed "What a shame. Talent like hers is a priceless gift."

"Whadda you want us to do, boss?"

"First, get Frank out of here. And clean up that mess. When you're done, get that car out of the parking lot. Tony, you go check out Miss Brownley's apartment. She was running scared when she bailed out of that window. A scared rabbit usually heads for his hole. Odds are she'll try to grab a few of her things and disappear. But she's a smart girl. Once she's had a chance to think clearly she may decide to go to the cops. I want you to find her first."

"Whadda you want me to do with her, boss?"

Carlo stared at the man for several seconds. "Kill her."

Lauren clamped her hand over her mouth and shrank deeper into her hidey-hole.

For a time after the lights had gone out and the men's voices had faded away, Lauren remained hunched in the cabinet, shivering from head to toe. Only darkness and silence surrounded her. Her own breathing sounded harsh to her ears and her heart still pounded like a wild thing against her ribs.

She strained to detect the slightest sound or movement, but all she heard was the faint whir of the heating system. Still she did not budge. It could be a trick. Carlo could be out there in the darkened lounge, waiting for her to reveal her hiding place.

Inevitably, however, physical discomfort began to

override hysteria. Lauren became aware of the cramping in her legs and it felt as though her hipbone were about to poke through her flesh where her side pressed against the back wall. It was also freezing, even though the heat was still on.

Lauren frowned, wondering how that could be. Then she realized that Carlo and his men had forgotten to close the window.

No matter how hard she tried, she couldn't stop thinking about that open window. It beckoned to her, teased her with the possibility of escape. The opening was small, but if she could somehow get up there she could squeeze through it, she was sure.

But if Carlo or one of his men was still out in the lounge they might hear her. Lauren gnawed at her lower lip. On the other hand, she couldn't stay hidden forever.

The debate went back and forth, but after a few moments she drew a deep breath and eased the cabinet door open, inch by inch.

Unfolding herself from the cramped space was excruciating, but finally she managed to roll out onto the cold tile floor onto her hands and knees. It took three tries to climb to her feet. Her muscles screamed in protest, and she had to clench her teeth to keep from moaning. She limped around the room several times, bending and stretching and twisting.

When the pain at last became bearable she peered through the darkness for something on which to stand. The only item in the room was the trash can beside the sink. Hip-high, it was made of metal and too heavy for her to lift, so she tipped it slightly and rolled it on its bottom edge to the window.

Glancing at the door every few seconds, Lauren grasped the windowsill, climbed up onto the can and stood with a foot braced on each side of the rim. When she threw one leg over the sill she lost a shoe and the can toppled out from under her. The crash against the tile floor set the cats in the alley to screeching and shot Lauren's adrenaline skyward.

She shimmied through the opening like a greased eel. She hit the ground hard, falling on all fours and scraping her palms and one knee, but she didn't feel the pain. Nor did she stop to find her shoe. Before the clatter in the rest room died away she lifted her long skirt and tore down the alley.

Two

Special Agent Sam Grey Wolf Rawlins knew something big was brewing the instant he walked into the office of the Senior Agent in Charge of the FBI's Denver Office, otherwise known as the SAC.

Harvey Weiss sat behind his desk fidgeting, while Sam's immediate boss, Charley Potter paced beside the window. Both men were puffing on cigarettes. So were Todd Berringer, David Owens and Roy O'Connor, the agents occupying three of the chairs arranged in a semicircle in front of Harvey's desk. Already a hazy blue cloud clung to the ceiling.

"Haven't any of you guys ever heard of lung cancer?"

Harvey looked up with a scowl. "It's about time you got here, Rawlins. Where the hell have you been?"

"Stuck behind a snowplow for the last thirty minutes. In case you haven't noticed, the storm dumped a foot of snow on Denver in the last few hours."

"If you didn't live up in that canyon in the middle of nowhere you'd be more accessible in situations like this.'' Harvey took in Sam's jeans and Stetson and scuffed cowboy boots, and his mouth pinched.

Sam ignored the comment and the look. If Harvey didn't like his living arrangements, tough. He couldn't survive in the city on a daily basis; he needed space to breathe. Anyway, he'd be damned if he was going to live in town just to make Harvey look good.

The SAC motioned toward the fourth chair in front of his desk. ''We're wasting time. Take a seat.''

Sam shrugged out of his parka and tossed it and his Stetson on the brass coatrack. ''Thanks, but I'll stand. The air is cleaner over here.'' Leaning against the jamb of the open door, he fixed his gaze on the fresh cigarette Harvey was lighting off the butt of his last one.

Harvey squinted at him through the cloud of smoke he exhaled. ''You nonsmokers are a pain in the ass. Besides, I don't know what you're complaining about. It was you Indians who introduced the white man to tobacco.''

''Yeah. My relatives call it the red man's revenge.''

Roy and Dave started to chuckle, but a look from Harvey silenced them.

The man never missed a chance to make a snide remark about Sam's Indian blood. Though Sam had never felt as though he truly belonged in either world, he was nevertheless proud of his heritage, Indian and white. Harvey's bigotry grated, but Sam never let his resentment show, not by so much as a twitch of a muscle.

"Funny, Rawlins. You're a real comedian. Now could we get back to what we're here for?"

Sam folded his arms and gazed steadily back at him. "Sure. But this had better be good. It's three in the morning and I nearly froze my ass off getting here."

Anger tightened Harvey's face, but before he could fire off a reprimand, Agent Berringer jumped in.

"Whatsa matter, buddy? Your car heater crap out again?"

A ghost of a smile flickered around Sam's mouth. Todd had missed his calling. He was a born peacemaker. The question was a transparent attempt to defuse the situation. "Not again. Still."

"Whadda you mean? Dammit, I told you weeks ago to send in a requisition and get that heater fixed," Charley growled.

"I did. Three times." Sam glanced at Harvey. "For some reason, my requests keep getting lost."

"Dammit, could we knock this off and get down to business?"

"Sure. Shoot."

"We got a call from the Denver P.D. about an hour ago. They have a woman in custody who claims she saw Carlo Giovessi murder Frank Pappano."

The three seated agents jerked to attention. Sam didn't turn a hair.

"No shit?" Dave, a rookie agent and the youngest

of the group, sat forward, so excited he was almost giving off sparks. Even his red hair seemed brighter than usual.

"Not only that. Her story also positively links Giovessi to drug running." Harvey took another puff and leaned back in his chair, looking as pleased with himself as if he had personally gotten the goods on the mob boss.

"Why'd Carlo whack his own man?" Todd asked.

"Well, it seems Frankie boy has been helping himself to his boss's merchandise. Carlo took offense."

"I'll bet."

Dave let out a whoop. "Man, this is great! We got the bastard now!"

"Yeah," Todd agreed, grinning. "It's about time we caught a break on this case."

"Who is this woman?" Sam asked quietly.

"Her name's Lauren Brownley. She plays piano at Carlo's Club Classico.

"The Denver cops have been keeping an eye on her for a while. So have our guys. Nothing serious, though. Just tailed her a bit, checked out where she lived and how she spent her time. The cops and our agents both believe she's Giovessi's latest mistress, but probably not part of his organization." Harvey tossed a legal-size envelope to Sam, and he caught it reflexively. "The dossier they worked up on her is in there.

"I didn't get all the details, but Ms. Brownley swears she saw and heard the whole thing—the murder, Frank's admission that he stole the drugs. Even the address of the warehouse where he stashed it.''

"Why would Giovessi's mistress rat him out?'' Sam asked.

Harvey spread his hands and shrugged. "Who knows why women do anything? Maybe she and Carlo had a falling out. Maybe she had something going on the side with Frank and she's looking to get revenge. What difference does it make? The important thing is, we got ourselves a witness.''

Todd gave a low whistle. "This is big. Looks like Dave's right. We're finally going to nail the bastard.''

"All of you keep your lips buttoned,'' Harvey cautioned. "I don't want any leaks this time. No one outside of the six of us is going to know anything about this until we have our witness stashed in a safe place. And I mean no one.

"Rawlins, you, Todd, Roy and Dave go to the police station and check out this woman's story. If the Denver cops have it straight, we'll take over the case. When we do, Todd, you and Roy take some backup and arrest Giovessi.

"Charley's already sent Sweeney to get a search warrant and we have a stakeout watching the warehouse. They'll arrest whoever shows up for the stash. If we get lucky, it'll be old Carlo himself. I expect he's still plenty pissed about Frank betraying him. He'll probably want to see for himself that his coke is there.

"Rawlins, I'm assigning you to guard the witness.

Dave will go along as backup. If you're satisfied this woman is giving us the straight skinny, hustle her out of town as soon as you can make the arrangements. Take her someplace safe and sit on her until the trial.''

"Send someone else. I've got more important things to do than baby-sit one of Carlo's little chippies.''

Angry color crept up Harvey's neck. He leaned forward and stabbed a nicotine-stained forefinger in Sam's direction. "You listen to me, Rawlins. This woman's testimony can put Carlo away for a very long time. Whether you like it or not, you're going to stay with her and see that she lives to give it, no matter how long it takes. You got that?''

"I'm already working on a case, remember? I'm close to cracking it.''

At once the room hummed with tension. The three agents shifted in their chairs and cleared their throats. Charley Potter's jaw clenched, and he stared at the floor.

Sam's assignment was one every lawman hated—digging up dirt on his fellow agents. Their office had been trying to build a case against Carlo Giovessi for years, but every time they thought they had him something would go wrong—key evidence disappeared, witnesses were killed, some minute irregularity in the investigation would mysteriously surface and Carlo's sleazeball attorney would get the case thrown out on a technicality. The whole thing had begun to smell of inside help.

There was nothing more hated within the Bureau than an agent gone bad—unless it was the guy who tried to ferret him out.

In law enforcement, teamwork was vital. No one wanted to believe that their partner or friend was dirty, and defenses went up when anyone started asking questions. Sam had tried to be discreet, but the word was out. Lately, with a few exceptions like Todd and Charley, everyone in the Denver office had been giving him the cold shoulder.

Which, Sam suspected, was one reason why Harvey had assigned the investigation to him instead of following proper procedure and turning it to the OPR, the Office of Professional Responsibility, which was the FBI's Internal Affairs division. The OPR was made up of all experienced investigators of supervisory rank.

Harvey claimed that he took it as a personal affront that an agent on his watch had sold out. He wanted the matter resolved in-house. Right now.

He justified that decision by pointing out that they had no hard proof that there *was* a mole—just suspicions and a string of coincidences. Never mind that the Bureau didn't believe in coincidences.

What the SAC really wanted, Sam suspected, was to turn every agent in the Denver office against him and make his life miserable.

Not that it bothered him particularly. He tended to keep to himself anyway.

"Nailing Giovessi is more important. Charley agrees with me. Hell, he recommended you for this job."

Sam shot his boss a hard look, and Charley raised his hands. "Now, Sam, before you say anything, hear me out. If this woman is Carlo's mistress, you'll have months to pump her for information that might help our case, including the name of our mole. It's worth a shot."

"That's right," Harvey agreed. "You never know what the man might've spilled during pillow talk. So consider yourself reassigned, Rawlins."

"Why me? Any one of a dozen agents could guard the woman."

"Because you've worked on this case longer than anyone else and you know it inside out. You know what we're up against. And I trust you. I don't particularly like you, Rawlins, but I trust you." Harvey took another long drag and sent a stream of smoke upward to join the cloud hovering around the ceiling. "Now get the hell out of here and go check out the woman."

Without a word, Sam plucked his hat and coat off the rack and walked out.

He was halfway down the hall when Todd sprinted up beside him and fell in step.

"Christ, Sam, when are you going to wise up and

stop butting heads with that guy? You know you can't win.''

''Is that what I do?''

''Hell, yes. You know damn well you do everything you can to get under his skin. Just look at you right now. You know what a stickler Harvey is about the dress code. Would it have killed you to put on a suit and tie before coming in tonight?''

''Screw Harvey. I had the weekend off. Plus I got approval to take a day of vacation. Officially I'm on my own time for another...'' He shot back the cuff of his flannel shirt and checked his watch. ''Twenty-seven and a half hours.''

''Yeah, well, you could've at least shaved.''

Sam dragged a hand down his sandpapery jaw and shrugged. ''I had a lazy weekend. So sue me.''

''You're one stubborn bastard. Look, I know you don't like the guy. I don't, either. But he is the SAC.''

Sam snorted. ''Harvey Weiss is a tight-assed, ambitious politician, not a lawman. His main concern— hell, his *only* concern—is making *Harvey* look good. He doesn't make a decision without weighing how it will affect his image and help with his next promotion. He probably plans to be running the Bureau by the time he's fifty.''

''Yeah, well, that may be. But that's all the more reason to do yourself a favor and stop baiting the guy.''

''Hey! Cochise!''

The bellow set Sam's hackles up and stopped him

in his tracks. Beside him, Todd lowered his head and groaned.

Sam turned slowly. His gaze shot past Charley, Dave and Roy to where Harvey stood in the doorway of his office, puffing on another cigarette. "Yeah?"

"Remember what I said. You get that gal out of Denver fast. I don't want any slipups this time. Take her out of state. Somewhere remote out of Carlo's reach."

"I plan to. Anything else?"

"Just be sure you keep in touch. You know the drill. You contact either me or Charley once a day without fail. No one else."

"Fine." Sam turned and walked the remaining few feet to the elevator and jabbed the button. The doors opened at once, and Todd darted inside, as though anxious to get out of the line of fire, but Sam paused and looked back at Harvey again.

"By the way, just so you'll know. Cochise was a Chiricahua Apache. My mother was a Navajo." Without waiting for Harvey to respond, he stepped into the elevator and smacked the down button with the side of his fist. "Asshole."

Lauren Brownley was not at all what Sam had expected. To his surprise, and annoyance, the instant he got a look at her through the two-way mirror he experienced the sharp pull of attraction. That had never happened to him before with a female witness, and it irritated the hell out of him.

Apparently he was not the only one affected. Beside him, Dave whispered, "Wow."

Todd gave a low whistle. "Oh, man, I think I'm in love."

"You? The stud of the Bureau?" Sam snorted. "I doubt it. In lust—now, that I would believe," he drawled.

"Whatever it is, I'm hooked. And you're going to spend weeks with her. Damn."

"I'd be glad to trade assignments with you."

Todd laughed. "Hell, Harvey'd have us both strung up by our balls. Still…it might be worth it. Damn you, Sam. You always were a lucky bastard."

Both Lieutenant John Dumphries and Detective Allen Morgan of the Denver P.D. chuckled.

"She is something, isn't she," the detective murmured.

"Mmm." Sam studied the woman through the mirror, noting every detail of her appearance.

She paced the interrogation room like a frantic animal, her arms crossed and hugged tight against her body. She was small, not more than five foot two or three, with a delicate build. Under the harsh light her auburn hair shone with copper highlights. Every time she reached the end of the dingy interrogation room and spun back, the long mane swung around her shoulders like a silk cape.

Sam watched her approach the two-way mirror. Her eyes were green, he noted when she stood just inches away. And her features were as delicate as the rest of her, though at the moment her skin was parchment-white.

Terror, probably, he mused dispassionately. And exhaustion, after being up all night.

She wore a floor-length, fitted black evening gown with long gauzy sleeves and a modest neckline. Not a bit of cleavage showing, he noted with surprise. A black velvet jacket, trimmed with black sequins, hung on the back of one of the chairs surrounding the table. The outfit looked more suitable for an evening at the opera than something a nightclub piano player would wear.

Her dress was smudged and wrinkled and the skirt had a hole torn at one knee, but its quality was evident, even to Sam's eye. With every step a long slender leg flashed in the skirt's side slit and the tear, revealing shredded sheer black panty hose and bare feet.

"What happened to her shoes?" Sam asked.

"Says she lost them getting away."

"She's not exactly Carlo's usual type." In the past the mobster's taste in mistresses had run to busty blondes with the fashion sense of Dolly Parton. Even barefoot, disheveled and agitated, there was an air of regal elegance about this woman, a certain refinement that all Carlos's other mistresses had lacked.

The lieutenant cleared his throat. "Well now, as to that, according to Miss Brownley she and Giovessi are just employer and employee. She says she works at Club Classico only on weekends and that during the week she's a music instructor at the University of Denver.''

Yeah, right, Sam thought, watching the woman pace the interrogation room. He'd glanced at her dossier on the way over. So this one was classy looking and happened to play the piano. Big deal. Carlos's mistresses always worked at his club in one capacity or another.

Speculation was, that was so he could keep his current plaything on a short leash, but personally, Sam thought he put them on the payroll to fool Mrs. Giovessi. If there was one person Carlo feared, it was his wife, Sophia.

''What have you got on her so far?''

''Not much. She's got no priors that we can find. All we have is her car license and her address. Our preliminary report, along with a transcript of her statement is in here,'' Lieutenant Dumphries said, handing Sam a file.

As he scanned the first page Detective Morgan grinned. ''Recognize the address?''

''Yeah, I recognize it.'' That was one of the first things he'd noticed while skimming through the Bureau's dossier on the way over to the station house. The apartment building Ms. Brownley listed as her address was a luxurious high-rise, owned by none other than Carlo Giovessi.

''Uh-huh. And our witness drives a shiny new Lexus.''

''Figures.''

Insofar as it went, the police report jived with the Bureau's findings. In addition to the information in the police report, agents had observed that the woman stayed at the club after hours alone with Giovessi every Friday and Saturday night. They'd also noted that Carlo visited her apartment every Wednesday evening and stayed for several hours.

Just an employee, my ass, Sam thought. His mouth twitched. He wondered what excuse Carlo gave his wife for those evenings? That he was a member of a Wednesday night bowling league?

"Our surveillance team has followed her to the campus several times. So she could be telling the truth about working there," the lieutenant went on.

Sam grunted. Their men had done the same, but because they had nothing to link her to any criminal activity, there had been no in-depth investigation into her background or employment. In the opinions of the agents who had tailed her, she was merely another of Giovessi's playthings who was probably taking a few university classes as a lark.

"Has anyone checked with the university to find out if she actually is employed there?"

"Not yet. We didn't want to start the investigation until you fellas had heard her story."

"Fine." Sam snapped the folder closed and nodded toward the interrogation room. "Let's do it."

Three

Lauren made another circuit of the dingy little room. Where was everyone? What was taking them so long?

She stopped at the front of the room and stared into the wide mirror beside the door. Were they watching her through there, the way she'd seen them do on police dramas on television? If so, why? Did they think she was lying?

Maybe Lieutenant Dumphries and Detective Morgan had gone to Club Classico to look for the body. If so, they wouldn't find it. By now Carlo's lackeys had disposed of all the evidence. She'd already told them that, but would they believe she was lying if they couldn't find anything?

Swinging away from the mirror, Lauren went back to pacing. As she circled the table she glanced around and shuddered. Dear Lord, what was she doing in this place? She'd never even been inside a police station before. How had her life degenerated to this?

Lauren made an aggravated sound and shot her reflection a disgusted look. "Because you're a fool, that's how," she muttered under her breath. "A naive fool. Face it, you have no one but yourself to blame for being in this mess.''

It wasn't as though the signs hadn't been there. Even as far back as two years ago when she'd been in the hospital and Mr. Giovessi had come to visit her, the nurses had hinted that he had a dark reputation.

She had brushed aside their subtle warnings, unable to believe that anyone with such impeccable manners could be anything but respectable.

Lauren sighed. No, that wasn't exactly accurate. The unvarnished truth was, she hadn't *wanted* to believe that Carlo Giovessi was anything but what he appeared to be: a nice, courtly old gentleman.

When Carlo had entered her life she had been lost and alone and completely vulnerable. He had been the only person to come to her aid. The only person who had been there for her when she had so desperately needed a friend.

So she had blanked out what she had not wanted to be true. And later she had ignored the obvious.

It had not been difficult to push aside her suspicions. Carlo had always treated her with a charming, old-world sort of respect and admiration. And as long as she was being completely honest, she might as well admit that it hadn't hurt that he'd been a devoted fan of classical music.

Groaning, Lauren raked both hands through her hair. Right. As though that automatically guaranteed good character.

What a blind fool she'd been.

She was operating on raw nerves, and when the door opened she jumped and whirled around. Relief poured through her the instant she spotted Detective Morgan. He had been kind and supportive earlier. His lieutenant, however, had been harsh and openly skeptical of her story.

Her tension returned when five other men followed the detective into the room. One was Lieutenant Dumphries, but she hadn't seen the others before. Three of the strangers were neatly attired in conservative suits and ties, but it was the other man, the taller of the four newcomers, who drew her eye.

His hair was thick and black as midnight. So were his deep-set eyes. Beard stubble shadowed the lower half of a face that could only be described as hawkish. He looked hard as nails.

His penetrating stare drew Lauren's nerves tighter, and she switched her gaze back to Detective Morgan.

"Detective, I'm so glad you're back. Have you arrested Mr. Giovessi yet? May I go home now?"

"No, not yet. Why don't you have a seat, Miss Brownley? This is Special Agent Sam Rawlins and Agents Todd Berringer, Roy O'Connor and Dave Owens from the FBI. They'd like to ask you a few questions."

"The FBI? But I don't understand. I didn't know the FBI got involved in murder cases."

"There's no reason for you to worry, miss," one of the FBI men replied, flashing a charming smile.

"Normally that's quite true. However, there are other factors involved here."

"What Agent Berringer is trying to say is, when a suspect is a known mob boss involved in drug dealing we're talking federal crime. We've been trying to put your friend Carlo away for a long time."

"Have a seat, Ms. Brownley." Agent Berringer held out a chair. When Lauren complied he poured her a glass of water from the pitcher on the table and said kindly, "Now then, why don't you start at the beginning and tell us what happened."

Lauren's hand shook as she took a sip of water. Her gaze darted to Detective Morgan. "I don't understand. I've been through this with the police already. Twice."

"And now you're going to go through it with us," the hawk-faced man stated without the least hint of sympathy. "For starters, let's get a little background information. How long have you worked at the Club Classico?"

"A little over two months."

"And how long have you known Mr. Giovessi?"

"I…well…I first met him two years ago."

"How did you meet him?"

"He came to visit me in the hospital after I had a car accident."

Sam looked up from the notes he was scribbling. "If you didn't know him, why did he visit you?"

"He knew of me. You see, at that time I was a concert pianist. Mr. Giovessi is a fan of classical music and he said he'd been following my career. I was in Denver on tour when the accident occurred. He read about it in the newspaper, and when he learned that one of my hands had been crushed and I might never play again, he came to the hospital to offer sympathy and whatever assistance he could.''

Agent Rawlins's gaze flickered to her left hand. Thin white lines crisscrossed the back like a road map. Self-conscious, Lauren laid her right hand over the left to hide the scars.

''And you had no idea who he was?''

''No. I told you, I was on tour. Until two days before the accident I had never even been in Denver before.''

''So why did you stay here? You obviously didn't lose the use of your hand. You still play the piano.''

Sadness flickered through Lauren. ''Yes, after several surgeries and over a year of physical therapy I could play. But not at the concert level. I'll never achieve that again. The flexibility just isn't there anymore. True, I can play better than most people, even now, but no longer as a virtuoso. I've toured for most of my life and had no attachment to any particular place. Denver seemed as good a place as any other, so I stayed.''

What she didn't bother to explain was, at the time she could not have afforded a bus ticket to the next town. Nor did she have any intention of doing so. It was too embarrassing.

''I see. So you're telling us that because Carlo

Giovessi is such a great music lover he offered to help you?''

Lauren darted him a wary glance, confused by his sarcastic tone. "I suppose so, yes.''

"Did he offer you financial help?''

She looked down at the glass of water and clasped her hands around it to keep them from trembling. "Yes. I thanked him, but I refused.''

"Really? Why would he even offer financial assistance? If you were a concert pianist, as you claim, surely you had money. I know classical artists don't earn as much as rock stars, but they don't work for pennies, either.''

Lauren bit her lower lip. So much for keeping secret the sad state of her finances. "I...that's true, but...by the time I left the hospital, my money was gone.''

"Yes, medical bills are steep these days,'' Agent Berringer put in.

"Yes. Yes, they are,'' she agreed eagerly.

It wasn't exactly a lie. Her medical bills had been astronomical, but her insurance had covered most of those. They certainly hadn't left her broke. Collin had taken care of that.

But these men didn't need to know about the most humiliating episode in her life. It had nothing to do with the crime she'd witnessed.

"I see.''

Agent Rawlins didn't believe her. Lauren could see

that in his cold stare. She quickly refocused on the glass cupped between her palms.

"According to Lieutenant Dumphries, you claim you're now a music instructor at the University of Denver. Is that right?"

"What do you mean 'claim'? I *am* a music instructor. Mr. Giovessi helped me get the job after I was released from the hospital. As I told the lieutenant and Detective Morgan, I only work at the Club Classico on Friday and Saturday evenings."

"And your apartment? Did he help you find that, too?"

Something about Agent Rawlins's tone grated. Lauren sent him a puzzled glance. "Yes. Yes, he did. Actually I don't know what I would have done if it hadn't been for Mr. Giovessi. He helped me get on my feet and put my life back together. He even arranged for me to have driving lessons and helped me find a car that I could afford."

"You didn't know how to drive? How old were you then? Twenty-four? Twenty-five?"

"Twenty-seven. And no, I had never driven before the accident. I'd never had to. When you're touring you're always met at the airport by a limo, and when I wasn't on tour my father or his assistant drove."

"How about before you turned pro? I've never met a teenager yet who didn't want to drive."

"Agent Rawlins, what you don't understand is I was a child prodigy. I've been touring since I was four years old. I can't remember any other life. During my teen years we were always on the road. Plus I rehearsed six or eight hours a day. When I wasn't rehearsing, I was either studying music or being tutored. There was no time for other pursuits. My father, who was my manager, saw no reason to make time for them. I needed to concentrate on my music.''

"A child prodigy, huh? Now there's a new twist." Sam stared at her, his expression disbelieving. "So you're saying your slave-driving father chained you to the piano bench and forced you to practice all day? Next you'll be telling me all he gave you to eat was bread and water."

"Don't be ridiculous. I said nothing of the kind. My father didn't force me to play the piano. He didn't have to. I love to play. Music is my life.

"My father took very good care of me. He guided my career and saw to everything so that I could concentrate on my music with no distractions. If anything, he was overprotective, but that's not a crime.

"Why are you asking me these questions anyway? What does my background have to do with Frank Pappano's murder?"

Agent Rawlins continued to scribble in his notepad. When he finished he ignored her questions and asked, "Where is this paragon of a father now? Why didn't he help you after the car wreck?"

Lauren fixed him with an icy look, but he didn't so much as flinch. "My father died ten months before the accident. After that, his assistant took over as my manager."

"What's his name?"

Panic fluttered through Lauren when she noticed Agent Rawlins scribbling in the notepad again. "Why do you need to know that? He had nothing to do with what happened tonight."

"Just answer the question, Ms. Brownley."

She glared at him, but it was a waste of effort. He merely stared back and waited. Finally Lauren huffed. "His name is Collin. Collin Williams."

"How can I get in touch with him?"

"I have no idea. Once he realized that I would never play on the concert level again he...he left."

"And you haven't kept in touch?"

Hardly, Lauren thought. "No."

"Ah, I see. So, you're saying you had no one to turn to after your accident, and that's why you took up with Carlo."

Lauren frowned. "I wouldn't have phrased it quite that way, but yes, I suppose so."

Agent Rawlins stared at her for so long she began to squirm.

"When I needed a friend, Mr. Giovessi was there. He was wonderful to me," she blurted out defiantly.

Suddenly remembering what she'd witnessed just a few hours earlier, the staunch defense sounded ludicrous, even to her own ears. Grimacing, Lauren groaned and cupped her forehead, massaging her temples with her thumb and fingertips. "It's...it's still difficult for me to believe he murdered Frank in cold blood. If I hadn't seen him pull the trigger I wouldn't believe it. He's always been so nice to me."

"Yeah. I'll bet."

Lauren looked up in time to see the men exchanging a cynical look. "Well, he *has!*"

"Oh, I'm sure he has. Carlo is known to be generous with the women in his life," Agent Rawlins drawled, somehow making even his agreement sound like an insult. "All right, why don't you tell us what happened last night."

"After the club closed I stayed for a while to play for Mr. Giovessi."

"Do you often give private concerts for him?"

"Yes. Every night that I worked at the club. Mr. Giovessi is a great lover of classical music. As I told you, my playing isn't perfect, but he understands. And he's a very appreciative audience."

She didn't bother to try to explain to this man that an artist needed an audience, how just knowing that someone was listening and being moved by the sounds you coaxed from the keyboard fired your creativity and inspired you. The job at the college was just that: a job, a means to support herself, but her soul cried out for more. To some small degree, the job at Club Classico assuaged her need to perform, but it had been Mr. Giovessi's deep appreciation for her music that had made her feel like a true artist again. Those evenings had saved her sanity.

"Go on," Agent Rawlins ordered, and Lauren drew a deep breath and tried to steady her nerves.

"Last night I'd been playing for a half hour or so when Mr. Giovessi stopped me. He didn't even let me finish the piece, which was odd. Usually he can't get enough of Chopin. But he said he was tired, so I told him good-night. Carlo went into his office and I left the building. But as I was about to get in my car I decided to go back inside and use the ladies' room before driving home. I was washing my hands when I heard the shots."

In detail, Lauren related the horrifying events that had followed. Several times Agent Rawlins or one of the others interrupted her to ask questions, and they made her repeat certain details over and over before they were satisfied, but finally she reached the end of her story.

"When I got to the street at the end of the alley I just kept running. I didn't know what else to do. After a few blocks I saw a police car and flagged it down. The two officers brought me here."

Agent Berringer put his hand on her arm. "That must have been terrifying for you, but don't worry, Ms. Brownley, you're safe now. We'll see that nothing happens to you."

"Thank you."

He looked up at Agent Rawlins. "Well? What do you think, Sam?"

The man's craggy face revealed nothing. His black eyes studied Lauren so long she once again had to fight the urge to squirm. Finally he looked at the other agent and nodded. "Go."

"We're on our way. C'mon, Roy, let's go have some fun. It's gonna be a real pleasure to slap the cuffs on old Carlo."

The door had barely closed behind Agents Berringer and O'Connor when Sam Rawlins tossed a pad and pen down on the table in front of Lauren, making her jump. "I have a few calls to make. While I'm gone, I want you to write down your sizes. Shoes, socks, slacks, shirts, skivvies, bras—everything from the skin out. And whatever toiletries you need beyond a toothbrush and toothpaste."

"Whatever for?"

"Because where we're going you wouldn't last five minutes in that getup."

"What do you mean, 'where we're going'? I'm not going anywhere with you. As soon as you arrest Carlo I'm going home."

Sam shot her a scornful look that made her feel like a backward child. "C'mon, lady. Do you really think after what you saw and heard that you can just waltz out of here and no harm will come to you? Hell, no one's that naive."

"But...if he's locked up—"

"Look, Carlo may be behind bars soon, but not all of his goons will be. Some of them are probably waiting in your apartment right now. Carlo knows that without your testimony we won't have much of a case, even if he's in possession of the drugs when we pick him up. Killing you is going to be his number one priority."

Lauren felt the blood drain from her face. "But...if that's true, won't...won't they still be after me, even after he's sent to prison?"

"Yes."

Agent Owens grimaced at his associate's bluntness, but when Lauren looked to him to refute the statement he nodded. "I'm afraid Sam's right. If convicted, Carlo will appeal. You can bet on it. If he's granted a new trial and you're not around to testify a second time, his chances of walking go way up."

"After the trial you'll have to disappear. Somewhere Carlo's men can't find you," Sam Rawlins said.

Lauren glared at him. "And just how am I supposed to do that?"

He shrugged. "You'll go into the witness protection program."

"Whaaat!" Lauren stared at him. He said it so matter-of-factly, as though it were no big deal. It was to her. She'd had her whole world taken away from her once already. She was only just beginning to adjust to the new life she'd made for herself. Now they were going to take that from her, too. "Oh my Lord." She dropped her head into her hands. "How can this be happening?"

Her head snapped up. "What...what if I refuse to testify?"

"He'll kill you anyway."

"Oh God. What am I going to do?" Trembling, she put her hand over her mouth and stared at Sam.

"It's simple. You can walk out of here, but if you do you're on your own. Trust me, you won't last an hour. Or you can testify and we'll do all we can to protect you, before and after the trial."

Lauren stared at him. Oh, that was wonderful. Just wonderful. All her life she'd been cosseted and looked after. She'd spent the last two years trying to overcome that and learn to fend for herself. It hadn't been easy, but she had finally begun to feel that she was making progress. She had sworn that she would never again allow herself to be dependent on someone else. Now, through no fault of her own, she had to put herself totally in someone else's hands. Again.

"So what's it going to be?"

Lauren's shoulders slumped. "Put that way, what choice do I have? I don't want to die."

"I thought you'd see it that way."

Agent Owens gave her a sympathetic look. "If you'll write down the names of family members, we'll notify them for you. Later, after Carlo is in prison and things have cooled down, we might even be able to arrange for you to visit with them in a safe place."

Lauren shook her head and stared at her hands. "There's no one. My father was the only family I had, and he passed away three years ago."

"How about a husband? Or fiancé?"

Briefly she thought of Collin, and her mouth twisted. "No. There's no one."

"Then it won't be a hardship for you to start over

somewhere new, will it?'' Sam stated with callous disregard for her feelings. ''So get busy and write down those sizes. I'll go make some calls. When I'm done, I'll gather everything we need and be back for you.''

Leaning down, he braced his palms flat on the scarred surface of the table and pierced her with a stare. ''And let's get something straight right now. If you want to stay alive, you're going to do exactly what I tell you, when I tell you. No arguments, no discussion. If I say jump, you jump. Got that?''

Lauren nodded.

''Good.''

''Wh-where are you taking me?''

His gaze slid to the detective, then the lieutenant and Agent Owen, and finally back to her. ''It's better that you don't know.''

A feeling of unreality enveloped Lauren as she watched Agent Rawlins stride out of the interrogation room. This couldn't really be happening. It had to be a bad dream. She would wake up soon.

''Uh...Ms. Brownley, you probably ought to get some rest while you can.''

Distracted, Lauren looked up into Agent Owen's earnest face. He was young and clean-cut, no more than twenty-two or three. Probably fresh out of college and whatever training school the FBI had for new recruits, she realized. He had sandy-red hair, guileless blue eyes and the florid complexion typical of a redhead—and he looked about as much like a federal agent as Elmer Fudd. This…this *child* and that unpleasant man were going to protect her from Carlo and his henchmen?

Lauren thought about the sinister-looking thug named Tony, and the others like him ready to do Carlo's bidding, and a shudder rippled through her.

"Ma'am?"

Lauren shook her head. "What? I'm sorry, did you say something?"

"I said you ought to rest while you can. When Sam gets back we'll be taking off. The lieutenant here says if you want to grab a little shut-eye you could use the couch in his office."

Lauren stared at him. She wanted to scream and rant and rave that none of this was fair. She didn't want to start over again. She didn't want to be a witness in a federal case. Most of all, she didn't want to leave the safety of the police station.

But that wouldn't change a thing. Like it or not, she was a witness and her life was about to change yet again. And there wasn't a thing she could do about it.

Left with no choice, Lauren fell back on the good manners and proper behavior that had been ingrained into her since childhood and replied dully, "That would be nice. Thank you."

Four

"**W**ake up."

Lauren bolted from a fitful sleep and found herself staring into the chiseled face of a man who was bending over her. Crying out, she scrambled to her hands and knees and tried to scoot away.

"Easy. Take it easy," Agent Rawlins ordered. "It's just me. Nothing to be afraid of."

The sound of his voice brought recognition. With an effort, Lauren subdued the rush of terror, but her breathing remained as rapid as a marathon runner's and her heart felt as though it were trying to club its way out of her chest. She put her hand on her breast and stared at him. Nothing to be afraid of? After all she'd been through, how did he think she would react, sneaking up on her like that? Besides, the man unnerved her.

She would choke, however, before she let him know that.

Gathering her composure, Lauren swung her legs over the side of the leather sofa and raked her hand through her hair, pushing the tangled mass away from her face. "You startled me. I guess I'm still a bit edgy."

"Looks like it." He shoved two huge department store sacks at her. "Here's a change of clothes and some other stuff. Put them on. The rest of what you'll need I've already put in a duffle. So get a move on. We need to get going."

Lauren glanced around. Lieutenant Dumphries had kindly let her nap on the couch in his office, but two walls of the room were glass and overlooked the squad room where the detectives worked. "Where? I can't get undressed in here."

He looked around and scowled, then nodded toward the door. "C'mon." Lauren grabbed her purse and evening jacket and scrambled after him. Feeling ridiculous and self-conscious, she padded barefoot through the squad room in her torn evening dress.

She noticed that he had changed out of his jeans and cowboy boots. He now wore wool pants and knee-high moccasins that looked handmade. The lower portions of the footwear was constructed of leather and from the ankles up a heavy canvas. They made no sound on the linoleum floor of the squad room as he wound through the maze of desks, moving with the supple grace of an Indian warrior.

Lauren shook her head and grimaced. She must really be exhausted to be having fanciful thoughts about this unpleasant man.

Agent Rawlins lead her down a dingy hallway and stopped in front of a door marked Women.

Instantly her face brightened. "Oh, good. I need to freshen up."

"How you look isn't important. You're not going to breakfast at the Ritz, you know."

"Agent Rawlins, for your information, I wasn't referring to cosmetics," Lauren replied in the coolest tone she could summon. "I need to wash up. It was filthy beneath that sink, and when I jumped out of the window I landed in some kind of awful muck. Unless you have some objection, I would like to get clean before we start out."

"All right, but make it quick. We have to get out of here. And be sure to put on those long johns."

Well. At least that told her one thing: they weren't heading south.

He leaned against the wall and crossed his arms in that age-old male gesture that shouted, "I'm waiting." Without a word, Lauren stepped past him into the rest room and locked the door with a satisfying snap.

Expecting the usual ladies rest room, she was surprised to find herself in what was apparently the changing room for the female officers. It contained not only the usual rest room fixtures but lockers and benches and, to Lauren's delight, a shower.

Quickly reaching behind her, she lowered the zipper on her evening gown and stepped out of the ruined dress. Holding it up by two fingers she gazed at the garment with regret. The elegant gown was the last of her concert clothes. Most of the others she had sold to a resale shop shortly after leaving the hospital.

With a sigh, Lauren dropped the dress into the trash can, peeled off her shredded panty hose and tossed them in as well, then stripped off her undies and stepped into the shower. Helping herself to the shampoo and shower gel she found on the shower ledge, she lathered herself from head to toe. The scrapes on her palms and knee stung like fire, but it felt so good to be clean again she didn't care.

When she stepped out of the shower and dried off she pawed through the sack and located a pair of panties and a bra. In addition the sacks also contained two pair of thermal long johns, one made of soft silk and the other of thick, scratchy wool, a heavy parka, fleece-lined gloves and snow boots, a sweat suit, two pair of thick socks, toothpaste and a toothbrush, the moisturizer and hand lotion that she had requested and a lady's deodorant stick.

Lauren hoped Agent Rawlins had sent one of the secretaries or a female agent to do the shopping. The thought of that harsh man purchasing panties and bras for her, even if they were the plain, serviceable kind, brought a blush to her cheeks.

Lauren held up a shapeless gray wool sweat suit and made a face. Charming.

At once she realized how foolish she was being. What was the matter with her? She was letting her dislike of Agent Rawlins addle her senses. There were men out there trying to murder her. She was so terrified she was sick to her stomach. What did it matter what the clothes he had chosen looked like? The sweat suit was clean and warm.

And she was still alive to wear it.

She dressed in the clothing, as instructed, but she was not quick about it. She felt safe in the police station, and wasn't in any hurry to leave. In the shower she had washed away the last of her makeup, but she didn't bother to apply more. Instead she rubbed her face with moisturizer and applied lotion to her hands.

She combed her damp hair away from her face and had started winding it into a French braid when a loud thump on the door made her jump and give a little shriek.

"Hurry it up in there," Agent Rawlins ordered. "You've got one minute. If you're not out by then I'm coming in after you."

"All right, I'm coming! I'm coming!" Lauren glared at the door. She knew the man was just doing his job, but did he have to be so abrupt? As quickly as possible, she finished braiding her hair, then snatched up her purse and the parka and gloves and headed for the door.

Outside, Sam checked his watch. With a curse, he straightened away from the wall and reached for the doorknob just as Lauren Brownley jerked the door open from the inside. The sight of her, scrubbed and shiny, her damp auburn hair pulled away from that perfect face in a simple braid, hit him like a fist to the gut, and he sucked in his breath. Instantly the sweet, erotic scent of a clean woman invaded his senses.

Desire slammed through him. Hot on its heels came anger.

Dammit, he had no business lusting after this particular female. She was a witness in a high-profile federal case, for God's sake. Worse, she was Carlo Giovessi's plaything.

"It's about time." He glared at her. "You showered and washed your *hair?* I thought you were just going to clean up a little? Dammit, woman, I told you to hurry."

"A shower seemed like the quickest way to get clean," she replied with the cool dignity of a princess, which irritated him all the more. Why the hell couldn't Carlo have stuck to his usual brassy women?

"Fine," he snapped. "If you're ready, could we go now?" Without waiting for a reply, he grasped her elbow and hustled her down the hallway toward a rear stair exit.

Practically trotting to keep up with his long strides, Lauren looked back over her shoulder in the direction of the squad room. "Where are you taking me? Aren't you going to tell Lieutenant Dumphries we're leaving? He said he would provide a police escort."

"We're going out the back way. Through the parking garage where the staff keep their personal vehicles. The fewer people who see us leave, the better."

Out of the corner of his eye Sam saw her shoot him

a startled look, and he realized that he had just added a new dimension to her fear. Good, he thought. He didn't get a charge out of scaring women, but if that's what it took to cut through that surprising naiveté of hers, then so be it. Maybe now she'd realize just how much danger she was facing.

"What does that mean? Surely you don't think someone with the Denver police poses a threat to me?"

He opened the door and shoved her into the stairwell without answering, but he felt her gaze on him and the increasing tension in the arm he was holding.

"Well *do you?*"

"Let's just say I don't believe in taking chances."

She whimpered, but he ignored the terrified sound and hustled her down the stairs.

He wanted to tell her to get used to it. Over the next few weeks, maybe even months, killing her was going to be the prime objective for a lot of nasty characters. If she was going to survive she had to learn to be suspicious of everyone and everything. If she was smart, even him.

Lauren stared at Sam Rawlins's hard profile. He frightened her almost as much as this hideous situation. The man didn't seem to possess normal human emotions. Certainly not fear. Or gentleness.

The nap and the warm shower had eased her nerves a bit, but now the tight knot began to coil in her belly again, and when an icy sensation trickled down her spine she shuddered. If Sam Rawlins noticed he gave no sign.

"Wh-where is Agent Owens? I thought he was going with us." At least, she fervently hoped he was. The prospect of being alone with this man for weeks on end was almost unbearable.

"He's waiting in the car."

They clattered down the last flight of metal stairs to the basement parking garage, but when Lauren stepped toward the door Sam jerked her back and shoved her up against the adjacent wall.

"Stay there until I tell you to move. And don't make a sound." He looked her over critically. "Put on the parka and pull up the hood so it covers as much of your face as possible. When I say ready, keep your head down and go. And I mean move. You got that?"

Lauren nodded mutely, too terrified to make a sound. She could barely breathe.

Sam waited until she fumbled into the parka, then flattened himself against the wall on the other side of the door. Her eyes widened and her heart almost jumped right into her throat when he pulled a gun from beneath his coat and held it pointed toward the ceiling beside his right shoulder. With his left hand, he eased the heavy metal door open a crack.

Apparently satisfied with what he saw, he eased the door a little wider and peered around the edge in all directions. "All clear?"

"Yeah. The place is empty," she heard Agent Owens reply.

Sam looked at Lauren. "Okay, let's go."

In a lightning fast move, he grabbed her wrist, hauled her from behind the door and out into the garage. Lauren had a brief impression of an unmarked gray car sitting a few feet away with the engine running and the rear passenger door standing open. Then she was being stuffed inside and shoved, facedown, onto the back seat.

"Cover up with this," Sam ordered, and tossed a heavy wool blanket over her. "And for God's sake, stay down." He slammed the rear door, jerked open the front one and jumped inside. "Go! Go! Go!" he yelled, and Agent Owens burned rubber peeling out of the parking garage.

Beneath the blanket, Lauren huddled in a ball and closed her eyes, shivering and praying. At any moment she expected some of Carlo's thugs to ambush them, to feel bullets punching through the car's metal exterior and ripping into her flesh, or that they would be overtaken and run off the road and they would all die in a fiery crash.

Instead there was nothing—just the sounds of normal traffic all around them and occasional terse comments between the two agents in the front seat. After twenty uneventful minutes, Lauren finally mustered enough courage to lift the edge of the blanket and peer out. All she could see was the backs of the men's heads. Sam Rawlins sat in the passenger seat, his head moving constantly as he kept a sharp lookout for trouble.

The sounds of traffic grew less and less until they all but disappeared. After what seemed like forever, the car turned off the highway onto what was apparently a country road and Agent Owens slowed their speed as they bounced over bumps and potholes. Gravel popped beneath the tires and banged against the car's undercarriage, and with every thud Lauren jumped as though she'd been shot.

Finally they came to a stop.

"Leave the engine running while I go check things out. Any sign of trouble and you haul ass outta here."

"Sure, Sam. Whatever you say."

"And you stay down back there, Ms. Brownley," he ordered. "Don't move until I say so."

"How're you doing, miss?" Agent Owens asked when Sam had gone.

"I'm…I'm okay." Out of habit she had started to say fine, but she wasn't fine. She was so scared she was afraid she was going to be sick.

"Don't pay any attention to Sam's gruffness, miss," Dave Owens went on. "That's just his way. He's a bit of a lone wolf, but there's no better agent within the Bureau. 'Course, I haven't been with the Bureau all that long, but that's what all the other guys say. So don't you worry, if anyone can keep you safe, it's Sam."

Too nervous to carry on a conversation, all Lauren could manage was a soft, "Mmm." Taking the hint, Agent Owens fell silent.

After a nerve-racking wait, Sam returned and

climbed back into the car. "Everything is go. Drive over to that green-and-white plane and park beside it with the passenger side next to the steps. Get as close as you can. Then you grab the bags while I get Miss Brownley inside."

"You got it."

As the car bumped over the uneven ground the sound of engine noise grew steadily louder, until it was almost deafening. Lauren realized that the plane they were about to board was waiting for them with the engines running.

The instant the car stopped Sam bailed out and jerked open the rear door.

"C'mon, move it."

Lauren felt exposed when he snatched the blanket off of her, but before she could protest he grasped her arm, hauled her out of the car and bundled her up the steps and into the plane.

The pilot sitting at the controls looked to be in his fifties. He turned around and flashed her a reassuring grin and a wave.

"That's Bob Halloran!" Sam yelled over the roar of the engines. "He's retired FBI and an old friend of mine, so you're in good hands! Take a seat and buckle up. We're already cleared for takeoff. Soon as we load our gear we're outta here."

He moved back to the open door, and caught the duffle bags that Agent Owens tossed to him. Then the younger man hurried up the steps, pulled them up and slammed the door closed behind him.

"Let's get this crate off the ground!" Sam yelled as he and Dave Owens made their way to the front of the plane.

Minutes later, Lauren stared out the window and watched the airstrip drop away. The plane banked and began a sharp climb, heading over the mountains to the west. Behind them, Denver's sprawl grew steadily smaller, fading into nothing more than a smudge on the pristine snow, then disappearing altogether.

Only then did Lauren's heartbeat slow to normal. She leaned her forehead against the cold window glass and closed her eyes. They had made it. She had gotten away.

Sighing, she settled back in her seat and willed her tense muscles to relax.

The plane was a six-seater—a noisy, bumpy little craft, so small that neither Agents Rawlins nor Owens could stand up straight inside it. Normally Lauren was frightened of planes, especially small ones, but at the moment all she could feel was relief.

She stared at the back of Sam Rawlins's head and marveled at the man's calm.

He sat up front beside the pilot. The two men were carrying on a conversation of sorts, though they had to shout to make themselves heard over the engine noise—something about a hunting trip they had taken together the previous year, but Lauren wasn't paying much attention. At least he was talking with his friend. That was more than he had done with her.

After whisking her out of the police station, he hadn't said a word to her the entire drive.

Not that she minded. Sam Rawlins made her uneasy. Just the thought of spending the next few weeks with him sent a shiver down her spine. What on earth would they talk about? Or perhaps they wouldn't talk at all. Maybe he would simply go about his business and give her the silent treatment, as he'd been doing all morning. She didn't know which would be worse.

The way her luck was running, she supposed she shouldn't be surprised that she'd gotten stuck with this taciturn man. If she had to hide out for months with a bodyguard, God alone knew where, why couldn't it have been someone pleasant...someone like that nice Agent Berringer?

At least Bob Owens would be with them. She glanced at the man sitting behind the pilot, hanging on every word of the conversation between the two older men. He was young, clearly a rookie, and he seemed eager to please Agent Rawlins. Still...he had been polite and pleasant to her.

Lauren leaned her head against the back of the seat and sighed. She felt as though she were trapped in a nightmare and couldn't wake up. Only two years ago she had been a rising concert star with a bright future ahead of her. She'd had a huge talent, a handsome fiancé whom she had thought loved her, who also managed her career, and plenty of money. Life had been wonderful. Then almost overnight her money, her future, and her fiancé were gone.

These days, during the week she worked for a pitiable wage as a college music instructor and played piano in a lounge on weekends. Or she had—until last night. Now she was on the run from murdering gangsters with a hard man who looked at her as though she were something he'd found under a rock.

If this was a nightmare, she prayed she would wake up soon.

Now that her situation wasn't quite so urgent, stress and exhaustion were taking their toll. Her scraped palms and knee still stung. Her eyes felt gritty and she was stiff and sore and achy all over.

In addition, her body felt heavy with fatigue, as though each cell were weighted with lead. Hardly surprising, she thought, yawning. Except for that restless doze she'd had at the police station, she hadn't slept in over twenty-four hours.

Snuggling down in the seat, Lauren gave in to her body's demand and closed her eyes. The drone of the engine lulled her, and one by one her muscles relaxed.

"What? What is it?" Lauren sat up with a start, her heart pounding. Disoriented and groggy, she didn't know where she was or how she'd gotten there. Her gaze darted around the interior of the small plane as panic gushed up inside her.

Then she spotted Sam Rawlins, and it all came rushing back. Uttering a low moan, she put her hand over her thundering heart and slumped back against the seat.

Her relief didn't last long. The next instant Lauren realized what it was that had jerked her out of a sound sleep. The drone of one of the plane's engines had been replaced with an erratic sputtering and coughing.

Gripping the seat arms, Lauren sat forward and yelled at the three men, "What's making that noise? What's wrong?"

Agent Owens glanced back at her, but the terror in his young face did nothing to ease her mind.

Sam twisted around in his seat and shouted, "We've developed engine trouble! Sit tight and keep your seat belt on!"

Engine trouble? Lauren's chest suddenly felt as though it were being squeezed in a vise.

She pressed her face to the side window and looked out, and her stomach dropped to the vicinity of her knees. They were much lower than she had expected. The treetops and rocks seemed only a few hundred yards beneath the plane.

The scenery was spectacular. They were flying over a majestic mountain range, but there wasn't a sign of civilization anywhere, only what appeared to be hundreds of miles of jagged peaks and high, fog-shrouded valleys, buried deep in snow.

"C'mon. C'mon, baby, don't quit on me now, sweetheart!" the pilot exhorted his aircraft.

Instantly Lauren's attention switched back to the front. The men's shouts had taken on an urgent quality. Bob Halloran was furiously flipping switches and checking dials on the cockpit control panel and shouting orders at Agent Rawlins, who was working like a demon to carry them out. Neither man's efforts had any effect. The sputtering and coughing grew worse, and the plane bucked like a rodeo bronc.

Lauren held on tight to the seat arms and fought back a scream.

"We're losing it! Dammit! We're losing it!"

"Losing it? Losing what? What do you mean? What are we losing?" Lauren shouted, but a glance out the window supplied the answer. She stared in horror as the right propeller slowed and stopped. "Oh my God, no! No!"

"How about the other one. Can we hold it?" Sam shouted.

"Not for long!"

Only then did Lauren realize that the erratic noise had not stopped. The plane's other engine was making the same sickening coughs and sputters. She leaned over to look out of the window on the other side of the cabin just in time to see the second propeller come to a stop.

The sudden cessation of noise was stunning. The only sound was the eerie whistle of wind flowing over the fuselage.

"That's it! We're going down, people!"

"Oh my God!" Dave shrieked.

Sam twisted around and shouted at Lauren, "Pull your seat belt tight. And put your head down! Do it! Now!"

She didn't hear him. Paralyzed with fear, Lauren

stared out the window at the snowy mountain side rushing up to meet them.

Then Sam was beside her. "Put your head down, dammit! And brace yourself!" Shoving her parka into her lap, he grasped the back of her neck and pushed her face into the down-filled coat.

"I see a clearing ahead!" the pilot shouted. "I'm gonna try for it! Come on, baby. Come on. You can make it. Just a little farther. Glide! Glide!"

Lauren wanted to scream, but her throat was so tight she couldn't make a sound. There was just the whistle of the wind and the pilot's desperate chatter.

"Here it comes! We're gonna hit! Oh, shit! We're gonna clip the trees! Hang on! Hang on!"

Something scraped the underside of the fuselage, and at once a series of jolts shook the plane. The repeated crack of splintering wood sounded like gunfire. Then the world exploded all around them.

The horrible screech of metal rending seemed to go on forever, like a banshee's wail. Lauren was thrown cruelly against her seat belt and slung from side to side, bouncing off the bulkhead, then Agent Rawlins, as struts snapped, and rocks scraped and tore at the plane's underbelly. The plane bounced and lurched and all around came the terrible sounds of grinding and crashing and shattering glass.

They slammed to an abrupt stop.

Then there was only silence.

Five

"Lauren? Lauren, are you hurt?"

She remained bent over with her face buried in the parka, clutching her ankles tight and praying.

Remotely she became aware of fingers pressing into the side of her neck. "Dammit, woman, answer me! Are you all right?"

"I...I don't know." She was afraid to move and find out. She couldn't believe they had survived, any of them.

"Sit up and let's see," Sam ordered.

Moving slowly, she obeyed and carefully rotated her head and tested her arms and legs. Though bruised and battered, everything worked. Something warm trickled down her temple and when she touched it her fingers came away covered with blood. She stared at it, shocked.

"You've got a cut on your forehead, but it doesn't look serious. Nothing seems to be broken. Put on that parka and let's get out of here. This plane isn't safe."

When Lauren continued to stare at her bloodied fingers, Sam grasped her shoulders and gave her a shake. "Snap out of it, dammit! Get a grip! We don't have time for female hysterics."

Lauren blinked at him and nodded, struggling for control. "I...yes. Yes, of course." While she fumbled into her coat Sam unbuckled his seat belt and stood up.

"Bob? How're you doing up there?"

He got no answer.

"Bob? Dave?"

Lauren paused in the act of hooking her purse shoulder strap over her head and looked toward the cockpit. Bob Halloran sat motionless, his head tipped back at a sharp angle, arms hanging limp on either side of the pilot's seat. Agent Owens lay across the seat behind Bob, his head and shoulders hanging out into the aisle. His eyes were open and vacant and he was bleeding from the nose, ears and eyes.

They had landed on an incline with the nose of the plane buried to the windshield in a snowdrift. Using the backs of the other seats, Sam pulled himself up to his friends. He touched the pilot's shoulder, and the man head lolled to one side.

Sam felt for a pulse. After a moment his jaw tightened. Turning, he bent over Dave.

"Dammit to hell."

Sam started back down the aisle. On his second step, the plane wobbled.

Lauren cried out and clutched the seat back in front of her.

"C'mon! Out! Now!"

"But what about Bob and Dave?"

"They're dead."

Lauren caught her breath. Her gaze darted forward to the two men, and she felt a rush of sadness and pity, and to her shame, gratitude that it wasn't her who had been killed.

"Will you get a move on! This baby's going over the edge any second."

She tried, but her legs were so wobbly she couldn't stand. With an oath, Sam hooked his arm around her waist and hauled her out of the seat.

The movement made the plane shift again and slide a foot or so. Lauren screamed, but Sam held her tight against his side and kept going. The exit door was stuck, and he had to release her to shoulder it open. The plane shuddered and shifted in response. Lauren shrieked and clutched the back of the last seat, certain they were going to topple down the mountainside at any second.

The door gave way, and Sam grabbed her again. The belly of the fuselage was buried up to the bottom of the door, but when they jumped out they sank in snow to their knees.

Lauren would have fallen if Sam hadn't held her. He half carried, half dragged her a few feet away from the wreck. When they were clear he dropped her as though she were a sack of potatoes, and Lauren collapsed onto her stomach, her face buried in the snow.

"Stay here," he snapped.

Sputtering and wiping snow from her face, she

struggled to her knees. Looking over her shoulder, she saw him heading back toward the plane. ''Where are you going?''

Bogged in the deep snow, movement was awkward. By the time she managed to scramble to her feet Sam was climbing back aboard the plane. ''Wait! What are you doing?''

''I have to get some things.''

''Are you crazy? You'll be killed! Get out of there! Come back!''

He paid no attention to her. The plane, or what was left of it, rocked under his weight. Lauren made a strangled sound and put her gloved hand over her mouth. She stared in horror at the empty doorway when he disappeared inside the wreck.

She couldn't believe it. The idiot was going to be killed.

The wind whistled around her, and something wet and cold touched her face. She looked up and realized it had started to snow.

Terrified, she hugged her arms around her middle and looked at the fearsome beauty that surrounded her. Snow-covered mountains stretched away in every direction. Rugged. Stark. Unforgiving.

The jagged peaks stabbed the pewter sky, the taller ones piercing the low-hanging clouds. Everything was gray and cold and silent. Eerie fog rose from the valleys like ghosts.

To one side, a swath of broken treetops marked the

path of their crash landing, the raw, splintered trunks an ugly scar on the pristine landscape.

Trembling, Lauren pressed her lips together and hugged herself tighter. If Sam went over the edge in the plane she would be alone in this frozen wilderness. She wouldn't last the night.

Sam reappeared in the door of the plane and tossed out two duffle bags. "Grab these and pull them out of the way!" he shouted.

Wading through the deep snow, Lauren hurried forward to do as he instructed. Sam disappeared again. Just as she grabbed the straps on the bags a screeching rent the air and the plane started a backward slide.

She dropped the bags and screamed. Horrified, she watched the twisted fuselage bump down the incline, hit a rocky outcropping and hang there for a few seconds, rocking, then tumble over the edge.

At the last instant a bag and another object flew out of the door and Sam leaped out after them.

The mountains echoed with the harsh sounds of the plane bumping and crashing down the slope. Then there was a horrendous explosion, and a fireball and plume of dark smoke mushroomed upward.

Crying hysterically, Lauren plowed her way through the snow to get to Sam. "Are you all right? Are you hurt?"

He picked himself up and dusted the snow off his parka. "Yeah. I'm okay."

He looked over the ledge and so did Lauren. About

two hundred feet below, the crumpled fuselage was enveloped in flames. "That was close, though."

Lauren didn't understand how he could be so calm. She stared down at the fiery wreck, and suddenly it was all too much. All the terror and helplessness and worry she had experienced in the last twelve hours came rushing up to the surface.

With an anguished cry, she whirled around and began to pummel Sam's chest.

"Hey! Cut that out! What the hell's the matter with you?"

"This is all your fault. You were supposed to protect me! Instead I was nearly killed! Again! Now we're going to die out here in this frozen wilderness. I should never have trusted you. You're a mean, cold, thoroughly unpleasant man. And you scared me half to death!"

Sam finally managed to grasp her flailing hands and haul her up tight against his chest. The fog of their breaths mingled as he put his face close to hers and growled. "Listen to me. *Listen!* We are *not* going to die. So *shut up!*"

"How can you say that? We're in the middle of nowhere with no provisions and no way to get out."

"We have provisions. We have Bob's survival pack and our gear. That's what I went back in for. And we *are* going to get out."

"How? Just how are we going to do that?"

"We're going to walk out."

"Have you lost your mind? You don't even know where we are."

"I know in a general sense. That's all we need."

He released her, and she stumbled back and landed on her rear. He picked up the backpack and put it on, then retrieved a rifle from a snowbank and slung the strap over his shoulder. "C'mon. Let's get the other bags. We need to get going."

"Where? There's no place *to* go?"

"We have to find shelter." He jerked his head toward the northwest. "There's a blizzard coming."

Only then did Lauren notice that it was snowing harder and the low clouds rolling in were a dark, angry color.

Without waiting for her, Sam strode away and scooped up the two duffle bags. He knelt in the snow and began transferring the contents of one bag into the other.

"What are you doing?" Lauren demanded, struggling to her feet.

"Consolidating. We can't carry both bags so I'm sorting out just the clothes and essentials we need and putting them into one bag."

The thought of her clothing and intimate toiletries packed in with this man's did not thrill Lauren, but she had more urgent things to worry about.

"There, that should hold us," Sam announced, rising to his feet. He dusted the snow off his pants and started walking away. "You carry the duffle," he ordered over his shoulder. "I'll carry the pack."

Lauren wanted to object to his tone, but a glance at the dark line of clouds changed her mind. Stopping just long enough to retrieve the duffle, she slung it over her shoulder—and almost toppled over from the weight. Determinedly she straightened and adjusted the bag's strap and scrambled after him.

"I still think you're a horrible man," she muttered.

"Yeah, well, you're entitled to your opinion. Just don't expect me to lose any sleep over it. And keep up."

"I thought if you survived a plane crash you were supposed to stay by the wreck and wait for rescue," she said to his back. "I'm sure I read that somewhere."

"The plane is a bonfire at the bottom of a steep slope. You'd break your neck getting down there. Besides, there won't be any rescue. No one knows where we were heading."

"No one?" she panted, struggling to keep pace with him. "Didn't your pilot friend file a flight plan?"

"Sort of."

"Sort of? What does that mean?"

"Let's just say he may have made a mistake, okay?"

"He falsified a flight plan, didn't he?"

"Look at it this way—at least Carlo's thugs don't know where you are."

"That's small comfort if we end up freezing to death on this mountainside."

"We're not going to freeze to death."

"Are you kidding? I'm freezing already. My toes feel like ice cubes."

He stopped so abruptly she almost bumped into him. "Did you put on the wool socks that were in the sack I gave you?"

"Of course I put them on. I don't usually wear boots without socks." Actually she'd never worn big clunky hiking boots in her life.

"Both pair?"

"Well...no, but—"

"Dammit! I told you to put on what was in that bag."

"You didn't tell me to put on both pair of socks! How was I supposed to know to do that? You didn't bother to tell me where you were taking me, and I certainly had no idea that we were going to crashland in this frozen wilderness, now did I?"

"What did you do with the extra pair?"

"I put them in my purse."

"Dig them out and put them on over the others." He snatched the duffle bag off her shoulder, unzipped it and pawed through the contents and pulled out another suit of wool long johns. The ones she had on were of silk and soft against her skin, but these were the thick, scratchy kind. "Here. While you're at it, put these on over the other pair," he said, tossing them to her.

"*What?* You mean *here?*" She caught the long johns reflexively, but held them clutched against her breasts. "You can't seriously expect me to strip down to my underwear right out here in the open. In front of you."

"I not only expect it, I'm ordering you to. Besides, I don't know what you're complaining about. I'm going to do the same thing. The temperature is dropping fast and I don't know how long it will be before we find shelter." He shrugged off the backpack and dug through the duffle bag again and pulled out another pair of long underwear. Shucking out of his parka, he dropped it on top of the backpack and bent over and started untying the drawstring that held the canvas tops of his knee-high moccasins snug to his legs.

"What are you doing?"

"What does it look like? Now get busy. We don't have time to waste."

He removed one moccasin and propped his socked foot on the duffle. "Work one leg at a time so you won't get your socks wet," he cautioned.

Straightening, he took off his vest and dropped it on top of the parka and went to work on the buttons of his flannel shirt. It soon joined the parka. When he unfastened his trousers, Lauren quickly looked away, but from the corner of her eye she saw him remove one leg from the pants, shove it into the long johns, then back into the pantleg. He pulled his moccasin back on and pulled up the drawstring and tied it.

Then he shifted his weight to that foot and repeated the process.

He darted Lauren a look. "I'd get busy if I were

you. If you're not out of those clothes by the time I'm done I'll strip them off you myself.''

Lauren sucked in her breath. Of all the arrogant, overbearing, insufferable... He'd do it, too. She could see it in his eyes and that hard, determined face. Since he was a foot taller than she was and outweighed her by a good hundred and twenty pounds, there wasn't much doubt what the outcome would be.

She was sorely tempted to tell him to go to hell. If she didn't need him to stay alive, she would. For a moment Lauren fumed, but she had no choice.

"Oh, all right! But I'm going over there behind those trees.''

"Don't bother. Trust me, I won't be overcome with lust at the sight of you in baggy drawers.''

Lauren lifted her chin. "I didn't think you would be. If you must know, I have to use the...the ladies' room.''

He pinned her with that dark stare and arched one eyebrow. "The *ladies'* room?''

Refusing to be intimidated, she stared back and tipped her chin up another notch. "Yes. Since I have to strip, I figured I may as well take care of that while I'm there.''

"Okay, fine. Just don't go too far. And remember what I said about keeping your feet dry,'' he called after her as she plowed through the snow toward a huge blue spruce tree whose snow-laden branches were bent down to the ground.

When she returned ten minutes later Sam was fully

clothed with the backpack strapped on and the rifle hanging from one shoulder. Giving her an impatient look, he tossed the duffle bag to her and nearly knocked her down.

"Pull up your parka hood," he ordered. "Keeping that fur ruff extended out in front of your face prewarms the air before you breath it in. It's easier on your lungs that way. Your breath will cause ice crystals to form on the fur. It's important that you brush it off periodically."

That said, without so much as a "c'mon," he turned and started off again.

Walking through the deep snow took torturous effort, even with him plowing a path ahead of her. Lauren struggled along behind him with her jaw clenched, her gaze shooting daggers at his back. That she had to be dependent on anyone for anything didn't set well with her. That she now had no choice but to trust her very life to this man was galling.

If the loss of her career and her fiancé had taught her nothing else, it was to take control of her own destiny. She had vowed that never again would she allow others to direct her life and make all her decisions for her. Now, here she was, tromping along behind this hard-as-nails man whom she barely knew, completely dependent on him for her very survival. Oh, how that grated.

Since being released from the hospital ten months ago, Lauren had continued her rehabilitation by working out in a gym three evenings a week. Overall, she was in superb physical condition—or at least, she had thought she was. However, at this altitude the air was thin, and every movement seemed to take twice the energy it normally required. Added to that, too little sleep and two brushes with death had left her exhausted, physically and emotionally.

Soon her breathing became labored and shallow and her heart chugged like a locomotive. Sucking in the frigid air made her lungs burn and her throat dry. With every step she panted and gasped for breath, but Sam would allow her only a few sips at a time from their canteen of water.

It irritated her that he didn't even appear to be winded. He kept the same steady pace with no apparent effort, his face set like granite.

Lauren struggled to match his speed, but the distance between them steadily lengthened. It was snowing harder and the wind whipped the flakes into a swirling frenzy and cut visibility to almost zero. Only ten feet ahead, Sam was merely a ghostly gray form moving through the driving whiteness.

She frowned at his back. Did he really know where he was going? Or were they just wandering aimlessly?

He looked back over his shoulder. "If you don't keep up you're going to lose sight of me and get lost."

"How...can I...keep up? You're walking...too...fast."

"So hustle."

She narrowed her eyes and tried to drill a hole in his back with her stare. After a while, though, even that took too much effort. It required all her energy and concentration to put one foot in front of the other.

It was bitterly cold and getting colder. Through the swirling snow, everything was gray and bleak. The only sounds were the crunching of the snow under their feet, the howl of the wind, an occasional snap of a limb under its weight of snow, and the heavy rasp of their breathing.

"I saw...a cave a few...few minutes back," Lauren gasped. "Wouldn't that make...a good shelter?"

"Sure. If you don't mind sharing it with a bear."

"Bear?" She shot a terrified look around and scrambled to close the gap between them. "There are...bears around...here?"

"Plenty of them. But don't worry, they're hibernating right now."

"Are there...any other...predators around that...I should...know about?"

Without breaking stride, Sam shrugged. "Mountain lions."

Mountain lions! Fear shot another blast of adrenaline through Lauren. Casting a frantic look around, she scooted in closer to Sam's back and picked up the pace. After that her gaze darted around constantly.

She had expected him to start down the mountainside, but it seemed to her that they were gradually climbing. He tramped on at a steady pace, like a man with a specific goal in mind. As they hiked Lauren glanced around at the inhospitable terrain.

"Is there something…in particular…we're looking for?"

"A few seconds before we crashed, I saw a log structure," he shouted above the howl of the wind. "It's probably an old abandoned mine, or if we're really lucky, the remains of a miner's cabin. There are hundreds of them scattered over these mountains. They're relics from the Colorado gold rush days in the 1800s."

"Are they still…ha-habitable?"

"Not in the normal sense, but any kind of structure that will provide enough shelter to get us out of the wind and snow and be a dry place where we can build a fire will help."

A fire? A fire sounded wonderful. A fire sounded absolutely fantastic. She was so tired her leg muscles were quivering and she was almost asleep on her feet. Oh, how she longed to lie down beside a warm fire and close her eyes.

Sam glanced over his shoulder at her again and his jaw clenched tighter. The mere sight of her filled him with a rage he could barely contain. Because of this woman he'd lost an old friend and a fellow agent. He tried to push the feeling aside, but he couldn't banish the mental image of Bob and Dave as he'd last seen them, vacant-eyed and slumped in death.

Sam tended to be a loner, but those few he counted as a friend, he valued. Bob Halloran had been the first close friend he'd made within the Bureau, and the best. Though seventeen years Sam's senior, they had formed a strong bond over the years they'd worked together. Outside of work they'd shared the same interests, and had gone fishing and hunting together numerous times. Bob was one of only a very few men whom Sam had trusted absolutely.

Dave Owens had been a green rookie, which was why Sam hadn't objected to him working this assignment with him. He figured the kid hadn't been with the Bureau long enough to have been corrupted, and therefore wasn't on Carlo's payroll. He'd been an eager, idealistic young man who'd had the potential to become one hell of an agent.

Now both men were dead—their lives forfeited in an attempt to save a mobster's mistress—a woman who traded her body and self-respect to a vicious old man in exchange for creature comforts.

Granted, she was vital to their case. With her testimony they could finally nail Giovessi. But at what cost? So far, two good men had died trying to keep her safe.

He glanced over his shoulder again, and his mouth twisted. He probably should have mentioned the mountain lions when they first started out. At least now she was no longer lagging behind.

Sam knew she wouldn't be able to keep going much longer, though. Up until now she'd been running on adrenaline, but she was gray with exhaustion and so wobbly she could barely keep her balance. If he didn't locate the cabin soon he'd have to carry her.

To keep her moving he shouted over his shoulder, "The cabin is just ahead." At least, he hoped to hell it was, and that his eyes hadn't been playing tricks on him.

"How…how do you…know that?"

"When I spotted it from the plane I noticed it was on a massive rock outcropping. I took a compass sighting on the rock formation when we started hiking, before the storm hit in earnest and reduced visibility."

She dragged along in his wake and didn't bother to answer, as though even that much effort was too much for her.

They rounded the base of a gigantic boulder, and when the swirling curtain of snow parted for an instant the structure came into view. Perched precariously on the edge of the rocky outcropping above them, a derelict old mine shack clung to the mountainside, the remains of its sluice box dangling down the slope.

This, Sam realized, was what he'd seen from the air. As a shelter it was next to worthless. So many boards were missing from the outer walls you could see right through the ramshackle building. The damned thing would probably crumble if you stepped into it, he thought. Not that it mattered. Lauren would never be able to climb that sheer rock face, and time had obliterated the trail.

The snow swirled again, and Sam caught a glimpse of something.

"There!" he shouted over the wind, pointing. "I think I see a cabin!"

Six

To the right, tucked back against the base of the rock formation just a few feet away, another structure was barely visible through the swirling snow.

Lauren gave a moan of gratitude and stumbled toward the shadowy shape, but Sam grabbed her arm and stopped her. "Not yet. Wait here while I check it out."

Dropping the duffle, he unhooked the rifle from his shoulder, worked the bolt action to chamber a round and cautiously pushed open the plank door. Instantly the leather hinges crumbled, and the door fell into the room with a crash. Sam grimaced. If any creature had taken up residence inside, that should have run it out. He paused and listened, but there was no scuttling or rustling coming from inside.

Sam stepped into the cabin in time to see a chipmunk scurry out through a hole in the chinking. After a quick check turned up no other critters, he went back outside and picked up his duffle bag and motioned to Lauren. "All clear."

"Is it safe?"

"Yeah. It's been partially protected from the elements by the cliff wall. For its age, it's in fair condition. There's a hole in the roof, but I can throw some brush over that. Some chinking is missing and the door fell in, and the inside looks like it's been a nest for chipmunks, but we can manage.''

Once inside Lauren sank to the filthy puncheon floor. ''Thank heavens. I don't think I could have plowed through that snow one more step.''

Sam shrugged off the backpack and dropped it, but he hooked the gun back over his shoulder. ''Don't go to sleep,'' he cautioned when Lauren started to lay her head down on the duffle. ''Not until I get a fire going in here. I'll go gather some wood. While I'm gone, go through the pack and see what kind of food supply we have. There should be a ground sheet in there. Spread everything out on that so we can take stock of what we've got to work with. While you're at it, you'd better clean up that cut. Knowing Bob, I'm sure there's a first-aid kit in that pack. And stay awake, dammit, or you'll freeze to death. At this temperature it wouldn't take long.''

''Okay, okay. You don't have to be such a grouch,'' Lauren grumbled. Sitting up again, she dragged the backpack closer and unzipped it.

There were plenty of trees around the cabin, and Sam was confident that Bob's survival pack included a small hatchet, but for the moment he stuck to gathering deadwood and brush. Once he had a fire going, he'd come back and chop branches.

He worked furiously, driven not only by the need,

but to hold at bay the anger and grief he'd been battling with ever since the crash.

He brought in several armloads of deadwood and brush, and when he was satisfied that he had enough to keep a fire going for a couple of hours, he propped the door back in place and braced it with a three foot long chunk of wood. Then he hunkered down in front of the stone fireplace.

Poking his head inside the firebox, he looked up the chimney and breathed a sigh of relief. Whoever had built the cabin all those years ago had mortared in a metal grill at the top of the chimney to keep birds and other animals out.

Sam crumbled a small mound of deadwood for kindling, stacked brush and the small twigs and limbs in a teepee shape over it, then looked over his shoulder at Lauren, who was hugging her upper body and rocking back and forth, struggling to stay awake. She had evidently found the first-aid kit, but her attempt to clean the cut had merely smeared the dried blood over her forehead and temple

"Are there any matches in those supplies? Or a fire starter of any kind?"

She gave him a blank look and blinked. "Um, I think I saw...yes, here they are." She picked up the box of matches and tossed them to him.

Within minutes a fire blazed in the hearth and Sam turned his attention to the contents of the backpack.

"Let's see what we have," he murmured. His gaze ran over the items spread out on the ground sheet, and he gave silent thanks to his old friend Bob's meticulous attention to safety and detail. "A pot and skillet, packet of utensils, matches, compass, binoculars, strips of waxed lamp wick."

Sam paused and stared at the last, a sharp stab of grief spearing through him. Bob never had been worth a damn at building a fire, and on every camping trip they'd ever made his friend had carried along plenty of the fire starter strips.

Gritting his teeth, Sam shoved aside the pain and the mental image of his old friend slumped in the cockpit seat and continued, picking up each item as he ticked it off.

"Ax, snare wire, sleeping bag, first-aid kit, three kinds of cord, both braided and twisted, a three blade folding knife, a fixed blade knife, waxed thread, sewing awl, a coil of light nylon rope. Looks like we've also got about fifteen pounds of food—freeze-dried eggs, meat, and meat and vegetable mixes, plus about a half pound each of jerky, beans, rice and oats. And a bottle of vitamins." Sam's mouth quirked. Bob always had been a health nut.

"How long will that last the two of us?" Lauren asked, giving the pile of packets a dubious look.

"Quite a while if we stay camped here. Once we start trekking out, our caloric needs shoot up. But supplemented with fresh meat, we'll get by."

"How are we going to get fresh meat? You can't go hunting in a blizzard."

"Ever heard of a snare? If I set eight or ten in about

a hundred-yard radius around the cabin, chances are good a couple will catch something.'' He patted his parka pockets, and an arrested look came over his face. Then he began to curse viciously.

Lauren winced. ''What? What's wrong?''

''I've lost my cellphone. It probably fell out of my coat during the crash. Dammit!''

He glanced at Lauren. ''I don't suppose you have one.''

''No.'' These days a cellphone was one of the many luxuries she could no longer afford.

''Figures.'' He picked up the ax and stood. ''There's just enough daylight left to chop the firewood and brush we need for tonight. While I do that, you can cook us something to eat.''

''You want *me* to cook?''

He stopped at the door and pinned her with a steady stare that somehow managed to convey utter disgust. ''Let me guess. You can't cook.''

''Well...''

''Oh, that's right, I forgot. You have other talents, don't you?''

A frown knit her forehead at his sarcastic tone. ''If you mean the piano, then yes. I am learning other skills, like cooking and keeping house. I'm just not very good at them yet.''

Sam glanced at the packages of dehydrated food. ''Just throw the contents of one of those packets in a pot with some water and boil it according to the directions.''

"But...the only water in the pack was in the canteen, and we drank all of that while we were hiking here."

Sam stared at her again and shook his head. "Damn, don't you know how to do anything? For God's sake, woman, look around you. There is snow everywhere. Scoop some up in the biggest pan and set it at the edge of the fire to melt. Keep doing that until you have a potful," he snapped.

Disgusted, he kicked aside the log bracing the door, opened it enough to slip out and pulled it back into place from the outside.

Lauren stared at the rough plank door, her feelings a churning mix of hurt, inadequacy and anger.

How was she supposed to know how to cook on an open fire? She hadn't even mastered the electric range and microwave in her apartment yet. Until ten months ago, when she'd been released from the hospital, she'd never so much as boiled water before.

Climbing wearily to her feet, she picked up the pot and skillet and headed for the door.

The instant she stepped out into the blinding storm she sucked in her breath. In just the short time they had been inside the blizzard had hit with a vengeance. The force of the wind nearly knocked her over. It howled like a banshee and whipped the snow in frenzied swirls. Darkness was falling, and between that and the storm, visibility was no more than a few feet.

Lauren looked around, straining to peer through the blowing snow for Sam, but it was hopeless. Fear trembled through her. How would he ever find his way back to the cabin in this?

No. No, she wouldn't think about that. Sam Rawlins was resourceful. He could take care of himself. Besides, he was too hard and mean to die.

Keeping her gaze on the weak light spilling out through the grimy glass of the cabin's sole window, Lauren took two steps and scooped up snow in both pans.

She packed the snow as tight as she could until it mounded high over the rims. When done, she straightened and looked around for Sam again with no more success than the first time, then hurried back inside.

Lauren was amazed at how little water a potful of snow produced. It took several more trips outside to fill the large pot, but at least the chore kept her busy and awake. Each time she tried not to look around for Sam, but she couldn't help herself.

After the last trip, she added more wood to the fire and pushed the pot closer to the coals. While she waited for the water to boil, she picked up a packet labeled beef stew. It weighed no more than a couple of ounces, and she didn't see how the contents could possibly make a pot of stew, but she turned the packet over to see the instructions.

It was so dark and the print was so small she scooted closer to the fire and leaned back against the duffle bag to read.

That was how Sam found her fifteen minutes later, slumped back on the duffle with one of the freeze-dried packets in the hand that rested on her chest, sound asleep. Beside her at the edge of the fire, a brimful pot of water boiled over, angrily hissing and spewing.

Her lips were slightly parted and the long sweep of her lashes lay against her cheeks like fans, but they could not hide the dark circles of fatigue beneath. The dried blood smeared over her forehead and down the side of her face just emphasized her pallor.

Sam's mouth thinned. She was a whore, a mobster's plaything. She had no right to look like a weary angel.

Bending his knees, he dumped the armload of firewood. It clattered and banged on the puncheon floor, raising a cloud of dust and a racket guaranteed to wake the dead.

''Wha—!'' Lauren jackknifed to a sitting position and looked around in bleary-eyed confusion.

''You fell asleep,'' Sam accused.

She blinked twice, then panic flared in her eyes, and he could see that for a moment she didn't know who he was or how she had gotten there. She started to scuttle backward away from him, but an instant later memory returned.

She slumped and released a huff of breath, raking her fingers through her hair, which had come loose from the intricate braid she'd fashioned that morning before leaving the Denver Police Station. Even so, it took her a minute to process his words.

"I...uh...I'm sorry. I was reading the instructions and...and I guess I dozed off."

"Dammit, I warned you about that."

"For heaven's sake, I didn't do it on purpose. In the last two days I've had a total of about five hours of sleep. In that time I've witnessed a murder, fled for my life, been in a plane crash and hiked through knee-deep snow. I'm exhausted physically and emotionally. Is it any wonder I fell asleep?"

It was a halfhearted protest, at best, but Lauren just couldn't muster the energy for a more heated reply. Her eyes burned and she was so tired and woodenheaded she couldn't think. It was all she could do to simply stay awake.

Sam was not moved. "I told you before we left Denver that when I gave an order I expected it to be obeyed. Fall asleep like that again, and you may not wake up. The fire has warmed the cabin up a little but it's still freezing in here. You have to stay awake long enough to get a hot meal in you and for me to build a shrub mattress for the sleeping bag."

"I'll try."

"Don't try, do it. And for God's sake, why did you fill the pot brim full?" he demanded, as globules of water continued to hiss and pop in the flames.

Grabbing a flannel shirt from the duffle bag, Sam used it as a hot pad to pick up the pot of boiling water. He poured some into the skillet, then carefully refilled the canteen.

"I...the instructions call for three cups of water. I wasn't sure how much that was."

"I see. So you filled the pot to the top."

"I, uh...I didn't find a measuring cup in the pack."

"No, and you won't find a food processor or a blender, either. Dammit, you're supposed to approximate three cups. That pot holds four times that amount. How the hell did you expect to add in the mix without the water running over?"

"Well, I...uh..."

"Never mind. Give me the packet."

Sam cut open the tough plastic with one of the knives and dumped the contents into the boiling water. After giving the contents a stir he put the lid on and stood up. "C'mon, on your feet. If you don't move around you're going to konk out again. You can man the door while I bring in the rest of the wood and brush. I piled it up just outside." He stopped and gave her a derisive look. "You can manage that much, can't you?"

Answering with a glare, Lauren climbed to her feet and staggered over to the door.

By the time the wood and the enormous pile of spruce brush were inside and more wood was added to the fire, the stew was ready. Bob Halloran's utensil packet consisted of two deep-dish aluminum camp plates that could double as bowls, two sets of lightweight forks and spoons and one large stirring spoon. Sam pulled the pot farther from the fire and dipped up stew into each plate, then handed Lauren one without a word.

They ate without speaking or even looking at each other. To her amazement, the thick broth actually contained chunks of meat, potatoes and other vegetables and tasted quite good. Better, in fact, than anything she'd managed to put together in her own kitchen so far. Of course, she was so famished, old shoe leather would probably have tasted delicious.

They polished off the pot of stew, each eating several helpings. When they were done Sam dumped his plate and spoon into the empty pot.

"Okay, now let's take care of that cut."

Lauren's hand automatically went to her forehead. "What do you mean? I've already cleaned it."

"Yeah, well, you'd never know it by looking." He took a sterile gauze pad from the first-aid kit and dipped it in warm water and gently swabbed the wound. When he began to scrub the rest of her face Lauren tried to pull away.

"What are you doing?"

"Be still. You've got blood smeared all over your face."

"Oh." She closed her eyes and bore his ministrations stoically, but his nearness made her nerves jump. He was too close. His breath feathered over her cheek, moist and warm. The sharp, fresh scent of the outdoors clung to him and mingled with the scent of male. His hands felt rough and cold against her face.

He applied an ointment to the cut and covered it

with a bandage. "There. That's better," he said, snapping the first-aid kit shut. Lauren opened her eyes and a relieved sigh escaped her as she watched him climb to his feet and move away.

"Do you think you can manage to wash up while I make a shrub mattress?"

Annoyance rippled through Lauren at his tone, but she tilted her chin and replied with a cool, "Of course."

She had no idea how she was supposed to accomplish the task with no sink, no dishwashing soap, no scrubber and only a skillet full of warm water, but she wasn't about to admit that to this man. He was scornful enough of her as it was without giving him more ammunition.

Gamely she picked up one of the plates and started to plunge it into the skillet.

"No! Not that way!" Sam barked, making her jump. He snatched the plate out of her hand and dumped it back into the stew pot, then hefted the skillet and poured a scant amount of water over the soiled plates. "Haven't you ever gone camping before?" he demanded, his voice hard with impatience.

"No. I haven't."

"Big surprise. Look, the object is to do everything as simply and efficiently as possible. You conserve water and don't make extra work for yourself. The skillet is clean and contains a supply of clean water that we may need later. The stew pot has to be washed anyway so you scrub everything out in it. It's just simple logic," he tacked on in a tone that said even a moron ought to be able to reason that out.

"Scrub? With what, exactly, am I suppose to scrub?"

Wordlessly Sam broke a twiggy shoot about four inches long off a bare clump of brush and handed it to her. "When you get them as clean as you can, take them outside and scrub them with snow to finish the job," he ordered and turned his attention to the pile of short spruce limbs.

Only anger and mortification kept Lauren from falling asleep on her feet. She wanted to believe that Agent Rawlins knew that and was being deliberately derisive to keep her stirred up and awake. That's what she wanted to believe, but deep down, she suspected it was dislike, not thoughtfulness that had prompted his comments.

While she scrubbed the pot and plates and utensils with vigorous anger, Sam returned their supplies to the backpack, then went to work with the spruce scrub. When Lauren had finished scrubbing the dishes she picked up everything and headed for the door.

"Wait a minute. Where do you think you're going?"

She stopped and cast a disgruntled look over her shoulder as he stood up and walked toward her. "You told me to scrub these out in the snow."

"Yeah, but first you tie on the safety line." He picked up one end of the rope that he'd left coiled on the floor beside the door. One end was tied to the door handle. With deft movements, Sam tied it around Lauren's left wrist. "This is so you don't get lost out in that blow."

"I really don't think this is necessary. I'm just going to step outside the door to finish cleaning the pots."

"Yeah, well, while you're out there…" He paused, his mouth twisting in a sardonic half smile. "You might as well use the 'ladies' room' again. That means going out away from the cabin. You can follow the rope back."

He turned and went back to the pile of brush. "As soon as I finish here we'll be turning in for the night."

Since she craved sleep even more than she had food, that was the most welcome news she'd heard all day. Lauren glanced behind him at the spot a couple of feet from the fire, where he'd been busily laying out rows of overlapping spruce boughs in roughly the shape of a twin-bed mattress. "Good. I'm more than ready for that."

While Sam held open the door, she darted outside into the teeth of the storm. The cold slapped her in the face like a giant icy hand and the wind almost knocked her down. Lauren put her head down and quickly went to work.

When she returned Sam was working on the last row of branches. Lauren had taken the time to pack the pot and plates high with snow. The last thing she wanted was to have to brave that storm for more snow again tonight.

Sam glanced up as she pushed the door open a crack and squeezed inside, carrying the pot and plates stacked one on top of the other and balanced against the front of her body, but he made no comment. She bumped the door back into place with her bottom, edged across the room as though she were walking a tightrope and placed the three containers close to the fire. She turned to find Sam spreading the silvery sheet over the mattress of spruce branches. When he lay the sleeping bag on top of that, she frowned.

"What are you doing?"

"What does it look like? I'm getting the bed ready."

"But you've put the sleeping bag on top of the mattress. Where are you going to sleep?"

Sam straightened and looked at her. "In the sleeping bag. The same as you."

"*Wha-aat?* You're out of your mind if you think I'm going to sleep with you."

"You don't have a choice. Neither of us does. We have one wool blanket, one space blanket and one sleeping bag between us and a fire that's barely putting out enough heat for us to survive. Hell, you could hang meat over in the corner right now and it would freeze solid in a few minutes."

"That may be, but—"

"Listen, why don't you just drop the virtuous maiden act, okay? Given who and what you are, it's a little ludicrous, don't you think?"

"What's that supposed to mean?" she demanded

huffily. Surely he couldn't know about her and Collin? There hadn't been enough time for him to dig that deep into her past relationships. Or relationship, she should say, since Collin had been her one and only lover.

Sam ignored the question. "Trust me, it isn't necessary. Lady, you could strip naked and beg and I still wouldn't be interested in you that way."

Lauren stared at him, quivering with so many conflicting emotions she was speechless. Anger, resentment and insult were uppermost, but at the same time she experienced a wave of relief so great her knees almost buckled.

She was trapped on this mountain in a raging blizzard for God knew how long, alone with a harsh, tough-as-nails man whom she barely knew. She was totally at his mercy, because without him she would surely die. If he were to turn sexually aggressive she could not possibly fend him off. They both knew that.

Under the circumstances, she knew she ought to be happy that he apparently found her repulsive.

And she was. Of course she was.

Still...he didn't have to be so blunt about it. She'd never thought of herself as the type to drive men mad with lust, but until now no one had ever treated her as though she were a troll. It was insulting.

"So don't just stand there looking like an offended virgin," Sam growled. "I'm tired, and I want to get some shut-eye, so get a move on. Take off your boots and crawl in."

Knowing he was right and that she was apparently safe from any sort of sexual advances did not make the arrangement any more acceptable, but Lauren was simply too exhausted to argue. She was ready to drop. If it meant getting some sleep, at that moment she would have cuddled up with Freddy Krueger.

Refusing to look at Sam, she unlaced her boots, tugged them off and slipped into the sleeping bag. She scooted over as far as she could, shifted a bit to find a comfortable position and with a sigh, closed her eyes. By the second breath, sleep had pulled her under.

Sam stared down at her. She lay curled on her side, facing the fire, her cheek cradled on her stacked hands, her face slack in utter surrender to her body's demand for rest.

The flames cast shifting patterns over her elegant features, throwing some into deep shadows and highlighting others with a golden glow, but even that could not disguise her exhausted pallor. The bandage on her forehead stood out in sharp contrast to her skin.

Her lashes lay against her cheeks like thick fans and loose tendrils of auburn hair curled around her face. Her luscious lips, bare of any trace of lipstick, were slightly parted. Between them he could see the edge of her teeth and the tip of her pink tongue. She looked utterly innocent and vulnerable.

Sam's mouth twisted. Which just proved that old saying that looks were deceiving, he thought and headed for the door.

A few minutes later he returned from answering nature's call one last time and found that Lauren had still not moved so much as a muscle. Her breathing was so slow and shallow he could barely make out the steady rise and fall of her chest.

Stepping around her, Sam hunkered down in front of the fire and stoked it with more wood. When the blaze was burning bright he unlaced his knee-high, fur-lined moccasins and tugged them off, then pulled out the felt liners that provided extra insulation and set them before the fire to dry out thoroughly.

To take full advantage of the meager warmth, he had placed the sleeping bag in front of the hearth and the supply of wood, close enough to both that he could reach over Lauren and toss more branches onto the fire throughout the night without leaving the bed. She might not appreciate that convenience, but he sure as hell did.

He skirted back around her, slipped into the sleeping bag from the other side and zipped it up. Turning onto his side, facing the fire and Lauren's back, Sam looped his arm around her waist and settled his body to hers, tucking his knees against the backs of hers and pulling her into the curve of his torso. Small and slender, she fit perfectly, her head tucked beneath his chin, her rump snug against his manhood, her body flush against his all the way from the top of her head down to her sock feet resting against his shins.

Sam shifted his head as a silky tendril of hair tickled his nose. With every breath its clean smell invaded his nostrils, a mix of subtle floral shampoo and sweet, clean woman.

Gradually her body heat began to reach him, seeping through the layers of clothing they both wore. Even through all that bulk, her womanly curves were apparent, and to his annoyance his body responded in the way any healthy heterosexual man's would.

Sam ground his teeth. Never mind that she wasn't one of Carlo's usual silicone-enhanced bimbos, she was still most likely the mobster's latest lay, and he had no business getting hot and bothered over her.

The lecture didn't help. Not one bit.

Not that Lauren seemed to mind. She was sleeping so soundly she didn't so much as twitch.

Sam gave a small, ironic snort. Hell, if anything, he should have been the one to complain about the sleeping arrangement, not her. God knew, if he'd had any other choice he would have taken it. Despite his body's mindless hormonal response, he didn't crave to be anywhere near this woman. As far as he was concerned, she was a job. Nothing more.

Though he was nowhere near as sleep-deprived as Lauren, it had been nineteen or twenty hours since Harvey Weiss had rousted him out of bed in the wee hours of the morning. Still, he could not sleep. Lying perfectly still, Sam stared at the fire, his mind worrying over their predicament.

He had to get her off this mountain alive and into a safe house, and he had to do it quickly. It wasn't going to be easy, particularly not with a pampered female with no outdoor skills. Or any practical skills at all, for that matter. Except maybe in the bedroom.

For the moment, they were safe—from the elements and from Giovessi's men. Lauren knew that, as well. Which was why she had relaxed so completely and succumbed to her body's demand for sleep.

However, what she didn't know, what he hadn't told her was, once the storm cleared that could change, and change rapidly.

She assumed the engine trouble that had caused their plane to crash had merely been an unfortunate twist of fate, and he hadn't bothered to tell her otherwise. But he didn't think so.

Bob had been a fanatic about safety checks and maintenance, and he had kept his aircraft in tip-top condition at all times. Both engines blowing within minutes of each other, almost an hour into the flight when they were over the most rugged mountain range in the state, was no accident.

And if someone had gotten close enough to sabotage the plane, they would have also planted a tracking device. It was a dead certainty that as soon as weather permitted, someone would come looking for the wreckage to confirm their deaths.

He had no intention of telling Lauren what he suspected, however. That knowledge would merely add to her anxiety and serve no useful purpose. For now, at any rate, what she didn't know, wouldn't hurt her.

Unconsciously Sam rubbed his chin back and forth

against the top of Lauren's head. Catching in his beard stubble, the clean strands of her hair slid back and forth against her scalp like slippery silk. As soon as the storm cleared he had to hike back to the plane and find and destroy that bug before Giovessi's men could locate the crash site. If he didn't beat them to it, when they found only two charred bodies in the wreckage they would know that he and Lauren had survived.

And they would come after them.

Seven

The next morning, as always, Sam awoke before dawn. Before he opened his eyes he became aware of a weight pressing on his chest. Sam frowned. Had the roof caved in and crushed them while they slept, pinning them to the floor?

Not daring to move in case he was badly injured, he cracked one eye open a slit—and sucked in a sharp breath.

He lay on his back and, with the total abandon of a child, Lauren lay sprawled on top of him, sound asleep.

With her cheek snuggled over his heart, her head rested on his shoulder and her hair spread out all around them. One of her arms curved around his opposite shoulder and the other lay limp against his side. Crooked at the knee, her left leg hooked around his right hip. The other nestled intimately between his.

And he had the granddaddy of all morning erections.

"Jesus."

Anger, disgust and unwanted desire twisted inside Sam. He tried to will away the arousal, but given the woman's provocative position, he knew that wasn't going to happen. "So be it," he snarled. "You play sex kitten, and you can't complain about the results."

Deep inside Sam knew that Lauren hadn't snuggled on top of him intentionally. She was exhausted and still sleeping like a log and wasn't aware of her actions. Either way, though, the result was the same, and he refused to feel guilty for his uncharitable thoughts.

Removing her arm from around his shoulder, he gave it a shake.

"Hey! Wake up!"

He could have been talking to the wall, for all the response he got. Spitting out a curse, he rolled onto his side and dumped her onto her back. Lauren sighed, curled into a new position and went right on sleeping.

Sam unzipped the bag, rolled out and sprang to his feet. He stared down at the sleeping woman with dislike, then swung away and stalked to the backpack, hunkering down to rummage through the contents.

Briefly he considered whipping up some scrambled eggs from the powdered mix, but another glance at Lauren changed his mind. He gathered the supplies he needed, then threw a couple more branches on the fire. When he had the blaze going again he shot another look at Lauren. She slept on with the innocence of a baby.

Jaw clenched, Sam stomped toward the door. Dammit! He had to get out of there. Now.

* * *

An hour later the fire had burned down to ashy embers and Lauren woke in a freezing cabin. Sitting up, she yawned and cast a sleepy look around, but there was no sign of Sam. She stretched hugely then brushed the tumbled hair off her face and glanced at her wristwatch. Her eyes widened.

Good Lord. She'd been sleeping for thirteen hours.

Lauren climbed out of the sleeping bag and pulled on her boots. She poked the embers with the iron rod the way she'd seen Sam do the night before, praying that she could stir the fire to life, because she hadn't the slightest idea of how to go about starting one from scratch.

A small flame leaped up, and Lauren quickly tossed a small branch on top of the glowing embers. The dead wood caught fire at once, and she exhaled a relieved sigh. She piled on more branches and twigs and in no time had a roaring blaze going. Feeling immensely proud of herself, Lauren pawed through her purse and pulled out a packet of tissue and a small bottle of antibacterial gel, stuffed both into her coat pocket and headed for the door. Tying the guide rope through a zipper ring on her parka, she wondered where Sam was, and immediately the same fears she'd experienced the night before fluttered through her. If something had happened to him—

No. No, she would not let herself worry about that. Sam could take care of himself. Hadn't he assured her of that? He was probably out doing some outdoorsman thing necessary to their survival. He would be back soon.

The temperature in the cabin had seemed cold, but it was nothing compared to the frigid conditions that met her when she stepped outside. The first slap of icy wind made Lauren catch her breath. Snow fell in a heavy curtain that made visibility impossible beyond eight or ten feet, and it showed no signs of letting up. On the flat the drifts came to above Lauren's knees. She plowed through powdery stuff as far as the rope would allow, looked around, and slipped behind the dubious protection of a tree to answer nature's urgent call.

When done she washed her hands as best she could in the snow then rubbed them with a dab of antibacterial gel and followed the rope back to the cabin.

The snow she had gathered the previous night had melted, but it didn't amount to much. She poured it all into the skillet, then took the pot outside and packed it full of snow.

She made several more trips, and by the time she had a pot full of simmering water her stomach was growling, and Sam still had not returned. Determined to fend for herself, Lauren picked up a packet of powdered eggs and read the instructions.

A short while later, she pulled the skillet from the fire and grimaced at the runny yellow glob in the bottom. Surely this wasn't right?

Screwing up her courage, she scooped up a spoonful, put it into her mouth and began to chew, tentatively at first, then with more gusto. It wasn't half bad. Either that, or she was so hungry her taste buds didn't care.

After eating a small portion of the funny looking eggs and a strip of jerky, she placed what remained next to the fire to keep them warm for Sam.

She tried to wait patiently for Sam to return, but she couldn't resist peeking at her wristwatch every few minutes. She scoured the plate she'd used and went back outside and gathered more snow. She read the directions on the backs of all the food packs, filed a fingernail she'd broken, neatened the sleeping bag and other supplies. She told herself over and over not to worry, but as the minutes ticked by her agitation grew, and by the time Sam finally returned she was a wreck and pacing the small cabin like a caged lioness. The instant he shifted the door open and stepped inside she whirled on him and demanded, "Where have you been?"

Sam paused in the act of shifting the door back in place and shot her a stony look. "Out setting snares." He looked her over, his dark eyes narrowing as he took in her fear and agitation. "Why? What's wrong?"

"Nothing. Everything," she snapped, twisting her hands together. "I didn't know where you were! You could have told me you were leaving the cabin and when I could expect you back."

Sam put the door in place and braced it with the chunk of wood. "You were sleeping like a baby when

I left. Anyway, I told you last night that I was going to set snares this morning.'' He shrugged and took off his gloves and stuffed them into the outside pockets of his parka, and with casual unconcern, walked over to the hearth and stood with his hands outstretched to the fire.

"But it's still storming out there! You were gone so long I thought something had happened to you."

He gave her a piercing look. "I see. Your concern wasn't for my safety so much as your own. You were worried about what would happen to you if I'd gotten myself badly injured or killed."

Anger and embarrassment brought a flush to her cheeks. Put that way, he made her feel small and selfish, which she was certain he had intended.

However, after a good night's rest Lauren was sufficiently recovered from the traumatic events of the previous day to have regained at least a portion of her spirit.

Ignoring the heat in her cheeks, she lifted her chin and glared at him. "That's not true. I would have felt terrible for you if that had happened. Just as I felt terrible for your friends. I feel sad for anyone who loses their life. But I will not let you make me feel guilty." The longer she talked the angrier she became. With every word her voice grew harsher and more clipped, in direct proportion to her building ire.

"Where the devil do you get off, criticizing me, anyway? I didn't ask to be here, you know. It wasn't my choice to witness a murder, or my decision to fly over the Rocky Mountains in the dead of winter in an unsafe small plane. Nor did I make it crash.

"Neither, I might add, did I ask to have my world turned upside down again and the life I've managed to build for myself snatched away from me. And I certainly don't want to freeze to death alone in this godforsaken wilderness! If that makes me selfish, so be it."

"I didn't say that."

"You didn't have to. Damn you, I have a right to be concerned for my own safety. You would be, too, if you were in my shoes. I have no survival skills. No knowledge of the area. I don't know how to cook or find food. I don't even know how to build a fire, for heaven's sake. If I had to strike out on my own I wouldn't have any idea which direction to take."

By the time she finished she was shouting. On some level Lauren knew that at least part of her anger was a delayed reaction to all that had happened to her during the last thirty-six hours, but she didn't care. One of the things she'd learned since the car accident that took away her concert career was to stand up for herself. And she'd had about all of Agent Rawlins's rudeness she intended to take.

Lauren had worked up a full head of steam and was braced for a battle, was half hoping for one, but her outburst seemed to have no effect on Sam. His expression remained closed. He didn't so much as blink.

"Yeah, well, don't worry about it. I'm not going

to get hurt." As though he'd grown bored with the conversation, he turned away, took two good-size branches from the dwindling pile of wood and tossed them into the fire, then poked the blaze into renewed life with the metal rod.

Lauren stared at him. "You can't be certain of that."

"As certain as it's possible to be." He put down the rod and turned to her again. This time his face wore a look of mild impatience. "Look, I was born out here. Since I was a kid I've gone hunting and fishing in these mountains, camped out for weeks at a time with my dad and with my mother's people. I know this area and I know how to survive in the wilderness. Let me worry about getting us out of here, okay? You just do as I tell you."

The last made Lauren grind her teeth. Arrogant bastard, she thought. As if she had a choice. Anyway, what did he think she'd *been* doing?

"Fine," she snapped. She plopped down onto the sleeping bag, dragged her purse near and dug around inside. "Oh, by the way," she ground out. "If you're hungry, I made eggs. The leftovers are in the skillet by the fire."

Sam glanced down at the yellow mess in the skillet, then back at her. "*You* cooked?"

"Yes, I cooked," she replied in an offended tone. Then she, too, glanced at the mess and grimaced. "At least I tried. I don't know what went wrong. I followed the instructions exactly."

Picking up the skillet, Sam examined the pale yellow goop without a word.

"They taste better than they look. Honestly."

He flicked her a look that clearly said they would have to and picked up the fork.

Sam ate the runny glob without comment, along with the strips of jerky she'd left in the pan. Lauren watched him, but it was impossible to tell by his expression what he thought of her efforts. When done, he poured a small amount of water into the pan. "Next time, don't use quite so much water," he commented, as he scoured the pan with the twig bundle.

Lauren glared at his back. She'd already figured that out for herself. Did he think she was stupid? "Thank you. I'll remember that," she replied, fuming. She hadn't expected any thanks from him, or praise for trying, but would it have killed him to be pleasant?

Ignoring her, Sam rummaged through the pile of brush. He tested several slender limbs for strength and pliability and tossed the most limber into a pile at the end of the hearth, as far away from where she sat as he could get and still benefit from the fire's warmth.

Lauren's mouth tightened. Who knew? With a hard-nosed male like this one perhaps it would have killed him to be polite, after all. The previous morning he had walked into the interrogation room at the Denver Police Station looking as though his face had been chiseled from granite, and it had yet to soften.

With quick, angry movements, Lauren pulled a

tube of hand lotion out of her purse and slathered the moisturizer on her face and hands. Casting Sam resentful looks out of the corner of her eye, she saw him cut two slender limbs down to about three and a half foot length and remove the small branches and twigs. He then placed the stripped stems side by side and bound their ends together, wrapping them securely with a length of nylon cord. When done, he cut another stick into two shorter pieces, about eight or ten inches each, and began to carve shallow notches in each end of both.

Lauren wondered what he was doing, but since he obviously intended to ignore her, she decided to return the favor.

After leaving the hospital, she had continued her physical therapy at a health club close to her apartment, and before long, experiencing the benefits of regular exercise, it had been a natural next step to expand her therapy into a full-blown regular workout regime. As with everything Lauren undertook, she applied herself to the fitness routine with the same determination and all-out dedication that she had to her music. Her entire life had been about focus and applying herself, and the workouts quickly became a routine part of her life.

Turning her back on Sam, Lauren spread her legs in a wide V and began her warmup stretching exercises. She touched the toes of each foot with the opposite hand, twisted from the waist as far as possible, bent to the sides and rotated her head, shoulders and arms. She climbed to her feet and bent and touched the floor thirty times, then, grabbing an ankle, she pulled her heel up behind her to touch her bottom, repeated the action a dozen times, then switched and did a dozen more with the other foot.

"Jesus! Can't you be still a minute? What the hell are you doing, anyway?" Sam demanded when she began to jog in place.

"Isn't it...obvious? I'm exercising. I...work out at a gym...three times...a week," she gasped between breaths. "To stay in shape...it's important to keep...to a regular routine."

Sam snorted. "I wouldn't worry if I were you. You probably got more exercise yesterday than you do in a month at your yuppie health club."

Lauren ignored the snide comment and kept on jogging. Let him poke fun. If they were going to hike down this mountain in knee-deep snow, she wanted to be as fit as possible. If the trek was anything like what they had done the day before, she was going to need every ounce of strength and stamina she could muster.

For an hour Lauren jogged in place and back and forth across the derelict cabin. Outside the grimy window the world had been reduced to a blinding white swirl of snow. The wind whistled in through the gaps in the chinking, bringing with it stray flakes, and now and then more found their way through the evergreen boughs that Sam had thrown over the hole in the roof. Except directly in front of the fire, the air in the cabin was cold enough to vaporize their breaths, but by the time Lauren stopped exercising and sat down on the sleeping bag again she no longer felt the chill.

She had intended to give Sam the same cold-shoulder treatment he was giving her, but the longer she watched him the more curious she became. While she had exercised he had somehow managed to pry the two long bound sticks apart in the middle and lashed one of the short sticks at right angles between them, about ten inches from one end to hold them open. Now he was doing the same thing with the other short piece at the opposite end. The longer Lauren watched the more intrigued she became, until finally she could no longer contain her curiosity.

"What are you doing?"

He spared her the briefest of glances and went right on working the twine over and around the joined sticks in an X pattern.

"I'm making snowshoes. We're going to walk out of here when this storm passes. With all that fresh powder out there, we're going to need these."

"Really? I've never walked in snowshoes before."

"Figures."

The sneer in his voice was too much. Ever since they'd met, his manner toward her had been harsh and distant, even downright hostile. For the most part, up until now, she had tread softly around him—partly because she thought it wise not to annoy the man who was essentially her bodyguard, but also because he made her uneasy. Something about this hard, remote man put her on edge.

However, if Lauren's experience with Carlo Giovessi had taught her nothing else, she had at least learned that ignoring a difficult truth or pretending it didn't exist just didn't work. From now on she intended to face her problems head-on...and Sam Rawlins's attitude was a problem.

Lauren cocked her head and gazed at him across the few feet that separated them. By now he had lashed both short sticks between the longer one, forcing them apart into an elongated oval with points at each end. Now he was weaving heavy nylon twine in an open, diamond-shaped pattern, overall.

"You don't like me very much, do you, Agent Rawlins?"

"No."

A startled chuckle bubbled from Lauren's throat. "Well. That was certainly direct and to the point."

She had expected denial, or at the very least, subtle evasion. Something like—"What makes you think that?" or "You're imagining things," or "I don't know you well enough to like or dislike you?"—Not a blunt confirmation.

Although...given her experience with Sam Rawlins so far, she supposed she should have been prepared for brutal honesty. Diplomacy and polite white lies were not this man's style.

"Would you mind telling me why? I mean, you barely know me, and I don't think I've done anything to you to cause such animosity. What, exactly, is it about me that you find so objectionable?"

"Does it matter? My job is to keep you alive so you can testify against Giovessi in court, not to be your friend."

"I understand that. However, since we're going to be spending a lot of time together, a little civility would be nice. But unless I know what it is about me that irritates you so much, how can I correct the problem?"

"You can't. The problem is, I don't have any respect for women who sell themselves to rich old men. Especially mobsters."

"Pardon?" Lauren shook her head, sure she'd heard him wrong. "What did you say?"

"You're Carlo Giovessi's mistress. In my book, that's the same as a hooker."

"Whaaat!"

"Oh, spare me the innocent denials, okay?"

"No, it is *not* okay! Because I most certainly am *not* Mr. Giovessi's mistress! I don't know where you got that idea, but you're wrong!"

"I don't think so."

"Look, I admit he helped me get on my feet after I left the hospital. He located an apartment for me and an affordable car, recommended me for the job at the university. Then a few months ago he offered me the job at the club. But those were just friendly acts of kindness. Being a music lover, he has a lot of admiration and respect for musicians, and he felt the accident that ended my career was a tragedy, so he did what he could to help. I explained all that at the police station. But Mr. Giovessi doesn't support me, and he most certainly is *not* my lover!''

''Sorry, but that righteous outrage just won't wash. All the evidence says otherwise.''

''Evidence? *What* evidence? Just because I worked at his club two nights a week that doesn't make me his mistress.''

''How about the fact that Carlo visited you at your apartment every Wednesday night?''

Surprise shot through Lauren. ''How…how do you know that?''

''Or that the two of you were alone together after hours at the club every Friday and Saturday night?'' he pressed, ignoring her question.

''I explained that at the police station, too. I play the piano for him those nights. That's also why he came by my apartment every Wednesday evening. Oh, I don't believe this!'' Lauren closed her eyes and pressed the heels of her hands to her temples. ''I just don't believe this!''

Too agitated to sit, she jumped to her feet again and began to pace. ''For two years I've struggled to become independent and learn how to stand on my own two feet, and now you're accusing me of being a…a *kept woman!* All because I gave a nice old man—or at least, someone I thought was a nice old man—a few hours of pleasure each week!''

''Yeah, I'll bet you did.''

"Not *that* kind of pleasure," Lauren snapped, shooting him a blistering glare. "I played the *piano* for him. That's *all!*"

"Yeah, right. And I'm supposed to believe that he doesn't support your upscale lifestyle?"

"My what? What upscale lifestyle? I work two jobs to support myself, and even at that I'm barely getting by."

"Uh-huh. What about that apartment of yours?"

Lauren gave him a blank look. "What about it?"

"The building belongs to Giovessi."

"What? I...I didn't know that." Stunned, Lauren stared into Sam's dark face, an uneasy feeling creeping up the back of her neck. She shook it off and tilted her chin. "But so what if he does? If you're thinking that I live there free, you're wrong. I pay the rent on that apartment, not Mr. Giovessi."

"Sure you do. It's just a coincidence that he always installs his mistress of the moment in the very same apartment that you're currently living in."

"I..." The statement caught her by surprise and sent a flash of disquiet through her, but she quickly tamped it down. "Yes. Yes, of course. It has to be. It's the only explanation."

"How much?"

"Pardon?"

"You heard me. How much rent do you pay?"

"None of your b—"

"How much?"

Lauren's mouth thinned, but she could see that he

wasn't going to give up until she told him. "If you must know, three hundred dollars a month. Not that it's any of your business."

"Three hundred!" Sam snorted. "Lady, the cheapest apartment in that building goes for ten times that amount."

"Ten..." The uneasy feeling threatened to turn into full-blown nausea, but Lauren shook her head. "No. You must be mistaken."

"C'mon, lady, Estes Arms is a luxury high-rise. One of the most prestigious addresses in Denver. There's a waiting list to get in there. You can't be naive enough to believe you could rent a place like that for a measly three hundred a month? You had to know that Carlo was subsidizing you. The only thing that surprises me is that he allowed you to pay any rent at all."

"Oh, dear Lord. I...I had no idea." Dazed and sick, Lauren sank back down onto the sleeping bag. "He told me the apartment was in a rent-controlled building. That was why it was such a bargain."

"Nice try, but we don't have rent-control in Denver."

"I...I didn't know that." Lauren shook her head and stared across the cabin, seeing nothing, feeling as though she'd been hit in the stomach with a battering ram.

"Right. And how do you explain that snappy little car you drive?"

"Mr. Giovessi found me a bargain—" The look

on Sam's face stopped Lauren in midsentence, and the sick feeling in the pit of her stomach intensified. "Are you saying...?"

"It's a luxury car, lady." He told her what the vehicle cost new, and Lauren moaned and covered her face with both hands.

"What an idiot I've been," she muttered against her palms. "What a total idiot. No wonder you thought... Oh, God."

Eight

Sam watched Lauren fall over onto her side on top of the sleeping bag and curl into the fetal position. She lay staring into the fire, the picture of despondent misery.

Unimpressed, he shook his head and went back to weaving fill-line across the snowshoe frame. If she hoped to gain his sympathy with that pitiful act, she was wasting her time.

For the next hour or so neither Sam nor Lauren spoke a word. He worked steadily the whole time. The only time Lauren moved was to turn back the top of the sleeping bag and burrow inside. Otherwise she lay motionless. If she hadn't blinked now and then he would have worried that she was dead.

By midday Sam had completed two snowshoes and had made a good start on a third when hunger forced him to take a break.

He rose and stepped around Lauren and built up the fire, then prepared a meal from one of the dehydrated packets. While he moved around the cabin, Lauren remained motionless and mute, her gaze still fixed on the flames.

Sam did his best to ignore her, but finally his patience came to an end. Hunkered down in front of the fire, he glanced over his shoulder at her, and his mouth thinned. "For God's sake, are you going to lie there all day moping?" he snapped.

"Maybe. What do you care?"

"I don't. But it's time to eat."

"I'm not hungry."

"Too bad, you're going to eat anyway. It's important to keep your strength up."

She looked as though she might argue, but after a pause she sighed and tossed off the cover and sat up, pushing the heavy fall of hair away from her face.

Sam dished up the meal and handed her one of the aluminum plates.

"I don't know what you're upset about. You have no one but yourself to blame. You made the decision to get involved with Giovessi of your own free will."

That earned him a quick, dagger look, but she continued eating and did not speak.

"C'mon. Did you think no one would ever know you were his mistress just because you worked at the club? Trust me, that job is transparent cover. Carlo always puts his women on the payroll."

"I told you— Oh, what's the use? Talking to you is pointless." She clamped her mouth shut and looked away, treating him to a flawless profile.

The frosty dignity in her tone almost made him smile. She sat there, cross-legged on the floor of this hovel, bundled up in long johns and shapeless, bulky winter garb, not a speck of makeup on and her mussed hair tumbling around her shoulders, eating camp food out of an aluminum plate...and still she managed to look and sound as regal as a queen.

Which just proved how deceiving outward appearances could be.

"Look, you're obviously uncomfortable that your secret is out, but what do you care what I think anyway?"

"Believe me, I don't."

"Then what the hell is your problem?"

She slanted him a pithy look. "Why should I tell you? You wouldn't believe me. You've already made up your mind about me."

"So convince me I'm wrong."

Lauren huffed and rolled her eyes. "Oh, right. I'm sure *that's* going to happen."

She went back to eating, and so did Sam. When they were finished, she picked up her plate and his and carried them to the hearth, where she poured hot water into the skillet and started scouring the pan and dirty dishes.

Sam watched her, a bit surprised that she had pitched in on her own without any prompting from him. He hadn't expected that, and it piqued his curiosity even more. "So, are you going to tell me why you're feeling sorry for yourself?" he said to her back.

She looked at him over her shoulder. "I'm not indulging in self-pity. If you must know, I'm furious with myself." Sparingly, she poured fresh hot water over the plates and spoons to rinse them, then set them aside. Picking up the skillet, she headed for the door. "Excuse me," she said, stepping around him. "I have to rinse this pan outside."

"Leave it. I'll do it later. Finish what you were saying. Why are you angry with yourself?"

Lauren sighed, but she set the skillet back on the hearth and resumed her seat on the sleeping bag. "Are you sure you want to hear this? For you to understand, I have to go back a ways."

Sam glanced out the window at the swirling snow beyond the grimy panes and picked up the snowshoe he was making. "We've got plenty of time. Shoot."

She plucked at the knee of her wool sweatpants, keeping her gaze on her restless fingers. "As I told you before, I was a child prodigy. My entire life was devoted to music. When I wasn't on stage, I was practicing."

"Because your father insisted," Sam tossed in. He didn't bother to hide the disbelief in his tone, which earned him another of her glacial looks.

"Yes. That's right. Although...that was never an issue between us. I loved playing and enjoyed practice. I still do, even though now..." She shook her head. "Never mind. The point is my father took care of everything else so that I could devote my life to my music. And by that, I mean everything. He paid all our bills, booked concerts, made all the arrangements and saw to all the mundane, everyday details of life, both when we traveled and during the infrequent periods when we were home.''

"And where was home?"

"An apartment in New York."

"What about your mother? Did she travel with you?"

"My mother died when I was born."

"Sorry."

"That's all right. You didn't know. Anyway, three years ago, when my father died of a coronary, I was shattered. That's when his assistant stepped in and took over his duties, and like my father, he saw to everything, too."

"That would be Collin Williams, right?"

She darted him a wary look, then stared down at her plucking fingers once again. "Yes."

"He was more than just your manager, wasn't he?"

Lauren's head snapped up. "What makes you say that?"

"You get a funny look on your face whenever his name comes up."

She lowered her gaze once more, but not before Sam saw the flicker of pain in her eyes. He waited, watching her, but she remained silent so long he decided to prod some more. "So, am I right? Were you and Collin lovers?"

"He was my fiancé," she replied in a voice barely above a whisper. "He proposed right after my father died. The car accident happened just three weeks before our wedding was to have taken place.''

"I gotta tell you, lady, if this is supposed to convince me you weren't involved with Giovessi, it isn't working. Seems to me you have a history of going from one male protector to another.''

Her head snapped up again. "I've done no such thing! That had nothing to do with it. I was in love with Collin! And he lo— That is…I thought he loved me, too.''

"So what happened? Surely he didn't break off the engagement just because your career was cut short?''

"Actually…yes. He did. I guess I was no longer an asset. Certainly I could no longer provide him with the life he wanted.''

"Which was?''

"Traveling the world, being a part of the music scene, basking in the reflected glory of a wife who was a rising star. You see, Collin enjoyed rubbing elbows with music patrons—the rich and famous and the society types who attend classical concerts.

"After concerts there were parties in my honor and we were wined and dined at the homes of some of the world's wealthiest families, or even invited to stay at their villas or on their yachts during periods between concerts. It was a heady lifestyle.''

She looked back at the fire. "And Collin didn't exactly break off our engagement. He just…left.'' Lauren shrugged. The gesture, meant to convey indifference, revealed a world of hurt instead. "And he took all my money with him. All but a thousand dollars, anyway. I guess his conscience wouldn't let him abandon me in a strange town completely broke.''

''He just cleaned you out and took off? While you were still in the hospital?''

Lauren nodded, and plucked harder at the knee of her sweats.

''Did you file charges against him?''

She shook her head. ''No. I told you, he paid all the bills and took care of everything for me. He had full power of attorney. There was nothing I could do.''

''That would make the case more difficult to prosecute, that's certain, but you could still have filed charges and had him picked up. Maybe even recovered some of your money. How much did he take?''

''That's just it. I have no idea.'' She grimaced. ''I feel like an idiot, admitting this, but up until the accident, I'd never paid any attention to the financial side of my career. I had never had to. First my father, then Collin took care of that. The money was just…there. If I needed or wanted something I had a credit card. Or I would simply tell Dad, or later, Collin, and he would get whatever it was I wanted.

''Then suddenly I found myself alone and practically penniless, in the hospital in a strange town, my career over. There was no one I could turn to. I had no relatives. There were tons of acquaintances all over the world, but we'd never stayed in one town long enough to develop any close friendships. Not only was I heartbroken, I was scared.''

I'll bet, Sam thought. On your own for the first time in your life. Must have been a terrifying prospect for a woman who'd been sheltered and pampered from the day she was born.

Provided she was telling the truth.

Lauren looked up, her green eyes awash with emotion, silently pleading with him to understand. ''I didn't know what to do or even where to start. I'd never had a job other than giving concerts. I'd never paid a bill or even written a check in my entire life. Cooking, cleaning, operating a washing machine, buying groceries—the kinds of things that most people learn as they're growing up—were a mystery to me. That's why, when Mr. Giovessi offered to help me get back on my feet, I accepted gladly.

''I made it clear that I wouldn't take money from him, and he seemed to respect that, but I didn't see anything wrong with accepting his help in other ways.'' She shook her head. ''What a naive fool I've been.

''Before I even left the hospital he'd gotten me the job at the college and found me a car and a place to live. Since I'd never rented an apartment or purchased a car before, the car payments and rent he quoted sounded reasonable. It didn't occur to me that he was absorbing most of the costs.

''Once I got over the initial shock and hurt of the accident and Collin's desertion, I vowed that I would never again allow myself to be dependent on anyone for anything or allow anyone else to run my life for me. I'd gotten a late start, but I'm an intelligent woman and I knew that I could learn whatever skills and knowledge I needed. It would just take time.''

Lauren huffed out a long breath. ''To think, I'd been congratulating myself lately for all that I've accomplished. I actually believed I'd become an independent woman. Now I find out that Mr. Giovessi has been subsidizing me all along.''

She shot Sam a resentful glare from beneath her lashes. ''If that isn't bad enough, now I'm totally dependent on you for everything, including keeping me alive. Is it any wonder I'm angry with myself?''

''If it's any help, I'm no happier about this arrangement than you are,'' Sam replied.

''Really? My, my, I never would have guessed.''

Ignoring her frosty sarcasm, Sam stared at her, searching her face for the slightest flicker of deceit or guile, but he found none. She merely sat there, glaring back at him, her expression a combination of mulish innocence and offended dignity.

Damn. Either she was telling the truth or she was one of the most accomplished liars he'd ever encountered. During his years with the Bureau he'd met plenty of the latter and damned few of the former, which made him skeptical of her babe-in-the-woods claim.

Lauren began to squirm under his piercing stare. ''You still don't believe me, do you?'' she blurted out finally.

Sam took his time replying.

"Let's just say I'm reserving judgment." He picked up the snowshoe and went back to work.

Lauren's mouth tightened. "Thanks so much for your understanding." She bounded to her feet, snatched up the skillet again and headed for the door. "I knew talking to you was a waste of time."

"Don't forget the safety line," Sam cautioned. He didn't bother to look up, but out of the corner of his eye he saw her spin around and glare. She stood so rigid she was shaking, and he knew she was considering heaving the skillet at his head.

"I wouldn't if I were you," he warned in a quiet voice.

Lauren stayed outside longer than necessary. Sam figured she was still fuming and was dawdling to spite him. Either that, or she'd taken time to "visit the ladies' room," as she so delicately put it.

One corner of his mouth quirked. Whatever else she was, the woman was no classless bimbo. Even under these primitive conditions she had the elegance and impeccable manners of a well-bred eighteenth-century lady. That she had even contemplated bashing a skillet over his head was downright comical.

The hint of a smile disappeared from Sam's face. Carlo had an old-world attitude about women. In his mind, they were either saints or sinners. Lauren was exactly the type that he might admire and put on a pedestal. Especially if her claim of being a musical genius was true. The mobster was fanatical about classical music.

But when it came to having an ornament on his arm or doing the horizontal mambo, old Carlo went for flash every time.

Sam scowled, not liking the direction his thoughts were taking him. He wasn't sure he believed any of her story. She could have made the whole thing up just to save face. Yet her bearing, the way she talked, those exquisite manners—everything about her— screamed class and privilege. Maybe she was just some spoiled high society debutante who had re- belled, and now she didn't want her family to find out that she'd sunk so low.

The theory was a stretch and it didn't quite set comfortably, but Sam ignored the pricks of doubt and continued his work. After a moment he glanced at the door again, then pushed back the knitted inner cuff of his parka and checked his wristwatch. Where was she? Dammit, she'd had more than enough time. Was she just standing around out there in a snit, freezing her ass off just to get back at him?

He'd give her thirty seconds. If she wasn't back by then he'd go find her. Hell, it wouldn't surprise him if the fool woman hadn't gotten the guide rope tan- gled in the underbrush and tied herself up.

He started to climb to his feet but sank back down when Lauren shifted the door from the outside and squeezed in through the gap. Snow clung to her from head to toe, making her look like a ghostly aberration. The flakes mounded on her shoulders and the top of her hood, and ice crystals clung to the fur ruff around her face and on her pants up to her knees. A layer of compressed snow and ice made the soles of her boots three inches thicker.

Lauren replaced the door and braced it with the log then turned and stamped her feet and brushed at her parka and pants. When done, she placed the skillet, mounded high with snow, on the hearth, stripped off her gloves and held her hands out to the fire. All without so much as glancing Sam's way.

"While you're there, throw a couple of handfuls of beans into that water to soak. We'll cook them for dinner later."

He still didn't look up, but in his peripheral vision he saw her stiffen and glare at him. Nevertheless, after a brief hesitation she stomped over to the pack, withdrew the small burlap bag of dried beans and did what he'd told her.

Sam kept his gaze on the fill-line he was weaving around and across the snowshoe frame.

When he reached a stopping point he put the work aside and rose. Using one of the knives, he cut a one-inch strip off the length of the ground sheet along one side then cut the strip into four equal pieces. He wound one piece through one of the snowshoes then put his foot on top and laced it over the toe, heel and ankle of his boot.

"That storm doesn't show any sign of letting up and we're running low on firewood," he announced as he worked. "I'm going to gather more while it's still light out."

"I'll go with you."

Sam stopped and looked at her. "What?"

"I can help," she asserted.

"You?"

Her chin tilted up in what he was coming to think of as her royal battle mode. "I may not be much of a cook, but I've got two arms. I can carry firewood. There's no reason why you should have to do all the work."

"You're serious?"

"Yes. We're in this together. I want to do my part."

He started to tell her to forget it, but the proud tilt of her head made him hesitate. He stared at her, torn, knowing that she would probably be more of a nuisance than a help. But pride was something Sam understood.

"All right, but I want you to wear the snowshoes. You need to practice walking in them anyway, and this is as good a time as any." As he spoke he began unlacing the shoe he had just strapped on.

"But what about you? There's only one completed pair."

"I'll manage. It's important that you get the hang of this now. As soon as this storm blows over, we're outta here. So come here and put your feet on these."

While he laced up the makeshift snowshoes Lauren leaned over him and watched his every move as though memorizing just how it was done.

When done, Sam rose. "Now hold on a sec." He

stepped over to the pack and pulled out a small coil of nylon cord. "Come here, so I can tie you to me."

Lauren lifted one foot high to step forward, then quickly put it down again and gave him a wide-eyed look. "What did you say?"

"Relax, will you. I'm not into bondage. This is just a safety precaution."

He tied the cord around his waist then stepped close to Lauren. Bending over to secure the other end through the metal ring on one of her zippered pockets, he heard her sharp intake of breath and felt her stiffen. He glanced at her face and his fingers stilled.

Their faces were mere inches apart. She was pale from the extreme cold, the tip of her nose, cheeks and chin slightly chafed and red, but not even that could really mar the porcelain-like texture of her skin. He was close enough to see the long sweep of each individual auburn eyelash, the spokes of variegated green that rayed out from her pupils. Close enough to catch her womanly scent. A pulse beat wildly beneath her left ear and her breathing was so shallow it was barely discernible.

Slowly his gaze ran over her face. A slight tremble vibrated her body, but other than that she stood absolutely motionless, her eyes wide and slightly out of focus, like a deer caught in headlights. Sam realized that she was experiencing the same sharp pull of attraction he'd been feeling ever since he'd first set eyes on her—probably for the first time, if the stunned look on her face was anything to go by.

Sam resented the feelings she aroused in him, but

he was human, and the discovery that the attraction wasn't one-sided sent a surge of satisfaction through him.

His gaze found hers, and for a few taut seconds neither could move nor look away. Awareness sizzled between them like heat lightning. A gust of wind briefly lifted the brush over the hole in the roof and a small flurry of snowflakes fluttered down between them. Neither noticed.

Sam's gaze dropped to her slightly parted lips, lingered, then returned once again to the madly throbbing pulse by her ear. The urge to place his lips against that tiny flutter, to taste her, was so strong it pulled at him like a powerful magnet. Mesmerized, he gazed at that delicate skin, and as his eyelids grew heavy he angled his head and leaned toward her.

Whether it was the infinitesimal widening of her eyes or the loud pop the fire made just at that moment that broke the spell, Sam neither knew nor cared. He was just grateful for the return of his senses.

Jerking back, he bent once again to the business of tying the cord to her parka.

"It's too easy to get disoriented in a storm like this one," he said in a brusk voice. "If you were to wander more than six feet from me you'd be lost, so I'm going to put you on a tether."

"I—" Lauren's voice broke, and she stopped to clear her throat. "I see. But, uh...but what about you?" she stammered. "You could get lost just as easily."

Sam breathed a sigh of relief that she had also chosen to pretend those sizzling few seconds had never happened.

"Not quite. I have a good sense of direction. Maybe that's because I'm half Indian. Also my dad took me hunting from the time I was a kid and taught me about the wilderness."

"You're part Native American? Really?" She cocked her head to one side and looked at him as though he were a fascinating new species. "I've never known anyone before who had Native American blood. What tribe?"

He glanced at her out of the corner of his eye, half expecting to see contempt or disdain. Or worse, patronizing acceptance. God knew he been exposed to it all. Even in their present, so-called enlightened world, there were still many who referred to him as a half-breed. At times, he suspected that his own father thought of him that way.

Lauren's guileless green eyes, however, held only amazement and a sort of childlike curiosity.

"My mother was Navajo," he said in a curt voice. He gave the knot a hard yank, straightened and shifted the door aside and strode out into the blizzard.

"Wait! Wait!" Lauren hurried after him, high-stepping in the awkward snowshoes. It was that or be jerked off her feet.

Nine

Over the next two hours they worked steadily and talked little. It was so cold, merely breathing was difficult. Sam plowed through the deep snow, seemingly oblivious to the bitter cold and the blinding swirl all around them, moving from tree to tree, chopping off small to medium-size limbs. Lauren clomped behind him with her head down, panting and shivering. She felt as though she had two boats strapped to her feet. Just staying upright took most of her concentration.

While Sam chopped at the trees with the small ax from the survival pack, Lauren stacked the branches into a pile, along with all the deadwood she could find. More than once, she was grateful that he had tied her to him. The tether was only about six yards long, but whenever she roamed more than a few feet away from Sam she lost sight of him.

Periodically, before moving on to another group of trees, they stopped and carried the wood they'd already gathered back to the cabin. Each pile required several trips, and by the time Sam decreed that they had enough Lauren was half-frozen and so exhausted from struggling with the awkward snowshoes and toting wood she could barely put one foot in front of the other.

Once back inside the cabin she slapped the snow off her parka and pants and collapsed onto the sleeping bag.

"Before you get too comfortable, hand over those snowshoes. I need them."

Lauren opened one eye and looked at him. "You're going back out? I thought you said we had enough wood."

"We do. I'm going to check the snares. With any luck, we'll have fresh meat for dinner."

She sighed and started to struggle to her feet. "I'll go with you and help."

"That's not necessary."

"No, I want to do my share."

"I appreciate that, but you don't have to help with everything. Besides, with the snowshoes I can make faster time. I'll be back in an hour or so."

Lauren opened her mouth to argue, but he stopped her with a raised hand.

"Look, if it'll make you feel better, I'll let you cook whatever we've caught."

He grinned at her horrified expression—actually grinned at her—a genuine, hold nothing back, dazzling grin that transformed his craggy face into a rugged handsomeness that shocked Lauren and made her heart give a little thump. His teeth were a startling white in his dark, beard-stubbled face, and the corners of his dark eyes actually crinkled.

"Don't worry, I'll show you how. There's nothing to it. You can start by moving those beans onto the coals so they can boil."

"I...um...okay." Feeling as though she'd just received a dizzying punch, she ducked her head and went to work untying the bindings on the snowshoes.

For several minutes after Sam had slipped back outside, Lauren sat staring at the door. Dear Lord. What was the matter with her? For two years, ever since Collin deserted her, she hadn't so much as looked at a man with anything but casual indifference. She simply hadn't been interested. She had learned her lesson there, thank you very much.

Now, twice in the span of a couple of hours she'd experienced a jolt like she'd been struck by lightning. All because of Sam. *Sam, for heaven's sake!* A hard-nosed, suspicious man who didn't even like her!

Well, it just wouldn't do. Even if she were interested in a romantic relationship—which she most definitely was not—it wouldn't be with this man.

It was the stress, she told herself. This nightmare situation they were in. She had read recently that people under duress acted and reacted in ways they never would dream of doing normally. That had to be it. The harrowing events of the last few days must have left her with something akin to battle fatigue.

Wound too tight to rest, as she had intended to do, Lauren added wood to the fire and repositioned the pot of beans, then turned to the most familiar and comforting thing in her life.

Though there was no piano handy, she could still practice. It occurred to her as she settled back down on the sleeping bag and pulled a good-size chunk of wood in front of her that she hadn't played a note in almost two days. That had to be a record. In the past, even when she'd had a cold or the flu or some childhood disease, she had played at least a few hours each day.

Which just showed how out of kilter her life had become.

Sitting cross-legged, Lauren placed her spread fingertips on the log, closed her eyes...and began playing. One piece blended into another, then another, as her fingers danced over the log, sometimes with slow, fluid grace, sometimes in a frenzy of power and emotion. All the while the stirring notes played inside her head.

When Lauren played the piano, even when only in her mind, she became so immersed in the music that she lost all sense of time and place and circumstance. She had no idea that Sam had returned until he spoke.

"What the devil are you doing?"

She jumped and her eyes popped open. "Sam! You're back already?"

"Already? It's dark out. I've been gone almost an hour longer than I expected. I hurried back because I thought you might be getting worried again. Instead I find you...what the hell *were* you doing?"

A self-conscious grimace twisted her mouth. "Piano practice. Oh, don't look at me like that. I'm not crazy. It's called visualization. I close my eyes and imagine that I'm sitting at a Steinway.''

"If you say so."

"No, really. I can feel the keys under my fingers and hear the music in my mind. In the past, whenever we flew from one concert date to another, I often did it."

"That must've been entertaining for your fellow passengers."

"You needn't be so snide. It *does* work. It's not as good as actual practice, I'll admit, but it's better than nothing. Daily practice is important to a pianist, but since the accident it's become essential for me. Otherwise my hand would be even stiffer than it already is, and I wouldn't be able to play at all."

He stared at her for a long time, his harsh face impassive. "And that's important to you? Being able to play? Even though your concert career is over?"

"Of course. I can't imagine not being able to play. I don't think I'd want to live if I couldn't play at all."

He continued to stare at her for so long that she began to feel uncomfortable. Finally he nodded and stepped around her and placed something on the hearth. "We're in luck. We had a catch in two of the snares."

"What is that?" she asked, wrinkling her nose.

"Snowshoe hares. I dressed them outside before I came in. We'll roast them over the fire tonight and I'll hang one in the corner to freeze for later."

"Hares? You mean...*bunny rabbits?* Oh, I

couldn't eat a bunny. I couldn't possibly. I'll just eat something from the pack.''

''You'll eat the hare, and no arguing about it. We need to conserve our food supply. Besides, snowshoe hare is a good source of protein and fat, and you're going to need plenty of both for energy when we're on the move. As it is, you're so thin you don't have any reserves. Now come here and I'll show you how to roast it.''

Reluctantly Lauren did as she was told. She winced and tried not to gag as she watched him remove his gloves and skewer the carcasses onto a stout limb about an inch and a half in diameter. He then wedged the end of a forked branch into a crack in the hearth floor and braced the skewer in the V notch.

Lauren jolted when he stripped off her glove and wrapped her hand around the branch, but if he noticed it didn't show. ''Hold the hare just above the flames and turn it slowly, like so,'' he explained, demonstrating with his hand over hers. ''All you have to do is keep it moving. Got it?''

''Um...'' She felt as though her brain had short-circuited. Acutely aware of that large hand clamped over hers, she had difficulty focusing on his words. ''I...uh...yes, I...I think so.''

''Good. Just keep doing that until I tell you to stop.''

For the next hour, while Lauren slowly turned the carcass over the fire, Sam worked on the last snowshoe. She tried to appear indifferent and not to look his way, but over and over her gaze was drawn to him, especially to his hands.

Funny, she hadn't noticed before how beautiful they were. Probably because he wore heavy gloves most of the time. They both did. His palms were broad, his fingers long and blunt with short, clean nails, and they moved with incredible grace and sureness as he wove the fill-line back and forth across the frame in a diamond pattern.

Was it the intimacy of their situation that made her so aware of him? Lauren wondered. After all, they were stranded here on this mountain alone together for who knew how long. Previously, the only man with whom she'd ever shared a bed or spent so much time alone had been Collin.

Peeking at him out of the corner of her eye, it occurred to Lauren that Sam Rawlins and Collin were about as different as any two men could possibly be.

Blond and blue-eyed, her former fiancé was shorter than average height and slight of build. Sam's Native American heritage was evident in his blue-black hair and dark coloring, and he had a tall, muscular build without an ounce of fat on him.

The differences went deeper than mere looks and physique, she realized. Since Collin had been trained by her father, Lauren supposed that he was an adequate business manager, although she had no way of knowing that for certain. In social settings and the elite world of classical music his charm, wit and sophistication served him well, but in this situation she knew that he would be useless—less than useless, really. Not only would Collin not have a clue of what to do, he "gave" orders; he did not "do." A snap of the fingers or a call to a service or the hotel concierge brought someone to perform menial tasks.

Sam, on the other hand, had knowledge and experience and did not hesitate to roll up his sleeves and do what had to be done.

He was hard and distant and sometimes curt, but he was also strong, skillful, knowledgeable and absolutely reliable.

Lauren wasn't sure she even liked him, but with somewhat of a shock, it occurred to her that she trusted him. If fate had seen fit to land her in this horrendous predicament she was just glad it was with Sam Rawlins.

The man could probably not only survive, but thrive, if he were stranded on a desert island with nothing more than a string, a safety pin and a stick of chewing gum.

By the time Sam pronounced the meat done, the delicious aroma had overcome any qualms Lauren had about eating hare and set her stomach to growling. Sam divvied up the food and they ate sitting cross-legged in front of the fire without speaking.

For the longest time, the only sounds were the scrape of utensils against metal plates, the incessant howling of the wind and the crackle of the fire.

Maybe it was stretched nerves or boredom, or maybe just plain curiosity, or maybe it was because in her world, when people ate together they exchanged pleasant dinner conversation. Whatever, Lauren could not bear the silence a moment longer.

"You said that you used to camp in this area. Does that mean you grew up around here?" she asked out of the blue.

Sam seemed surprised—whether by the question, or merely that she had spoken, Lauren couldn't tell. After studying her for a moment he finished chewing, swallowed and cut another chunk of meat. "West of here. On a ranch near Monticello."

"Monticello? That's in...?"

"Utah."

"Then we've left the state?"

"No, we're still in Colorado."

Lauren watched him and waited, growing annoyed. She had opened the conversation, hadn't she? The least he could do was keep it going. Sam, however, merely scooped up another bite of food and chewed in silence.

Her mouth set. Okay, fine. She'd do this the hard way. "Tell me about your parents."

This time his head came up sharply, his dark eyes narrow and suspicious. "Why should I?"

His biting tone startled a laugh from Lauren. "You don't have to act as though I'm trying to worm state secrets out of you. I'm just curious, that's all. And I thought it might fill the time, maybe help us get better acquainted. Anyway, it's only fair. You know all about me, so now it's my turn to learn about you."

"There's a difference. I'm FBI and you're a civilian and part of a criminal investigation."

"Oh, for heaven's sake! I'm the *witness,* not the accused. You seem to keep forgetting that. Anyway, I'm sick to death of all this stony silence. I know you don't have a very high opinion of me, and to be honest, I'm not overly fond of you, either. But since we're stuck with each other can't we call a truce for a while and just talk like regular human beings? Is that too much to ask?"

For her trouble she received another of those piercing looks. He lowered his gaze and took another bite. She had about decided he wasn't going to answer when he surprised her by saying, "What do you want to know?"

"Well, for starters, tell me about your mother. What's her name? What's she like."

"Her name was Mary Morning Star Zah. She was tiny and delicately built." He glanced at her again, a look of mild surprise flickering across his face. "Sorta like you."

"You said *was.* Do you mean...?"

"Yeah. She died when I was seventeen. Anyway, she was small, soft-spoken and shy. I guess it was a case of opposites attracting, because my dad is a big, rawboned man. Tough as old shoe leather and as hard and unbending as they come."

Ah, that explains a lot, Lauren thought. Like father, like son. However, intuition told her she'd best keep that observation to herself.

"How did they meet?"

"Back then, my grandfather was running the ranch. They'd had a poor hay crop that summer due to a drought around Monticello, but farther south they'd had plenty of rain, so my grandfather sent Dad there to buy hay from a Navajo rancher named John Zah. He was my mother's uncle, and she happened to be visiting him at the time."

"Was it love at first sight?"

"I wouldn't know. I wasn't there."

"Very funny." She shot him a reproving look, but she refused to let his sarcasm discourage her. "Well, I happen to think the whole thing is very romantic," she insisted. "It's not every day a man marries a Native American princess and carries her away to his ranch to live happily ever after."

Sam snorted. "Guess again."

"What do you mean?" A troubling thought occurred to her, and she frowned. "How did their families react to the marriage? Surely there weren't any objections?"

"Plenty. On both sides."

"But that's awful."

"Maybe, but both my grandfather Rawlins and my mother's people worried that Mary wouldn't be happy living totally in the white man's world." Sam shrugged. "As it turned out, they were right."

"Oh, no. You mean the marriage didn't last?"

"Nope. She stuck it out as long as she could, but

she missed her family and reservation life. I was four when they split.''

"Oh, dear. So I guess after that you grew up on the reservation with your mother.''

"You'd think so, especially since the Navajos are a matriarchal society that believe the children belong to the mother. But my old man wasn't about to let her take me away from him. Or I should say, from the ranch. I was a Rawlins and his only child, and Rawlins men had worked the Double R for over a hundred years.''

Sam's fork clattered against the empty metal plate. He rolled to his feet in one fluid motion and dumped the dishes into the pot of water, then squatted down on his haunches to scrub them.

"I'll wash up later. Please, finish your story," Lauren urged.

He kept on scrubbing, and when he was done with his plate he reached for hers. "There's not much else to tell," he said finally. "Both my parents sought custody, but since the decision was made in the white man's court by a white judge, my father won.''

Though he spoke in his usual controlled way there was a harder edge than usual to his voice, revealing his anger and resentment.

"You weren't happy with your father?" she probed.

"I wasn't unhappy." He glanced up at her and his mouth took on a wry twist. "God, don't ever play poker. Not with that face. You might as well have your thoughts printed across your forehead. There's no reason to look so troubled. My dad didn't abuse me or neglect me. We just didn't get along. We still don't.'' Sam shrugged. ''It happens. It's no big deal.''

''You quarreled a lot?''

''Locked horns on a daily basis like two bulls.''

''Over what?''

''You name it. We couldn't agree on a single thing, and nothing I did pleased him. After a while, I stopped trying.'' His mouth twisted. ''Actually, to tell the truth, I went out of my way to annoy him.

''He hated it when I visited my mother, so I spent a lot of time on the reservation, even after she died. In my teens I started wearing moccasins and let my hair grow long and wore it in a braid just to infuriate him.''

''And did it?'' Lauren asked quietly.

''Oh, yeah. He ordered me to cut it, but I wouldn't, even though I actually preferred to wear it short. I guess you could say we're both strong-willed.''

More like stubborn, Lauren thought, fighting back a smile. Except for taking the skillet outside to rinse it in the snow, Sam finished washing up and sat cross-legged before the fire and picked up the snowshoe again. Tipping her head to one side, Lauren studied him while he worked, her woman's intuitive radar tingling. ''You think your father resents your Indian blood, don't you?''

She hadn't meant to voice the thought aloud—somehow it had just popped out before she could stop it—but she knew instantly by the look he flashed her that she was right.

Those dark eyes stabbed into her like icicles and his face seemed to turn to granite. He stared at her in silence for an uncomfortably long time, but finally he went back to weaving fill-line.

Lauren knew she should let the matter drop, or at the very least, change the subject. Sam obviously was not going to answer her question. But for some reason, she just couldn't. "You indicated that your father expected you to take over the ranch someday, but obviously you didn't. Don't you like ranching? Was that the main problem?"

"Damn, you're a nosy little thing, aren't you? Persistent, too."

"I guess I am." Lauren waited, then gently prodded, "Well?"

"Actually, I love ranching. Taking over the Double R was what I always wanted to do, what I assumed I *would* do someday. Just not on my dad's terms."

"So what happened?"

"After our last big argument, right after I graduated from college, I decided I'd had enough and walked out. Within a week I had applied to the Bureau. That was sixteen years ago. I've never looked back."

"But surely you eventually made up with your father? Please tell me you two are okay now."

"We're not at each other's throats, if that's what you mean. Probably because we don't communicate that often."

"You don't talk to your father?" Lauren stared at him, stunned.

"I didn't say that. I give him a call two or three times a year—usually on his birthday and the holidays."

"When was the last time you visited him?"

"Look, I told you, we don't get along, so what's the point? Every time we're together we just end up in an argument."

"But…he must be an old man by now. How could you—"

"Let it go. It doesn't concern you." Though his voice was soft, its deep timbre carried a warning. So did the steel in his eyes. When he was satisfied that he'd silenced her he went back to work.

"I'm sorry. You're absolutely right, of course. But truly, I wasn't passing judgment. It's just that my father and I were close and I miss him so much and…well…I can't imagine being estranged from him."

"Not all families are the same."

"Yes, of course. You're right. Please forgive me. I shouldn't have stuck my nose in."

Clearly he had not expected an apology. He stared at her again, trying to decide if it was genuine and whether or not to accept. Finally he nodded and lowered his gaze once again to his work. "It'll soon be time to turn in. I suggest you take a last trip outside," he said without looking up.

"All right," Lauren agreed in a subdued voice. She

rose and fastened the cord around her waist and tied on the snowshoes. She felt terrible about stirring up such a bitter issue. No matter how much Sam tried to brush the matter aside as unimportant, it was obvious that the rift between him and his father was painful.

Feeling strangely depressed, she slipped out the door and headed for the stand of trees. Odd, how quickly you could become accustomed to something, she mused as she trudged, head-down, through the icy darkness. Only twenty-four hours earlier she had been terrified to trek out here alone, with visions of all manner of wild beasts waiting to pounce on her flickering through her mind. Now it seemed routine. Or maybe she was just too down to care.

Lauren took care of her business in as short a time as possible and hurried back to the cabin. The instant she stepped back inside Sam tossed the bottle of vitamins to her and ordered her to take one.

When she took off the snowshoes, he put aside his project and strapped them on and, without another word, disappeared outside himself, taking the pan of dishwater with him.

Shaking her head, Lauren watched him go. She took the pill then brushed her teeth and slathered lotion over her face and hands. After she brushed her hair, she pulled off her boots and scrambled into the sleeping bag.

Settling onto her side, she stared at the fire, a painful knot of emotion lodged in her chest. Sam was right; his relationship with his father was none of her business. They were not friends, after all. She was merely a witness he'd been assigned to protect. She should just butt out.

Still...she couldn't stop thinking about what he had told her, or help but be sad and horrified that he was estranged from his father.

Like her, Sam had grown up with only a father for most of his life. If anything, that should have drawn the two men closer. It certainly had worked that way with her and her father. No matter how hard Lauren tried, she couldn't conceive of a disagreement so rancorous that you would voluntarily cut yourself off from a parent.

Her own father had been a stickler for perfection and a bit of a slave driver, but she had loved him dearly, and he her. Her chest ached at the thought of the emotional void between Sam and his sole remaining parent. It just wasn't right, she thought, as a huge yawn overtook her.

Lauren settled her cheek into a more comfortable position atop her stacked hands, her eyelids drooping as the day's activities began to catch up with her. She was drifting off when a gust of freezing wind announced Sam's return. Only then did she give a thought to their sleeping arrangement.

The night before she had been too exhausted to worry about that aspect of their situation. Now, however, as she lay with her eyes closed, pretending to be asleep and listening to him moving around the cabin, her nerves began to jump.

She was being foolish, she knew. There was nothing sexual about their sleeping together. It was necessity, pure and simple, just as he had informed her the night before.

The man was an FBI agent doing his job, and that job was to keep her alive, whatever it took. As long as they were stranded in these mountains, that included keeping her from freezing to death.

Besides, he certainly wasn't lusting after her. He couldn't have made it any plainer than he already had that he didn't even like her. She was just a job to him, an assignment. She had nothing at all to worry about.

Despite the pep talk, Lauren lay awake, every muscle in her body tense, waiting for him to slip into the sleeping bag beside her. She heard him shake out a vitamin from the bottle, and a few moments later brush his teeth. After that there was only the crackle of the fire and the moaning of the winds, and a steady, whispery sound. Frowning, she tried to identify the source.

Curious, Lauren opened her eyes a slit, but all she saw was the fire. She raised her head an inch or so and turned it, and discovered Sam, sitting mere inches away, once again fashioning a snowshoe.

"I thought you said it was time to turn in?"

"I want to finish this first. With any luck this storm will pass and we'll need these shoes tomorrow." He glanced up and scowled. "Go to sleep."

Sam saw the offended look that flickered over her face. Then came that proud lift of her chin. "Yessir.

Of course. Whatever you say, sir,'' she snapped. Her head dropped back down and she flounced over onto her other side.

Sam gritted his teeth. Damn. He hadn't meant to snap at her. He was angry with himself. He stared at the top of her head, his mouth grim. Dammit, he couldn't believe he'd actually told her those things. He never talked about his personal life to anyone.

Well, almost never, he silently amended, remembering a tedious, nightlong stakeout he and Todd had been on together years ago. The combination of boredom and sleep deprivation must have numbed his brain. Eventually their desultory talk had turned personal and he had revealed that he and his father had never been on the best of terms. He'd regretted the slip at once, and being one of his few close friends, Todd had known that. Tactfully he'd never mentioned the matter again.

When Lauren had urged him to talk he had gone along with her for a couple of valid reasons. First of all, because she was right. If he got them off of this mountain alive and to a safe place they were going to be together constantly for possibly the next couple of months. It made sense, and it would certainly make their situation more bearable, to establish some sort of casual rapport.

His other reason was less concrete, more a gut feeling he could no longer ignore. Because, God help him, he was actually beginning to believe that she was exactly who and what she claimed to be. Not totally convinced, but getting there.

Sam cursed under his breath. He had pegged her as Carlo's woman because everything pointed in that direction. It had seemed so obvious that he hadn't seriously considered any other possibility. The way he should have. The way he'd been trained to do.

But the longer he was around her the more he realized that there were just too many little things that didn't add up. She was bright and observant and willing to learn and insisted on pulling her weight. That, he realized, stemmed from her determination to be independent. Who the hell ever heard of an independent mistress?

And then there were those exquisite manners of hers. He could easily picture her rubbing elbows with princes and prime ministers and society's upper crust.

Not exactly the qualities you expected to find in a bimbo mistress, or even a lounge piano player.

The trouble was, he hadn't *wanted* to believe her story. He still didn't. Their situation was too precarious—and too damned close for comfort. If they managed to survive, they were going to be alone together for weeks, maybe even months—just the two of them.

As long as he believed that she was Carlo Giovessi's whore, the sharp pull of attraction he experienced around her was an irritating nuisance, but nothing he couldn't handle. If he accepted that she was the innocent she claimed to be, he wasn't so sure.

In his fifteen years with the Bureau, he'd always

kept a professional distance between himself and the witnesses and suspects in all his cases. Not only was it the smart thing to do, it was Bureau policy, and he'd never had a problem with it...until now.

So what was it about this particular woman? What made her different? No logical answer came to mind, and for Sam that just made the situation all the more frustrating.

He was good at solving puzzles. His analytical mind liked to examine all the facts and clues, all the various motivations and possibilities, and piece them together into a complete picture that gave him, if not solid answers, at least a good educated guess.

His reaction to Lauren, however, had nothing to do with logic.

Sam sighed and raked his hand through his hair. He could be in trouble here real fast, he thought with a frown.

He strung the last fill-line and tied it off, giving the knot a hard jerk. He put the finished snowshoe with the others and added more wood to the fire. When it was blazing he looked over his shoulder at Lauren. Fatigue had overcome her anger and she was fast asleep.

Sam tugged off his knee-high moccasins, removed the felt liners and placed them in front of the fire, then lifted the edge of the sleeping bag and slid in beside Lauren. Turning onto his side, he looped his arm around her waist and fitted the front of his body snugly to the back of hers.

A curling strand of her hair tickled his nose. Sam captured it and tucked it behind her ear. Sighing, Lauren wiggled her bottom and shifted into a more comfortable position.

Sam groaned. He stared down at the top of her head. In the light from the fire her auburn hair blazed. And it smelled wonderful, like wildflowers and shampoo. And woman.

Sam's jaw clenched, and he focused his gaze once again on the fire. Oh, yeah, he was definitely in trouble.

Ten

Sam awoke with a start. Like a stag in the forest, he raised his head, listening.

Something was different.

The fire had burned down to glowing embers and a few weak flames, its faint glow extending no more than a foot or so in front of the hearth. Once again, Lauren lay sprawled half over him, sound asleep, but he knew that wasn't what had disturbed him.

Sam lay motionless, alert, his eyes searching through the darkness around them. Then he saw the patch of moonlight spilling in through the grimy window, and he knew.

It had stopped snowing.

"Dammit!" He shoved Lauren off of him, jerked down the zipper on the sleeping bag, and rolled out, bounding to his feet. Heart pounding, he stuffed the warm felt liners into his knee-high moccasins. How long ago had it stopped snowing? Jesus!

He paused long enough to give Lauren's shoulder a rough shake. "Wake up," he commanded. Hopping on one foot, then the other, Sam rammed his feet into the tall moccasins.

Lauren raised her head and blinked at him as he drew up the drawstrings at the top of his footgear and tied them securely over his pant legs.

"Wha...what is it?" She pushed her hair out of her face and cast a bleary look around, confused. "It's still dark. What're you doing up?" she mumbled.

"Get up. It's stopped snowing. We're getting out of here."

Lauren sat up and looked around, her eyes growing wide and frightened. "We're...we're leaving? You mean...right now?"

"Not right this minute, but soon. First I have to hike back to the plane."

"You're going all the way back there? But...why?"

"I forgot something." He squatted down and started lacing on a pair of the crude snowshoes. Dammit, he had to find and destroy whatever homing device the saboteur had planted before he and his cohorts located the wreck.

"But that will take a couple of hours."

"Not quite. I can make it faster on my own. While I'm gone I want you to pack up all our supplies and gear. So haul your butt out of that bed and get busy."

"All right, all right," Lauren grumbled. "You don't have to be so obnoxious." Shivering she climbed from the limited warmth of the sleeping bag and stuffed her feet into her boots and tied them.

"What are you doing?" Sam demanded when she picked up several pieces of wood.

"What does it look like? I'm going to build up the fire."

"No. No fire. Let those coals burn down."

"No fire? Why not?"

"I have my reasons. Just do as I tell you."

"But it's *freezing* in here right now. Without a fire it will just get colder. Anyway, how are we going to cook breakfast?"

"We don't have time for that. Just grab some jerky." He stomped his feet to test the snowshoe bindings, then dug into the bag of jerky, extracted a few pieces and stuffed them into a pocket on his parka.

"You're going to be gone for hours. You expect me to sit here in the cold?"

"Get used to it," he replied. He picked up the rifle and headed for the door. "You're going to be even colder when we start hiking out of these mountains. Anyway, if you stay busy you won't get that cold, and I figure it'll take you hours just to pack. It does most women."

"Very funny. I still don't see why I can't build up the fire. We have the wood right here. Anyway, since you're going to be gone so long, I could use the time to heat water and have a bath of sorts."

The statement jerked Sam to a halt. He spun around. "Are you *crazy?* Dammit, woman, get three feet away from that fire and it's a deep-freeze in here. You'd have hypothermia before you could finish."

"If I built up the fire really big—"

"No! Absolutely not."

"But I need a *bath!*" Lauren wailed.

Despite the urgency and worry that gnawed at him, Sam almost grinned. It was the first time that she had whined about anything, and damned if she didn't look like an adorable, pouty little girl, with her hair all tousled, her chin stuck out, standing there glaring at him.

From the start, he'd expected her to give him nothing but grief every step of the way, especially after the plane crash, but she'd gritted her teeth and done what she had to do without complaint, and under the crudest and most difficult of conditions. She'd even made herself useful.

Everyone had their breaking point, though, and apparently two days without a shower was Lauren's.

"So do I, but it'll have to wait," he replied heartlessly.

"But—"

"I said no. That's it. End of discussion. Just do as you're told. I mean it." He clomped to the door and lifted it aside, but before he stepped out into the fading darkness he stopped and jabbed one gloved forefinger at her. "Remember what I said. No fires, no cooking. And absolutely *no bathing*. You got that?"

"Yes. I've got it," she snapped back. "I'm not deaf, you know."

"Fine. I'll be back as quickly as I can. Be ready to move out."

Sam stepped outside and propped the door back in place, shutting off the sight of her outraged face.

He took off at once, leaving the cabin behind within seconds. Without Lauren in tow Sam traveled at a fast clip, alternating between rapid walking and trotting in that unnatural, hopping gait made necessary by the snowshoes.

He thought about Lauren as he went. He'd hated to be so hard on her, but it couldn't be helped. There was no way of knowing when the snow had stopped falling, and by now whoever had sabotaged the plane could already have an aircraft out looking for them. He couldn't run the risk of them seeing smoke from their fire when they flew over.

They would come. Sam had no doubt about that. They had to. The only way to know for certain that their targets were dead would be to check out the wreckage. When they found only two bodies they would fan out and start searching.

But he didn't want to tell Lauren that. Not unless he had to. She was frightened enough already.

He hadn't missed the flash of fear in her eyes when he'd told her they were leaving, or the way she had paled. He even understood it. As crude as the old derelict cabin was, as primitive as they were living, as harsh as the conditions were—Lauren felt safe here, miles from anywhere, hidden by the storm and secluded by the rugged wilderness. Plus, no one knew they were there, or how to find them.

Or so Lauren believed.

No sense in taking that small comfort away from her unless he had no choice.

She was no dummy however, and she had already figured out that once they left this place and returned to civilization, she would be in many times more danger of losing her life than she was here. More people meant more risk of being recognized, and the higher the likelihood of Giovessi's people finding her.

Without breaking stride, Sam pulled a stick of jerky out of his pocket and bit off a chunk. Eating was a necessity—his body needed fuel—but he chewed the tough meat without conscious thought, his mind occupied. Lauren was the primary target, but Sam had a gut feeling that the saboteur had wanted him dead, as well.

The whole thing had probably been orchestrated by their mole. Sam knew in his gut that he was close to nailing the dirty agent, and the bastard probably knew it as well. It was just a matter of time. No doubt he had seen a golden opportunity to eliminate not only the witness against his mob boss, but Sam, as well. Two birds with one stone.

If, as Sam suspected, the plane had been sabotaged, that meant that the turncoat in the department was one of the five other men who had been in on the meeting in Harvey's office.

Sam's eyes narrowed at the thought, but he pushed on at the same rapid pace. He eliminated Dave right off. Not only had he been too new to the job to have been corrupted, he'd been a gung-ho, true-blue type, full of shining ideals that had not yet been corroded by the daily grind and the things he saw on the job. Besides, no way would the kid rig the engine to fail, then get on the plane. That left Harvey Weiss, Charlie Potter, Todd Berringer and Roy O'Connor.

He didn't know O'Connor that well, but he'd always considered him to be a straight-arrow. The same could be said for Sam's boss, Charlie.

Todd had a glib tongue and an eye for the ladies, but when it came to the job he was a by-the-book kind of guy—an approach that Sam thought lacked initiative and in his opinion was not always effective, but probably had his friend on the fast track for promotion—something that Sam knew would never happen in his case. He was considered a lone wolf. At times a rogue wolf.

Despite their basic differences, however, or maybe because of them, he and Todd had been friends a long time.

That left Harvey.

Sam didn't like the guy, and he had to admit that made him lean in that direction, but until he had proof, all four men were suspect.

Hell, every agent in the Denver office was a suspect. There could be, and probably were, more than one man—or woman—working for the mob boss.

Dawn arrived so gradually Sam barely noticed. A golden glow backlit the mountain peaks to the east and darkness gave way to a soft pearly light, but it would be another couple of hours before the sun cleared the crests.

The silence was absolute. Nothing else stirred. Sam's heavy breathing and the rhythmic crunch of his snowshoes on the fresh powder sounded shockingly loud in the pristine stillness. He pressed on doggedly, stopping only twice to take a drink of water and check his compass.

Slightly over an hour after leaving the cabin, he cut through a stand of trees and arrived at a spot about three hundred yards above the crash site. Sam stopped, breathing heavily, his eyes scanning the clearing and the ledge at its far side where the plane had gone over into a ravine. Cautiously he moved to the edge of the trees. The silence was so magnified he was sure that if it weren't for his own labored breathing he'd be able to hear a chipmunk sneeze.

Finally, satisfied there was no one around, he stepped out of the trees and started sidestepping down the steep slope. He'd barely gone a yard when he heard the distinctive *whop-whop-whop-whop* of a rotary engine approaching from somewhere behind him.

"Holy shit!"

Sam scrambled back up the incline and made a dive for the base of the nearest spruce tree just as the helicopter rose up over the ridge above him.

Hitting the snow with an *"oomph!"* he rolled beneath the low-hanging branches, weighted down with snow. The thick spruce needles shielded the ground at the base of the tree from most of the snowfall. Sam scooted on his belly into the natural hollow, in as close to the trunk as he could get and flattened himself into the snow.

Damn. Had they spotted him? Breathing hard, he lay perfectly still, his heart thudding.

The chopper's engine roared overhead, barely clearing the treetops. The tree above Sam and all the neighboring ones waved and whipped in the rotor wash, dumping bushels of snow on him. For a moment it seemed to Sam that the bird hovered overhead, and he hugged the ground tighter.

The chopper went on by and the earsplitting engine noise abated somewhat. Sam wriggled forward on his belly and cautiously raised his head just far enough to see over the rim of the shallow crater.

Through the spruce branches he watched the chopper circle out over the deep ravine. It hovered for a time, and Sam could see men peering down at the wreckage at the bottom. The ravine was too narrow for the chopper pilot to risk flying down to the site. Sam waited, every muscle in his body tense, hoping they would decide that no one could have survived the wreck.

"Yeah, right. You should be so lucky," he muttered to himself when the chopper circled back and set down in the clearing, the blade wash kicking up a cloud of snow.

Though he knew they could not spot him, Sam instinctively drew back a bit when the chopper door opened. The first man jumped out and hit the ground in a defensive posture, crouched, his rifle held at the ready against his shoulder, the barrel sweeping the area. Four more men followed, all assuming the same stance and spreading out in a semicircle, their backs to the chopper and the drop-off beyond it.

The pilot killed the engine and the rotary blades slowed and drooped, and the cloud of snow it kicked up began to settle. Moments later the man joined the other five.

Sam watched and waited, his hand on his rifle, every muscle in his body tensed. From that distance he couldn't see their faces well enough to recognize any of them, but the chopper was FBI.

The first man out, the one who seemed to be in charge, swept the area several times, then looked up the slope at the stand of trees.

Sam stopped breathing.

The man's gaze seemed to focus on the tree where Sam lay hiding. He stared at the same spot for several seconds. Watching him through narrowed eyes, Sam pulled his rifle closer.

One of the other men said something, and the man turned to answer, ending the tense moment. He shouted something to the others and they all relaxed and turned back to the chopper and started hauling out ropes and rappelling equipment.

Sam had seen all he needed. He wriggled backward on his belly and squirmed out from under the tree on the side opposite the clearing. Cautiously, he climbed to his feet and started backing away, through the tree branches, keeping his gaze on the activity below. The men in the clearing were busy hauling out equipment and most had their backs to him. He doubted they could spot him for the trees, anyway, but he carefully edged backward. When he could no longer see the clearing he spun around and took off for the cabin at a run.

Dammit! he thought viciously. If only he had gotten there an hour sooner. Now they were going to have to run for it.

And pray for a little luck.

Sam double-timed it all the way back, pushing himself mercilessly, his lungs working like a smithy's bellows, his breath rushing in and out with a harsh, rhythmic rasp. By the time he reached the cabin his arm and leg muscles were screaming.

He burst through the doorway, paying no attention when the old planked door crashed to the floor.

"Sam!" Lauren jumped and gaped at him, her face pale with shock. "You're back so early! Did you change your mind about going to the plane?" she asked innocently.

He skidded to a stop, his chest heaving. She sat cross-legged on the floor as close to the glowing remains of the fire as she could get.

"No. I...went," he gasped. He glanced at her bare hands. Her long, slender fingers were still spread over the chunk of wood. "Piano practice is...over. It's time to...haul ass outta here."

He darted a look around, pleased, and a little surprised, to see that everything was packed as he had instructed and the duffle bag and pack were stacked beside the hearth with the other pair of snowshoes leaning against them. He hadn't been certain that she would be able to pack everything as compactly as it had been before, but apparently she'd been paying closer attention than he'd thought.

He grabbed the snowshoes and tossed them to her, leaving her no choice but to catch them. "Put those on. And hurry it up. We don't have much time."

"For heaven's sake, what is your rush?"

"Just *do* it!" he snapped. Sam stepped just outside the door, scooped up a double handful of snow and came back in and tossed it on the embers of the fire, then went back out for more.

"All right, fine." She stood up and positioned her feet on the snowshoes, then squatted down to lace them on.

Sam moved back and forth, dumping snow on the embers. When he was satisfied that they were smothered he put the rifle down and snatched up the backpack and slipped his arms through the straps and hooked the rifle strap back over his shoulder.

"Did you find what you wanted at the plane, by the way?"

"No. There were six men in a helicopter already there."

"*What?*" Lauren looked up at him, her face lighting up. "You mean we're being rescued? Why didn't you tell me? That's wonderful!"

She finished tying bindings and shot to her feet. Slinging the duffle bag over her shoulder, she clomped toward the door as fast as she could. "C'mon, let's go. Oh, I can't wait for a hot shower and a real bed," she said fervently.

"Forget it. We're getting out of here on our own."

Lauren stopped and gaped at him as though he'd suddenly grown a second head. "What do you mean? Why in God's name would we do that when there's a rescue party waiting? I don't understand."

"You don't have to. If you'll recall, before we left Denver I made it clear that you were to follow my orders—no questions, no arguing. When I say jump, the only thing I want to hear from you is 'How high?' That's it." He grasped her shoulders and turned her back toward the door and gave her a little push. "Now move out. And hurry."

"No! I won't." She grabbed the sides of the door frame and tried to dig in her heels, which, of course, was impossible in the unwieldy snowshoes. "Why should I, when there are men with a helicopter waiting to fly us out of these mountains?"

"Dammit! Those men aren't here to rescue us, you little idiot! They're here to kill us."

She looked over her shoulder at him, her eyes as big as saucers. "Wha-what?"

Her face went slack with shock, every vestige of color draining away. Sam relinquished his hold on her shoulders and stared down at her, his mouth grim.

"They came to verify that we were dead," he said

in a voice only a fraction less harsh. "And when they discover that you and I aren't—which I'm sure they have by now—they'll try to find us and finish the job."

Lauren began to tremble. She slumped against the door frame for support. Pressing her hand against her midriff, she closed her eyes. "Carlo's men," she whispered. "Even here. Oh God."

Her eyes snapped open. "Wait. How can that be? How did they find us? How did they know about the crash and where to look?"

Sam just looked at her. She was quick, he'd give her that.

"Best guess? Someone sabotaged the plane. They probably made an educated guess that we'd head west, away from heavily populated areas. They timed it so that we would go down in the mountains, one of the most rugged and inhospitable places you can find, especially in the dead of winter. Case in point— if the weather hadn't prevented it, those guys would've been here two days ago.

"I figure they planted a homing device on the plane so that they could track us and verify the kill. That's what I was going back to retrieve from the crash and destroy."

"How can you be so sure of all this? Did you recognize them?"

"No."

"Then why do you think they mean to harm us?

What if those men are agents from your office who really are here to rescue us?''

"Look, you're just going to have to trust me on this. I don't have time to explain right now. We have to get out of here. So move it."

"But—"

"Dammit, woman! I figure we've got an hour at most before they find my trail and track me here. I'm not wasting another minute arguing with you. So get your ass moving. Now!"

"I still don't—"

Bending from the waist, Sam stuck his face to within an inch of hers. She flinched back, and he saw her pupils widen and a flicker of fear chase across her face.

Good. Maybe now she'd listen.

"Lady, you either get moving or so help me I'll deck you and throw you over my shoulder," he growled. "One way or another, we're getting the hell outta here right now. Your choice."

She swallowed hard, but after a moment's hesitation she tilted her chin and huffed, "Oh, very well, I'll go. But I don't like it," she tacked on defiantly.

"Tough." He put his hand in the middle of her back and shoved her out the door.

"Hey! You don't have to be so rough."

"This way." Ignoring the complaint, he directed her into the stand of trees to the right of the cabin. "Go! Go! Go!"

Lauren fumed every step of the way. This was

crazy. Why were they risking their lives this way? Someone else at the FBI office had to have known where they were going. That would've told them where to look when she and Sam didn't show up at their destination. Wouldn't it?

She wanted to argue that point with Sam, but she didn't dare. The look in his eyes when he'd threatened her with brute force had told her that he wasn't bluffing, and she didn't relish the idea of being coldcocked and carted off like a sack of feed.

A few yards into the trees, the ground began an upward slope that made the going even more difficult. Constantly nudging and prodding, Sam hustled Lauren through the spruce and aspens at a punishing trot. All along the way, as they ran he reached out to either side and behind them and shook the snow off tree limbs to cover their tracks as best he could. "C'mon. Move it! Move it! Get the lead out!"

"I'm going as fa-fast...as I ca-can in these sho—"

She stopped abruptly when the woods ended and she found herself staring at a steep rocky slope. Bending over, she braced her hands on her knees and struggled to catch her breath and shoot Sam an annoyed look over her shoulder. "Now...what?"

"Now we start climbing." He bent and started untying his snowshoes. "First, though, we take these off. Use the bindings to tie them to the duffle bag." He looked up at her and scowled. "Don't just stand there. Get busy."

"You *can't* be serious. You expect me to... cl-climb up there?"

"It's not as bad as it looks. There's an old trail hacked out of the rocks that leads to the mine shack. Above that is a fairly level bench of land that we can follow around to that cut west of here."

Lauren straightened and craned her head back to look up. About a hundred feet above their heads an abandoned mine building clung to the mountainside, its broken flume dangling out in air. The bench he wanted to reach was another hundred feet or so above that. "All the way up there? That's almost straight up. We'll never make it."

"We'll make it. We have to. Quit wasting time worrying about it and just do it. And get those shoes off. And take off your gloves, too. You'll need to get a good grip in places."

"Why are we doing this? Wouldn't it be easier to go that way?" she asked, pointing to the south, where the mountain sloped downward toward a high open meadow.

"That's the point. They'll expect us to take off that way. I even left a false trail before I came back to the cabin. It won't fool an experienced tracker for long, but it may give us a little extra time. We need all the breaks we can get.

"Anyway, that meadow is farther away than you think. Before we could get across that open stretch they'd have us lined up in their crosshairs."

Lauren winced. Now there was a pleasant thought.

"They won't be expecting us to go this way, and tracking someone over rock is more difficult—even rock with snow on it. I'm hoping, by the time they figure it out, we'll have bought ourselves even more time."

Still unconvinced, Lauren bit her lower lip and looked doubtful. Nevertheless, she did as she was told.

Sam already had his snowshoes tied to the backpack by the time she stood up, and he took hers from her and quickly secured them to the bag she carried. When done, he pulled a short length of nylon rope from the pack and tied one end around her waist and the other around his. "Okay, let's move out."

The trail had long since grown over with scrub, and in places it had been altered by rock slides and was mostly covered with snow, to the point that Lauren couldn't make out a path at all. Sam, however, had no such difficulty. He set a grueling pace, climbing with the speed and agility of a mountain goat. Tethered to him, Lauren had no choice but to keep up as best she could.

Huffing and straining, she clambered over boulders and struggled up steep grades on which the merest toeholds had been chipped out by some long-ago miner. More than once she slipped on icy spots and loose rocks. Each time she cried out in terror but somehow she managed to grab hold of a nearby bush or tree branch and arrest her slide. Even so, if it hadn't been for the safety line she knew she would have probably tumbled down the mountainside.

Another slip was followed by a shriek, and Sam scowled at her over his shoulder. "Keep it down, will you? Sound carries a long way in these mountains."

"I can't...help it," she gasped. "Nearly falling to my death tends to frighten me."

"You're not going to fall. The rope will prevent that. Just watch where I step and do what I do and you'll be okay."

He turned back before she could answer, and Lauren ground her teeth and aimed a blistering look at a spot between his shoulder blades. What did he *think* she'd been doing? She'd been trying to mimic his every move, but the difference in their heights, and therefore their strides, did not always make that possible.

It took perhaps twenty minutes of hard scrabble climbing to reach the old mine shack. By that time Lauren was winded and her palms were scraped and stinging. She had assumed they would take a rest break at the abandoned mine shack, but Sam forged on without so much as a pause. She wanted to protest but pride kept her silent. That and a lingering wariness of his black mood.

For the first seventy-five or eighty feet above the mine shack the going was arduous, even more so than on the so-called trail they had followed the first half of the climb. At various times, Lauren found herself clinging to the mountain by her fingertips and climbing up impossible grades, often pulling herself up by grabbing onto bushes and small trees.

The higher they went, the more difficult the ascent became, especially for Lauren. Sam's moccasins seemed to give him a surefooted grip, but her heavy boots, though they protected her feet from the sharp rocks, made the climbing awkward for her.

Lauren was concentrating so fiercely she hadn't realized that Sam had stopped until she climbed up onto a ledge beside him.

"We'll never make it up this," he said, craning his neck back to look up.

Pressed as flat as she could get to the rock-face, Lauren clutched the granite slab in a death grip. Carefully she tilted her head to follow Sam's gaze and saw that above them, all the way to the bench, was a perpendicular cliff face. To her eye, there didn't appear to be so much as a fingerhold in the smooth rock.

"We'll have to make our way around this outcrop and find a better spot," Sam announced.

"What, on this?" Lauren looked down at her feet. The shelf of rock on which they stood was no deeper that her boots. The heels of Sam's moccasins hung over the edge a good two inches and all there was to hold on to was this smooth, curving rock. It had been scary enough climbing up here, but the thought of edging sideways on this tiny ledge made her blood run cold. "No. No, we can't. That's suicide."

"We don't have a choice. Before too much longer we're going to have company, and we're sitting ducks up here. C'mon, let's go." Extending his left arm, he ran his hand over the rock-face until he found another fingerhold, then, slowly, carefully, sidestepped to his left, pushing the snow off the ledge with his left foot as he inched away from her.

Lauren hugged the cliff-face, too terrified to move, watching him. Her cheek was flattened against the icy rock, the hardness of it grinding her flesh against her cheekbone, but she bore the pain rather than loosen her grip.

The tether grew taut, and Sam looked back, surprised to see that she hadn't budged. "What are you doing just standing there?" he snapped. "Move."

"I...I can't."

"Yes, you damn well can," he growled. Then he must have seen the hellish fear in her eyes because when he spoke again the timbre of his voice had dropped, become deeper, gentler, more persuasive. "You're a strong, intelligent woman, Lauren. A survivor. You can do this."

"No, I—"

"Lauren, listen to me. These past few days you've done a lot of things you probably never thought you could do. You can do this, too. Just reach out and find a fingerhold, then slide your left foot over. C'mon, Lauren," he coaxed. "You can do it."

He held out his right hand, and his dark eyes locked with hers, willing her to come to him. "C'mon, baby," he whispered.

Maybe it was his tenderness, or the mesmerizing quality of his stare, or the steely strength he exuded.

Lauren didn't know, but something in her responded. Trembling, hesitant, she did as he instructed.

"That's it. You're doing fine. Just take it nice and slow. Atta girl."

She inched along, hugging the cliff, her heart pounding like a jackhammer against the rock, a knot of ice lodged in her chest. Her insides were trembling like gelatin.

Then she made the mistake of glancing down.

Spread out far below them was a sea of treetops and a bird's-eye view of the cabin, which, from there, looked like a child's toy.

Her head spun and her stomach dropped. With a cry, she froze and squeezed her eyes shut and clung even tighter to the cliff-face. "Oh God. Oh God. Oh God."

"Don't look down! Don't look down!" Sam ordered.

Now you tell me, Lauren thought, biting her tongue to keep from screaming.

"Look at me. C'mon, Lauren, open your eyes. That's it, that's it," he encouraged when she reluctantly obeyed. "Now focus on my face and don't look away. Just look at me. And don't think about where you are," he ordered in a velvety voice.

Screwing up her courage, Lauren stared into those dark eyes and moved ever so slightly to the left again.

"That's it. Just take it nice and slow. You're doing fine. C'mon. It isn't far. Just a few more steps," he coaxed, moving to his left just out of her reach. "You're doing great. Keep going. A little more is all— No! Don't look down! Keep your eyes on me. That's it. Thata girl.''

It seemed to take forever, like some terrible nightmare that had her in its grip and would not allow her to wake up. As they inched along, with Sam coaxing and encouraging Lauren every step of the way, the ledge climbed steadily, making the going even tougher. Finally they maneuvered around the curve of the rock-face and found themselves in a V-shaped area where two formations met and the ledge ended. The juncture was rough and jagged, but mercifully it had an inward slant and offered handholds.

"I think we can get to the top here," Sam said. He looked at Lauren. "Ready?"

Ready? she thought on the verge of hysteria. *Ready?* Lord, have mercy, she would *never* be ready for this. Never in a million years. She was clinging to a steep cliff hundreds of feet above the treetops, for Pete's sake.

Flattened against the rock-face, she clung to its rough surface like a limpet, so frightened she could barely breathe. Oh God, oh God, oh God.

She didn't want to move. But she couldn't stay here. As though to emphasize that point, the wind kicked up, buffeting her cruelly, as though trying to peel her away from the rock's surface, bouncing the dangling snowshoes against the backs of her thighs. Left with no choice, she screwed up her courage and managed the merest of nods. "I...I'm ready."

"Okay, here we go."

Sam reached up and grabbed a jagged rock with

one hand and started climbing, finding and testing hand and toeholds, working his way steadily upward. He was about ten feet above her when the rope began to tauten again.

"C'mon, Lauren. We're almost there. Just a little more to go."

Lauren tried to swallow, but her throat was too dry.

"Reach up with your right hand. There's a rock you can get a good grip on above your head."

Pressing her lips together, she drew a shuddering breath. With her arms spread wide to either side, she was barely holding on by her fingertips. The thought of letting go with one hand terrified her. She wasn't sure she could do it.

"C'mon, Lauren. It's the only way."

She whimpered and squeezed her eyes shut, but after a while she slid her hand slowly upward, and sure enough, about a foot above her head her fingers curved over a sharp edge. It was the most secure hold she'd had on anything since they'd started this climb, and she gripped the rock so tightly her knuckles whitened. Cautiously she slid her other hand up and found another handhold.

"Pull yourself up and throw your leg over the edge," Sam encouraged, pulling up on the rope to take part of her weight and assist her.

Straining with all her might, Lauren did as he instructed, and hoisted herself upward, trying not to shudder when her feet lost contact with the narrow ledge.

"Okay, now grab that sharp rock just above you to your left."

With Sam a few feet above her, directing her every move, Lauren slowly inched her way toward the rim. She concentrated on one move at a time, all her focus and energy zeroed in on what she was doing. She didn't notice how close they were to their goal until Sam gave an explosive sound somewhere between a grunt and a groan, and she looked up in time to see him drag himself over the top.

Panic assailed her when he momentarily disappeared from her line of vision. Then he poked his head over the edge and grinned down at her, his face full of male triumph. "Made it. Now you. Hook your fingers in that crevice and step up on that slab of rock, then reach up and grab the trunk of that sapling."

She did as he instructed, but no matter how hard she tried her fingers were a few inches shy of the tree. "I...can't...reach it," she gasped.

"Try again."

She rose up on tiptoes and stretched her body as far as she could, but it was no use. "I...can't. I'm too...short."

"Damn."

Lauren resumed her precarious fingertip hold on the crevice and scanned the six feet or so of mountainside between her and Sam. There was nothing else to grab hold of but that one scrawny spruce sapling.

The wind still slapped at her and her fingers were beginning to cramp. She didn't know how much longer she could hold on. She whimpered without realizing it, and gazed pleadingly up at Sam.

"Don't panic," he ordered. "You're okay. We'll just have to go to Plan B."

Leaning out over the edge of the precipice, he wrapped the safety rope around his wrist, gripped it firmly and pulled it taut. "Now, I want you to grab the rope at about your shoulder level with both hands and at the same time brace your feet against the slope and lean back."

"Lean back?" She glanced fearfully over her shoulder. "Are you crazy?"

"You'll be okay, I promise. As I pull you up you 'walk' up the side."

"Walk?" she said weakly. "I don't think this rope will support me."

"Sure it will. Trust me, babe. I won't let you fall."

She didn't have any choice. She closed her eyes and said a quick prayer, then began to count. One. Two. She took a deep breath. Three.

She grabbed the rope with both hands and screamed as she felt her upper body tilt backward, but somehow the soles of her boots found purchase on the slope. Then she was being pulled upward.

It wasn't easy. Her bare hands were so cold they hurt, yet the rope burned her palms. The strain on her arms and shoulder muscles was excruciating, but she set her jaw and forced her feet to move.

"You're doing great. Just a little more," Sam grated out.

The muscles and tendons in his neck stood out and

his face was red from exertion, but, hand over hand, he pulled her steadily toward him. When her head was within three feet of the top two things happened—the thin rope began to fray and she lost her footing.

There was no time for more than a gasp of fright from Lauren before Sam's hand whipped out and clamped around one of her wrists. The next thing she knew she was dangling in space by one arm.

"Be still," Sam snapped. "Don't kick. I've got you." He frowned. "Jesus, woman, you can't weigh a hundred pounds soaking wet. It's a wonder you don't blow away."

In one quick, continuous motion, he plucked her up and over the top as though she were a sack of feathers and rolled with her away from the edge. When they came to a stop Lauren lay sprawled on top of him.

For a moment she clung to him with her face buried against his chest, gasping and shuddering.

Sam rubbed his hands up and down her back. "It's okay. You're safe now. You made it. Shh. Shh. You're all right, little one. It's over."

He had only a second's warning. A low rumble started deep inside her, almost like a cat's purr, but the sound increased steadily in volume and intensity as it rose in her throat. When it erupted in a shriek of pure rage she hauled off and socked him.

"You *jerk!*"

Eleven

"Hey!" Sam yelped.

Lauren pummeled him with both fists. "Idiot! Imbecile! You nearly got me killed! *Again!*"

"Dammit! Will you knock it off and listen to m— *Oof!*"

"No! I won't listen to you! You got me into this mess! You and your brain-dead friends in Denver." Lauren rammed her fist into his gut, too furious and shaken to do anything but lash out. "You risked my life. And for what? Those men were probably here to...rescue us...just like I said," she gasped out between blows. She struck out blindly with both hands, slapping and pounding with all the pent-up fear and anxiety that had been building for days. "We could have flown...out of here in...a helicopter if you would just...listen to...reason! But, no. You don't...trust anyone, so we had to climb this...stupid mountain!"

"Hey! Cut it out, before I have to hurt you."

"Ha! Just try it!"

Sam grabbed her wrists, but then Lauren began to kick and thrash. When her knee came too close for comfort, he wrapped his legs around hers, scissor-fashion, and rolled her onto her back. Pinning her hands deep in the snow on either side of her head, he held her down with the weight of his body.

''You little hell-cat.'' He glared down into her furious face. ''Will you calm down for a second and let me—?''

''No!'' She bucked her hips. ''Get off of me, you oaf! I don't wa—''

His mouth closed over hers, swallowing the rest of the tirade.

Shocked to her core, Lauren froze, her eyes wide, as though the touch of his mouth on hers had short-circuited her brain. The stunned reaction lasted only a moment. Then all the raging passion still churning inside her came boiling back to the surface. Her heart took off at a thundering gallop, and she kissed him back, matching the punishing kiss with a fury and ardor that equaled his.

The kiss was hot, greedy, devouring—an eruption of emotion and need. Their mouths plundered, giving no quarter, each taking what they wanted, demanding more.

Sam released her wrists to cup one hand around her face while the other slid downward to her breasts. Encountering the bulky parka, he made a frustrated sound.

Lauren grasped his head between her palms, knocking aside his parka hood and knit cap to winnow her fingers through his hair and explore his scalp, the shape of his head. The thick, ebony strands felt like warm silk slithering through her chilled fingers.

They strained together, driven by a need neither understood nor expected. It was instinctive, desperate, irresistible. Primal.

The flare of fierce emotions burned bright for several seconds, but gradually the kiss forged into something deeper, stronger—a hot and searing pleasure so intense it took Lauren's breath away and made her feel as though her bones were melting.

She clung to Sam and returned the kiss with a simmering passion that matched his, even while on some distant level she was shocked and appalled by what was happening.

This was the last thing she had expected—or wanted, she told herself. Sam didn't even *like* her, for Pete's sake. Nor did she care much for him, except in a purely practical way. He was, after all, an excellent man to have on your side in a crisis. But he was also hard and cold and distant, even downright unfriendly, and his opinion of her was about as low as it could get.

Yet…she could not summon the will to stop what was happening. The pleasure was too great, the need too compelling.

Sam groaned. He felt as though his world had suddenly shifted on its axis. Nothing was as it should be, and he had a hunch that it might never be again. That possibility terrified him.

The kiss had been an impulse, one of those things

that just happens before you can stop it. Borne out of anger, it should have been a punishment, even an insult for Lauren, and nothing more than a meaningless encounter for him, but it was none of those things. The feel of her, the softness of her lips, the sensations he was experiencing, all rocked him to his soul and left him weak and shaken...and desperate for more.

This was insane, he told himself, as his tongue mated with hers. They were in a tight spot. There was no time for this. They had to make tracks out of here, fast.

Even as the thoughts went through his mind he deepened the kiss, unable to resist her mouth or the extravagant sensations that throbbed between them.

Finally, though, common sense prevailed, and from somewhere he found the strength to pull away. Their lips clung, parting with exquisite slowness as he raised his head.

Except for their heaving chests, neither moved. Sam's dark eyes fixed on Lauren and narrowed. Damn. She looked sexy as hell, her face relaxed and flushed, her lips a bit swollen and still wet from his kiss. He winced when he noticed that around her mouth her delicate skin was red and abraded from his beard.

They were both breathing heavily, their breath mingling between them in a white fog. Through the mist, Sam watched her eyelids flutter open. She gazed up at him, her green eyes still clouded with passion and slightly out of focus. The sight nearly drove Sam over the edge again. He ground his teeth and waited.

"Why——" Her voice broke, and she cleared her throat and licked her lips. Sam had to stifle a groan. "Why did you do that?" she whispered.

He stared at her for a long time. Finally he shrugged. "I had to shut you up someway."

Even before all the words had left his lips he regretted the comment. Hurt flashed in her eyes, and Sam cursed silently. He could have kicked himself, though a part of him accepted that it was probably for the best. Even if she wasn't Carlo's mistress, she was still a witness and his responsibility. He had no business touching her.

He watched the passion fade from her eyes and her mouth tighten. Before she could lash out again he rolled off of her and sat up. "Let's get going. We've wasted enough time already."

"Why you insufferable——"

Lauren scrambled to her feet, only to have Sam grab her arm and jerk her back down again.

"Wha——?

"Just shut up and stay down," Sam commanded in a gruff voice, shoving her roughly down, flat on her belly. Keeping his hand clamped around the back of her neck, he ignored her squirming and held her in place and flattened himself in the snow beside her.

Lauren sputtered and spit snow out of her mouth and swiped the icy globs off her face. "What do you think you're doing?" she snarled. "Let go of me."

Ignoring her struggles, he raised his head cautiously and peered over the edge of the drop-off. "You think I worry for nothing? Take a look down there. That's the reason we made this climb."

Releasing her, Sam slid one arm out of the backpack and scrounged inside for the binoculars while Lauren raised her head and peeked over the side.

Far below, three armed men eased out of the woods and moved cautiously into the clearing.

"Still think they're here to rescue us?"

"Okay, so they're carrying rifles. That doesn't mean they're the bad guys," Lauren insisted, but the uneasiness in her voice came through all the same.

"Just watch and see what they do." Looping the binocular strap around his neck, Sam raised the glasses and scanned from one man to the next. They had on ski masks and their parka hoods were up. Identifying any of them from that distance and angle was impossible.

The leader signaled to the other two, and they spread out across the small clearing. Crouched low, they moved with stealth toward the cabin, weapons ready.

At the cabin they pressed their backs to the log walls on either side of the door. The leader again gave a hand signal, and he and the man on the other side of the door rushed inside. Instantly the sound of automatic weapon fire erupted.

Lauren gave a startled cry and jumped back, unconsciously scooting closer to Sam. "Oh my God!"

The staccato sound went on for several seconds. Sam's eyes narrowed and his mouth thinned into a grim line. The bastards were spraying the inside of the cabin with bullets. If he and Lauren had been inside they wouldn't have had a chance.

The shooting stopped as quickly as it began. Seconds later the men came back outside. They scanned the clearing again, then huddled together for a discussion. After a few minutes they spread out and began searching the ground for tracks.

Lauren lowered her head and buried her face against her crossed arms, shuddering. "They found me. Even here, in the middle of nowhere. Oh God, they're going to kill us."

"Like hell they are."

"Oh, right. And just how are you going to stop them?"

"For starters, we're going to outrun them. It'll take them a while to find our trail. They will, eventually, but by then we'll have gained more time. There's no place between here and the crash site for that chopper to land and pick them up, so those three will either climb up after us or hike back to the chopper and hunt us from the air. Either way, by then we'll have a couple of hours lead on them, and we're going to make the most of it. If we can beat them back to civilization, we can shake them. So, c'mon, let's go."

"Hunt us from the air!" Lauren squeaked. "Dear Lord, we won't have a chance!"

Ignoring her, Sam scooted backward through the

snow a few feet until he was far enough from the edge of the cliff that he was out of sight of the men below. Sitting up, he scowled at Lauren as he untied his snowshoes from his backpack. "C'mon, get over here and put those snowshoes on. Let's go, let's go!"

She did as he ordered, simply because she had no other choice. "This is hopeless. We're going to be sitting ducks if they come after us in the helicopter."

"Not really. Spotting someone from the air is a lot more difficult than it looks. We'll keep to the trees, and when we hear the chopper coming we'll dive for cover."

Sam knelt on one knee, then the other as he wound the lacings over and around his boots. "Anyway, they won't be able to sustain an aerial search for long. These mountains are too remote and that chopper's fuel capacity isn't that great. The pilot will probably do a sweep or two, then head back to base and leave the others to track us on foot. I'm sure they came prepared for the possibility."

He stood and stomped his feet to test the bindings. Lauren finished tying hers and did the same. Sam watched her, and when he was satisfied he turned and headed for the thick stand of fir trees that blanketed the bench of land and most of the mountain slopes below ten thousand feet. "C'mon. Let's go."

"Go where? If they found us here, they can find us anywhere."

He stopped and looked back, fixing her with that inscrutable stare that sent little tingles dancing along her spine. "Don't make the mistake of crediting Carlo with more power than he has. He's a mob boss who controls a small army of thugs. That makes him a dangerous man, but he's not omnipotent. The only reason his men found us is because we have at least one agent in the Denver office who's on Carlo's payroll. Maybe more."

"*What!* You *knew* this? Then how on earth did you think you could keep me safe?"

"Besides myself and Dave, only four others knew about you. Four trusted agents who I thought were clean. I was wrong. At least one of those four is dirty."

Just saying that out loud made Sam's gut clench. Dammit, he would have trusted every one of those men with his life. Even Harvey.

"How did they—?"

"We don't have time for this discussion right now. You have a right to know what's going on, and I'll answer your questions later, but right now it's time to get the hell outta Dodge."

"What's the point? They'll find us, somehow. There's no safe place to hide."

"I know a place. Trust me, Lauren. I'm going to do everything I can to keep you safe. I won't let anyone hurt you. You have my word on that."

"Ah, yes, how could I forget? You need me to make your case against Mr. Giovessi, don't you?"

"There is that," he answered finally. "But now it's personal, too."

"You mean because they almost killed you, too, while trying to eliminate me?"

"No. That's part of the risk you take when you sign on as an agent." He stared at her, unblinking. "For what it's worth, I wasn't honest with you before. I didn't kiss you to shut you up. I kissed you because I wanted to. Because I've been wanting to ever since the moment I first saw you."

He turned and walked away toward the woods, leaving her standing speechless, staring after him with her jaw hanging open.

She was so stunned she couldn't move, or even think at first. Then he disappeared into the woods, and she jolted. "No, wait! *Wait!*"

She might as well have saved her breath. Sam ignored her and forged on at a pace just under a trot. Lauren hurried after him as fast as she could, almost tripping several times in the awkward snowshoes before she caught the rhythm.

She followed along behind him, her gaze drilling a hole through the back of his parka. Darn him. He was the most aggravating, enigmatic man. How could he make such an astounding statement, then turn and walk off?

He hadn't meant it. Of course he hadn't. She'd figured out that much. He'd just said that to snap her out of the despondent mood she'd sunk into and get her mind off of those men.

The devil of it was, it had worked.

Lauren narrowed her eyes and glared at his back. Oh, you're good, Rawlins. Very clever.

Sam set a grueling pace. He broke into a run wherever he could, eating up the ground with that awkward, side-to-side, rocking hop and making it look easy.

For Lauren, just keeping up took tremendous effort and concentration. She had to take three or four steps to every two of his, thanks to the difference in their sizes.

Added to that, it was bitter cold, and getting colder. Lauren's breathing quickly grew rough and rapid, her lungs working furiously. With every raspy breath they burned like fire.

Sam didn't stop. When she gasped that she needed water he merely passed the canteen back to her and kept going without breaking stride.

Before long Lauren forgot about Sam's stunning statement. She forgot about the men who were tracking her. She forgot about the cold and the unforgiving wilderness all around them. Her entire focus centered on putting one foot in front of the other as quickly as possible without tripping herself.

Lauren had believed that she was in good physical condition, but after almost two hours of the relentless pace, she was exhausted. Positive she had reached the end of her rope, she opened her mouth to protest that she couldn't move another step when they heard the distinctive *whop-whop-whop-whop-whop* of a helicopter approaching.

Halting, Sam swung around and held out his hand to her. "Here they come! C'mon! C'mon! Hurry!"

It was amazing what fear and adrenaline could do. Lauren trailed him by about twenty feet, but she shot forward as though she were rocket-powered, her fatigue forgotten. The instant she was within reach Sam grabbed her hand. He jerked her to the ground, wrapped his arms around her and rolled them beneath the low hanging branches of the nearest fir tree.

When they came to a stop against the trunk, Lauren lay on her back with Sam sprawled on top of her. He raised his head and listened. "Here it comes!" he shouted in her ear. Then he lowered his head and did his best to cover her completely with his body.

The helicopter grew steadily closer until it was about a hundred feet directly above them. The noise was deafening. Overhead the tree they were under and all the surrounding ones swayed in the rotor wash and dumped snow.

Clutching Sam's back, Lauren closed her eyes and sent up a silent prayer. It seemed to her that the craft hovered over them for a few seconds. Expecting to feel bullets ripping through her flesh at any second, she held her breath.

The impression must have been a trick of nerves, because the chopper continued on in a zigzagging course, clearly still searching.

Sam and Lauren remained absolutely still, clutching each other tightly and listening to the engine noise fade into the distance. When it was no more than a soft rumble, Sam raised his head, listening.

"Do you think they're gone?" Lauren murmured.

"For now." He looked down at her. "You okay?"

"Yes, I...I'm okay. A little shaken, but at least I'm still alive. We both are."

"Yeah," he agreed in a throaty murmur.

In an instant, everything changed.

Adrenaline ran high, and the taut quiet that surrounded them still quivered with danger and anxiety, yet with that one word awareness sparked between them like arcing electricity.

Sam's dark eyes roamed slowly over Lauren's face, and when his gaze met hers she felt her heart skip a beat. The crackling current sizzled between them, skipped along her nerve endings, making them jump and tingle.

She became conscious of the intimacy of their position, that Sam still lay stretched out on top of her, that their faces were so close she could feel his warm breath on her face, see, for the first time, the slightly darker pupils at the centers of his black eyes, see each stubby hair of his emerging beard, each individual eyelash that rimmed his midnight-black eyes.

See the heat in those ebony depths.

A thrilling little shiver rippled through Lauren.

Sam's broad-shouldered torso completely covered her much smaller one, pressing her deep into the snow. Even through their bulky parkas she became suddenly, acutely aware of the differences in their bodies—Sam's big, whipcord lean and tough. And utterly male. Hers small and soft and delicate.

Her heart beat in her chest like a wild thing, and through the layers of down and padding she could feel his thundering a deep counterpoint rhythm.

His gaze locked with hers—searching, intense, hot. Lauren could not have looked away had her life depended on it. Raw desire that he made no effort to hide tautened his rough-chiseled face beneath the stubble.

Trembling, Lauren stared back. So many emotions tangled inside her, tightening her chest and clogging her throat. She could barely breathe.

They were stretched out in deep snow, and the thin mountain air around them was so cold it was almost crystalline, yet her body felt flushed and hot, feverish.

Sam's gaze dropped to her parted lips. She saw the pulse in his temple jump, and so did her heart.

"Sa-Sam...we...that is...."

"You're so beautiful," he whispered.

Surprise shot through her, and immediately her brain scrambled. "I..." Staring at him, wide-eyed, she exhaled a shuddering breath and circled her dry lips with the tip of her tongue.

His gaze zeroed in on the tiny action, and she saw his pupils flare. Then his eyelids grew heavy, and his head tilted to one side.

Lauren's heart took off on a snare drumroll, and as his head began a slow descent her own eyelids fluttered shut and a sigh fluttered through her parted lips.

Sam's mouth had barely touched hers when his head jerked back and he went taut and still.

"What—?" Lauren began, but before she could express her shock and hurt she heard the ominous sound. "Oh dear God. They're coming back! They *did* see us."

"Be still," he ordered when she tried to scramble out from under him in full-blown panic. Raising up on one elbow, he flattened his other hand across her chest to hold her in place and looked up, his head cocked, listening.

The noise came closer and the trees began to sway, and Lauren cringed, but the chopper passed overhead without pause.

Sam looked down at her, his face stern and commanding. "Don't move until I tell you." He waited for her agreement, and when she merely continued to stare up at him, he raised both eyebrows. "Understand?"

She nodded and swallowed hard. "Ye-yes."

He studied her a moment longer, then nodded. He rolled off of her and shrugged off the backpack.

Squirming on his belly, he moved to the outer edge of the overhanging, pulled the rifle off his shoulder and peered out through the branches. He raised the binoculars he still wore around his neck and tracked the craft. "It's okay. They're just searching in a crisscross grid. When they found our trail, they probably calculated approximately how far ahead of them we were, and they're searching a radius of that distance in every direction. They can't keep it up for long, though. Soon they'll be too low on fuel and have to head back to base. All we have to do is sit tight and wait them out."

"Thank God." Lauren closed her eyes with heartfelt relief. "If they have to give up the search we'll be safe. There won't be anyone hunting us down to kill us."

"Not quite." Sam lowered the binoculars and looked over his shoulder at her. "There are only two men in that chopper."

"Two? But you saw..."

"Right. There were five men at the wreckage. That means there are now three tracking us on foot."

Lauren felt her face blanch. Sam turned back and focused the binoculars on the helicopter again, slowly moving the glasses from side to side as he followed the craft's zigzagging sweep. "I suggest you start praying that chopper pilot is the cautious type and will head back to base pretty damn quick. For every minute we're pinned under this tree, those three hired guns are getting closer."

Twelve

Every second that ticked by seemed an eternity. After twenty minutes Lauren was wound so tight she thought she would surely fly apart at any second. She could barely restrain herself from bursting out from under the cover of the tree and running for her life.

The helicopter was far enough away now that its engine noise was no more than a distant buzz, but Sam still tracked the craft with the binoculars.

"There they go. They're packing it in and heading back."

"At last." She closed her eyes and exhaled a long breath.

"Let's go." Sam grabbed the backpack and scrambled out from beneath the branches. Needing no second urging, Lauren wriggled out right behind him.

How long had they been hiding? she wondered, falling into step behind him. Thirty minutes? Forty-five? She had no idea. It had seemed like forever.

And the whole time the men on their trail had been gaining on them.

As they tramped across the snow she could not stop

herself from checking over her shoulder every few minutes.

They broke out of the trees into a clear area. "Let's go! Let's go!" Sam took off at double-time. Lauren didn't object, although she had to hustle just to keep him in sight. Nor did she complain when the slope became steeper. Better to risk her neck in a fall than to take a bullet.

For hours they trekked over rough terrain. At times they were forced to remove their snowshoes to negotiate drop-offs and rocky outcrops, then stop and put them back on to cross patches of fresh powder over three feet deep.

Lauren had never attempted anything so strenuous. She panted and gasped every step. Her lungs burned and her breathing grew so rough and raspy it hurt her throat. Her shoulders and back ached from carrying the duffle bag and her legs felt like lead. Still, she ignored the pain and fatigue and forged on. Somewhere behind them were three assassins.

They ate their noonday meal of jerky and an energy bar on the go. Sam kept the same grueling pace for hours, stopping only rarely to take a compass reading or peer through the binoculars. Lauren took advantage of the infrequent stops to take a drink of water and catch her breath, leaning against a tree or rock, whichever was handy. She didn't dare sit down. She wasn't sure she would have the strength to get back up.

After endless hiking and scrambling over boulders and sidestepping down steep slopes, often snagging the ends of tree limbs to stop themselves from tumbling, Lauren was moving like an automaton, numb to everything but the need to keep going.

When twilight descended she assumed they would soon make camp, but Sam showed no sign of stopping.

"S-Sam! Wh-when are we go-going to stop for the n-night?" she panted.

"We're not," he called back. "The moon is close to being full. The moonlight...reflecting off the snow will provide a lot of illumination...which means it's unlikely those guys...behind us will stop," he explained between breaths. "That means we have to keep going, too."

Lauren looked around at the lengthening shadows. "Isn't that d-dangerous? Will we...be able to s-see?"

"Not well, but under the circumstances...night travel is a risk we have to take."

Great, she thought tiredly. One more thing to worry about.

A short time later they reached a thick stand of trees and Sam announced that they'd take a short break. Bending from the waist, Lauren braced her hands on her knees and struggled to bring her breathing under control.

"There's a good clump of scrub oak over there you can use for cover. Better shake a leg and take care of business while you can," Sam warned.

Lauren didn't have the strength to object to his tone

or even to comment. Without a word, she straightened and trudged for the brush to answer nature's call.

By the time she returned Sam had built a minuscule fire and melted enough snow to prepare one of the dehydrated packets. Lauren shot a fearful look around. "Do we have time for that? Shouldn't we keep going?"

"We need fuel, and a hot meal will warm us up and keep us going longer. Besides, those guys have to eat, too."

When she met Sam he hadn't shaved in several days. Now, after four days on the run, he had the beginnings of a thick beard. His hair had grown also, Lauren realized. A swath of it fell across his forehead, thick and arrow-straight and shining with the blue-black sheen of a raven's wing. In the firelight his skin had a golden bronze hue, and as she studied his hawk-ish profile she was struck by how obvious it was that he had Native American blood. Funny. She hadn't noticed that before—not even afer he'd told her about his mother.

There was just something about him, an attitude as much as his physical appearance, she reasoned. Sam looked natural squatting on his haunches before the fire—tough and competent, even a little dangerous. A primitive alpha male. Dominant. Sexy.

A delicate shiver rippled through Lauren. She looked away from his craggy profile and hugged her arms across her middle.

"It's ready," Sam announced. He pulled two

spoons from the backpack and handed one to her, then he held up the pot between them. "Dig in. And eat fast. We're outta here in five minutes."

The hot stew tasted delicious, and the warmth of it sliding down her throat was pure heaven.

Lauren was almost giddy with fatigue, and as she and Sam wolfed down the contents of the pot she almost giggled when she thought of all the elegant dinners she'd attended during the course of her career.

"Something funny?"

She glanced up and found that Sam was eyeing her.

"No. Not at all," she denied. Ducking her head again, she scooped up another bite, and fought down the urge to laugh hysterically as she pictured how horrified all those posh music patrons would be if they could see her now, hunkered down in the woods in the snow with a scruffy, bristly-faced man, gobbling a reconstituted meal out of a metal pot.

They finished off the last few bites and Sam gave the pot and spoons a cursory rub with snow and stuffed them back into the pack. After kicking snow over the small fire, he surprised Lauren by helping her to her feet. Still holding her hand, he studied her face in the fading light. "You okay?"

The concern in his voice surprised her even more and sent a queer sensation dancing over her skin and, absurdly, brought tears to her eyes.

Annoyed with herself, she blinked the moisture away and shook her head. "Yes. I'm fine. I'm ready when you are," she said, reaching for the duffle bag.

Full darkness descended moments after they set off again. The pale moonlight reflected off the snow in a bluish glow that was eerily beautiful.

They pressed on at a steady and only somewhat slower pace for the next few hours. By ten Lauren was nearly asleep on her feet. She followed Sam like a zombie as they carefully picked their way down a steep slope. Her movements were so stiff and uncoordinated it took only one small misstep to bring disaster.

She was so exhausted she barely cried out, but her small yelp alerted Sam. He stopped and looked back just as Lauren tumbled past him. She went head-over-heels down the slope, rolling and bouncing, arms and legs flailing like a rag doll.

"Jesus!" Sam's heart stopped, then took off again like a rocket. *"Lau-reeen!"*

Throwing caution to the wind, he scrambled after her in a loping sidestep, leaping down the mountain-side and sending snow cascading down in front of him.

Lauren crashed into a clump of brush about forty feet below where Sam had stopped and came to an abrupt halt. He kept his gaze on her motionless form and felt an icy hand squeeze his heart.

"Hold on! I'm coming! I'm coming!" Panting, his heart pounding, he clambered down the last few feet and dropped to his knees by her side.

She lay on her back with her eyes closed, her arms outstretched. Frantically Sam jerked off his gloves and ran his hands over her arms and legs, her ribs, testing for broken bones. Mercifully she seemed to be in one piece. The cut she'd received in the plane crash was the only visible injury he could find.

He unzipped her coat and spread the edges wide, then bent and pressed his ear against her chest. Relief poured through him when he heard the slow, strong beat of her heart. "Thank God," he muttered.

"Lauren? Lauren, talk to me." He brushed her tangled hair away from her face and patted her cheek smartly. "C'mon, open your eyes."

Her eyelids fluttered. "Wha...what happened?"

"You fell."

"Oh. Right," she mumbled. "I think I caught my snowshoe on the edge of a rock."

"Try to move and tell me if you hurt anywhere."

Cautiously she obeyed, turning her head slowly from side to side, rotating her shoulders. "I think I'm just a little shaken and bruised."

"Well, that's it. We're going to have to stop and get some rest."

"Oh, but—"

"We don't have a choice, Lauren. You're dead on your feet. It's too dangerous to keep going." He looked around. "There's a cluster of boulders over there against a cliff-face. If we camp in among them they'll probably hide our fire. If they don't, it's at least a defendable spot."

Lauren winced at that, but she held her tongue.

Sam looked at her again with concern. "Can you walk?"

"I...I think so."

When he rose she took hold of his arm and gamely struggled to her feet. After taking a few cautious steps to test her legs, they headed for the rocks.

Luck was with them. In the cliff-face behind the boulders Sam located a small, shallow cave. It was only about five or six feet deep and they both had to stoop to get inside, but it offered protection from the wind and would reflect the heat from a fire.

When Sam announced he was going to gather brush and firewood, Lauren immediately offered to help, but he overruled her. "No. You just stay here and rest."

"But—"

"Dammit, Lauren, you just took a nasty fall."

She opened her mouth to argue, but he hooked his gloved hand around her neck and pressed a hard kiss on her cold lips, silencing her. When he raised his head, he stared deep into her startled eyes, and murmured, "I know you want to do your share, but this time, humor me. Let me take care of you. Okay?"

"O-okay," she said meekly. He didn't know whether she was too stunned or too tired to argue. At the moment, he didn't much care. He just wanted to get a fire going and let her sleep.

"Good." Sam pulled the flashlight from the backpack and shined it into the cave. "We're in luck. No critters. Here, you take this," he said, handing her the flashlight. "Go on in and sit down. I'll be back before you know it."

It took him close to a half hour to gather the minimum he needed. When he returned, Lauren was curled on her side at the back of the cave with the lit flashlight still in her hand, sound asleep.

Kneeling beside her, he studied her pale face, and a strange sensation curled in his belly. He bent over and brushed a tangled lock of hair off her forehead and took the flashlight from her limp hand.

Working quickly, Sam arranged the spruce boughs into a mattress shape. He hadn't gathered as many as he would have liked, but it was imperative that he get her warm as soon as possible. Besides, he hadn't wanted to leave her alone any longer than absolutely necessary.

Within minutes he had the bed set up, and he scooped Lauren up and placed her into the sleeping bag. She didn't stir or make a sound. He would have been worried if he hadn't felt her breath on his cheek.

He zipped her into the bag, then turned his attention to building a fire just inside the cave opening within reach of the bed and stacked the remainder of the wood close by. When he was satisfied with the fire he took the coil of wire from the pack and left the cave.

The cave could be reached only by winding through the jumble of boulders. About twenty feet from the entrance, Sam strung a trip wire across the path, anchoring each end with a stack of small stones.

If the wire was disturbed the pile would come tumbling down. As security, it wasn't much, but at least the clatter would give them a few seconds' warning.

Back in the cave, he placed the rifle and his handgun within easy reach next to the sleeping bag before climbing in and pulling Lauren into his arms.

"Wake up. Breakfast is ready."

Lauren tried to turn away, but Sam gave her shoulder a shake.

"C'mon. Move it."

She moaned. It seemed as if she'd just closed her eyes. Prying her eyelids open a slit, she squinted against the light of the fire, then fixed her bleary gaze on the darkness beyond. "It's still the middle of the night," she groused.

"It'll be dawn soon. And when it is, our friends will be on the move."

The statement had the effect of a bucket of cold water in her face. Lauren shot out of the sleeping bag as though it was suddenly on fire.

In less than fifteen minutes they were on their way.

The strenuous hike the previous day had left her sore and bone weary, but Sam made no concessions. He kept up the same punishing pace, leaving her no choice but to do the same.

An hour or so of steady hiking worked out most of her aches and pains and she got her second wind. Though far from easy, the trek began to seem less arduous than it had the day before. She actually began to feel proud of herself for the way she was coping.

All right, so she was still dependant on Sam to keep her alive, she admitted to herself grudgingly. That galled her, but there was no denying it. Or any way around it. Without him, she wouldn't have a clue. But, by heaven, at least she was no helpless wimp.

A couple of hours after daybreak they descended into a high valley. Sam stopped and surveyed the area from the edge of the trees. Except for a few spruce and bare aspens and boulders dotted here and there, the valley was a long expanse of open snowfield, crisscrossed by a few animal tracks.

It occurred to Lauren that all the mountains looked much the same to her. For all she knew, they could have been wandering in a circle.

"Please tell me you know where we are," she said.

"I know." He pointed toward the end of the valley. "There's a pass between those two mountains. On the other side is another valley, lower than this one and more accessible from the highway that runs between Durango and Silverton. There's at least one vacation cabin there, maybe more by now. It's been a couple of years since I hunted in this area. If we can reach that cabin before dark, we'll spend the night there."

"If we'll be that close to a highway, why not keep going until we reach it?" Lauren questioned. "We might be able to hitch a ride." She'd never hitched a ride in her life, but she was willing to give it a try. "You said yourself that those men probably gained on us last night. If we stop for the night again, they may catch up.''

"First of all, I said the cabin was more accessible to the highway. That doesn't mean it's close by or easily reached. In the winter, unless you hike or ski, the only way in and out of that valley is by snow-mobile or helicopter. Anyway, we don't have a choice. Haven't you noticed? There's another storm coming in from the west.''

"What?'' Lauren's head snapped around toward the direction he'd indicated, and a fresh surge of fear rippled through her. A line of low-hanging dark clouds engulfed the distant mountaintops. And it was heading their way.

"We'll have to hole up somewhere, and so will they,'' Sam continued in his usual unperturbed voice. "Only I mean for us to do it in comfort this time. While those bastards are freezing their asses off, we'll be in a cozy vacation cabin. C'mon.'' He headed out, motioning for her to follow.

"We'll keep to the trees,'' he said over his shoulder. "It would be quicker to cut straight across the valley, but we can't chance being caught out in the open with no cover.''

By noon it had started to snow, but Sam wasn't displeased. "With any luck, the snow will cover our tracks before those guys get this far. That could buy us a little time.''

By the time they worked their way around the valley perimeter it was midafternoon, and Lauren was feeling the effects of two hard days. Though the valley floor was only a thousand feet or so below the pass summit, once they started climbing she began to flag in earnest.

Her legs hurt, her feet hurt, her back hurt, and if she wasn't mistaken, she had blisters on both feet. She was so exhausted her head felt as though it were packed with cotton, and she barely had the energy to put one foot in front of the other. And she was cold to the marrow of her bones.

The higher they climbed, the colder it became and the harder it snowed, shrouding the mountains in a veil of white, yet Sam pressed on with surefooted confidence. Lauren dragged after him, every step misery. By the time they reached the pass summit and started down, she was staggering with fatigue.

Sam watched her out of the corner of his eye, his concern growing. She's on the verge of collapse, he thought, noting her paleness and unsteady gait.

"You've been doing great. Don't fizzle out on me now," he cajoled. "I know you're tired, but it's just a little farther. The cabin is at the base of this slope. You can make it."

"Don't...worry 'bout...me. I'll...I'll make it."

"Sure you will. You're one tough la— Whoa!"

Lauren tripped and would have fallen if he hadn't caught her. "Easy, there. My heart won't take watching you fall again." Taking the duffle bag from her, he hooked it over his shoulder, then put his arm around her waist and pulled her close. "Here, lean on me."

"Not...nes-sary. I'm okay," she insisted, her voice slurred with fatigue. "I can make...it...on my own."

"Sure you can," he drawled. "Look, being independent is a good quality, but now's not the time. You're just making this harder. So give it up, because we're doing this my way."

"I'm...fine. I don't need..." Her cheek came into contact with his chest, and with a moan she closed her eyes and leaned against him.

"Damn fool stubborn woman," Sam growled between clenched teeth.

Though Lauren made a valiant effort to stay awake and on her feet, he half carried her the rest of the way.

The storm intensified into a raging blizzard as they picked their way down into the valley. The wind screamed like a banshee. Snow fell in a solid white curtain that shifted and swirled in the blow like a frenzied white dervish.

Sam struggled through the maelstrom with Lauren clamped to his side, cursing and blessing the storm at the same time. If it was snowing this hard on the other side of the pass he knew there was a good chance their pursuers had lost their trail. But even if they hadn't, he doubted that they had reached the pass summit as yet, which meant they would be forced to stop and wait out the storm in a makeshift shelter.

So would he and Lauren if they didn't find that cabin.

They had barely reached the bottom of the slope when the gloom faded to darkness, making the going much more difficult. Sam headed in the general direction of where he remembered seeing the cabin, silently praying that he wouldn't miss it in the darkness and swirling snow.

He was about to give up and build a shelter when he spotted the structure through the shifting snow. "Yes!"

When they reached the A-frame he propped Lauren against a porch post and unlaced her snowshoes, then his. Then he took a small tool from his wallet and squatted down on his haunches in front of the door to pick the lock.

"There. We're in."

Lauren blinked several times and struggled to focus her eyes. "G-good," she said through chattering teeth.

It was only slightly warmer inside the cabin and dark as a tomb. Sam dropped the duffle bag and backpack onto the floor and pulled out the flashlight and shined it around. The cabin was small—a main room, which contained a kitchen and eating area on one side and sitting room on the other, what appeared to be a bedroom and bath at the rear and a sleeping loft overlooking the main room. Sam was relieved when the beam of light revealed a good-size wood-burning stove in one corner of the main room and, next to it, an overflowing wood box.

"Great. I'll start a fire. Just hold on a little bit longer," he said to Lauren over his shoulder as he fed wood into the stove's firebox. "This place will warm up in no time."

Within minutes Sam had a good fire going. "There, that should do it," he announced, brushing off his hands as he rose. "These stoves put out a lot of heat. You'll start to feel—"

Turning, he saw Lauren curled up in a ball on the sofa, sound asleep.

Not even the warm glow from the fire could disguise her pallor or the exhaustion in her face. As long as her lashes were, they couldn't completely hide the dark circles beneath her eyes. As Sam studied her he felt something shift and expand inside his chest.

He squatted down beside the sofa and trailed his fingers over her cheekbone and jaw, tucked a strand of hair behind her ear. "Okay, little one. After the day you've had, I guess you're entitled," he whispered. Then his mouth quirked, and he gave a little snort. "Day, hell. You've had a godawful week."

But she'd weathered it like a champ and done what she had to, he admitted. Better than a lot of strong men would have. And with only a minimum of complaint, which he also had to admit, was justifiable. For all her diminutive size and fragile appearance, Lauren Brownley was a strong, capable woman.

"Well, c'mon, little one. Tonight you're going to

sleep in a real bed.'' Rising, Sam scooped her up into his arms and, flashlight in hand, carried her into the bedroom at the back of the cabin.

The cabin showed a woman's touch, he realized, shining the flashlight around—floral bedspread and matching curtains, a mountain of ruffled pillows piled against the head of the large brass bed, dried flower arrangements and candles all around. That meant there had to be some women's clothing somewhere.

With a sweep of his arm, he dispatched the mound of pillow to the floor. After laying Lauren down on the bed, he lit two candles and opened dresser drawers until he found one containing a stack of folded nightgowns. There was a nightgown in the duffle bag out in the main room but this was quicker.

The gown he'd grabbed was high-necked and long-sleeved, made of white flannel with tiny pink roses embroidered on the yoke and trimmed in pink satin ribbon. It looked like something his granny would wear and was about as sexy as a flour sack, but it would keep her warm.

With quick efficiency, Sam removed Lauren's parka, boots and socks, frowning at the blisters on her feet. Damn. Those had to hurt, yet she hadn't said a word. He shook his head and went to work on the sweatshirt, wool pants, then both sets of long johns. Through it all, she slept on without so much as stirring.

When Sam had purchased clothes for Lauren four days prior he had deliberately chosen cotton briefs, the kind that old ladies wore, and plain, serviceable bras. He had assumed that just imagining her in them would be a turnoff, but when he had her stripped down to nothing but those uninspiring undies his breath caught. He stared, mesmerized. He had seen women in bikinis who didn't appeal to him this much. She was so small and dainty and so beautifully curved.

Muttering a string of oaths, Sam rolled her onto her side and unhooked her bra. He tried not to look directly at her breasts, but even an oblique glimpse of those small, perfect mounds made his mouth go dry for a second.

Then he noticed the angry red marks on top of her shoulders and others encircling her torso. After four days of constant wearing, the bra had chafed her skin, he realized.

Grim-faced, Sam snatched up the afghan from the foot of the bed and tossed it over her, then picked up a candle and stomped into the adjacent bathroom, where he rummaged around until he unearthed a first-aid kit. He returned to the bedroom and applied the antibiotic cream to her blisters and red marks with as much detachment as he could muster. Then he put the nightgown on her and tucked her into the bed beneath the pile of thick quilts. Lauren sighed and burrowed her cheek deeper into the pillow.

Sam stared down at her, his chest so tight it felt as though it were being squeezed in a vise. What the hell was the matter with him?

Annoyed with himself, he turned abruptly and strode back into the main room. After stoking the fire he checked the window and door locks and for good measure stacked canned goods from the kitchen in front of both front and back doors and hung pots and pans by strings from the curtain rods in front of each window.

He discovered that there were two double beds in the loft. Good, he told himself. He would sleep there. For tonight, at least, there was no reason for them to share a bed. Even if the impossible happened and those three goons managed to get this far in the storm, at the first sound of forced entry he could be down the stairs in seconds, ready to protect her. They both needed some space, anyway.

Yet, when Sam finished setting up the security measures, he stripped down to his skivvies and crawled into bed beside Lauren, and when she sighed and turned to him in her sleep he put his arms around her and pulled her close.

Sam rested his chin against the top of Lauren's head and stared into the darkness. He was beat, but his troubled thoughts wouldn't let him sleep. From the moment he set eyes on this woman he had been fighting the inexplicable attraction he felt for her. He had tried to dislike her and had treated her with deliberate contempt and rudeness, but the gut-wrenching feelings refused to fade. Even when he'd believed that she was Giovessi's plaything, he'd still wanted her— and not merely sexually. There was something about her that made him itch to hold her in his arms and claim her for his own. He'd never felt that way about any woman before, and it brought a flutter of panic to his chest.

He'd lusted after many women, had bedded his share of them. He was, after all, a healthy, thirty-seven-year-old man. However, his past encounters had been purely physical. His feelings for those women had been pleasant and in some cases there had been affection, however fleeting. Still, he'd never before felt this strong sense of...of...connection and rightness, this unrelenting desire.

Sam huffed out a disgusted snort. Hell, Rawlins, you might as well admit it. Where this woman is concerned, you've lost the battle. But then, how could he not have?

He had expected her to be a spoiled, useless, not too bright bit of fluff, to whine and complain and be helpless—in general be a royal pain in the butt.

He should have known better. From the beginning, when she'd been an unsuspecting witness to murder she'd kept her head and shown surprising intelligence and resourcefulness in the way she'd escaped Carlo and his thugs.

Since then she'd continued to surprise him. She was not only bright, she was quick to learn and adaptable. If she didn't know how to do something, she watched him intently and absorbed the lesson. And if her efforts were less than perfect, she doggedly kept right on trying. In all the ways that mattered, she pulled her own weight and shared in the chores without prompting.

That, he supposed, he could chalk up to her determination to stand on her own two feet and depend on no one else, and he could certainly understand and respect that. He'd been a loner most of his life, himself.

But there was more to Lauren than that. For the last two days she'd gamely followed him over some rough terrain without a word of protest. Sam's mouth twitched again. Well...unless you counted the wall-eyed fits she had after the plane crash and again after climbing up that sheer cliff-face. Apparently her way of dealing with stress was to let off steam in one burst.

Anyway, he could hardly blame her. Both situations had been dicey as hell.

Absently he ran his hand up and down her back. He knew she was terrified of the assassins on their trail, yet she'd held herself together and kept her head when others would have fallen apart.

Lauren shifted and released a long, shuddering sigh. Once again, a hint of a smile tugged at one corner of Sam's mouth, and he stroked her back again. For such a tiny package, there was one hell of a lot of grit in this woman.

Thirteen

Lauren arched her back and stretched. Slowly she opened her eyes, blinked to focus—then jackknifed to a sitting position.

Her gaze darted around the unfamiliar room, her heart knocking against her rib cage. Where was she? Puzzled, she looked down at the flannel nightgown she wore and frowned as she realized that she had nothing on underneath it but her panties. How...?

She looked around at the big, comfortable bed. When her gaze landed on the dented pillow beside her own, she frowned.

A small noise from the next room made her jump and brought her gaze snapping around to the doorway. Cautiously she tossed back the quilts and climbed out of bed. She looked around for a weapon, then tiptoed barefoot across the hardwood floor to the dresser, picked up a heavy pottery vase by its neck and held it like a club.

Two things occurred to her as she crept toward the open doorway. First, wherever she was the place was blessedly warm. Second, the delicious smells drifting from the next room were making her stomach growl.

At the bedroom door she stopped and peeked around the frame, and caught her breath. A strange man stood in the kitchen, stirring something on the stove.

She must have made a small sound, because he looked up and spotted her. "Morning. I was beginning to think you were going to sleep the clock around."

Lauren's jaw dropped. "Sam?" She stepped around the door frame and into the main room. "Oh, my goodness, you shaved! I didn't recognize you."

It was the first time she'd seen him without at least a three-day growth of whiskers, and she was stunned by how attractive he was. He wasn't exactly handsome, but his rough-hewn face had the sort of sharp-edged masculinity that was far more appealing than mere conventional good looks. Just the sight of him did strange things to her insides.

"Yeah, well, it seemed like the thing to do. Who knows when I'll get another chance."

He glanced at the vase in her upraised hand and cocked one eyebrow. "I hope you're not planning to bash my head in with that thing."

"What? Oh." She quickly jerked her hand down and felt her cheeks pinken. She was so rattled by her reaction to him she had forgotten she had the vase. The almost teasing tone of his voice added to her confusion.

"I, uh...when I woke up I...I didn't know where

I was, and I couldn't remember how I got here. I still don't."

"I'm not surprised. You were asleep on your feet when we found this place."

"I'll, uh…I'll just go put this back," she announced self-consciously, and darted back into the bedroom. She took a moment to compose herself, taking several deep breaths and willing her nerves to settle. What on earth was the matter with her? It was just Sam. They had been stranded alone together for days. They'd even slept in the same sleeping bag. Sharing a bed with him was no different. She glanced at the dented pillow and rumpled bed again. Somehow, though, it was.

All because of those kisses he'd given her. She frowned at her reflection in the mirror above the dresser and raked her fingers through her tangled hair. Or had he kissed her? Had she been so delirious with fatigue she had imagined that?

Lauren shook her head. No. No, he had definitely kissed her. Twice.

But so what, she told herself. It hadn't meant anything, after all. People do all kinds of things under stress that they wouldn't normally do. It would be foolish to read too much into a couple of kisses.

Squaring her shoulders, she went to join Sam. "Please tell me that's coffee I smell," she said, sniffing the air.

"Yeah. Want a cup?"

"Are you kidding? I'd kill for a cup of coffee."

Actually she was dying to make a trip outside, but she hadn't had a cup of coffee in five days, and the aroma was just too tempting to resist.

"The mugs are in the cabinet and the pot's on the stove," Sam said, tipping his head toward the counter to his left as he continued to stir the contents of the skillet.

Lauren scooted around him in the small kitchen and retrieved a mug and poured herself some coffee. Leaning back against the counter, she took a sip and closed her eyes and sighed. "Oh my, this is wonderful."

Sam cast her a quick look, a ghost of a smile twitching his mouth, but he said nothing.

Lauren sipped the coffee in silence for a few minutes, but the niggling discomfort wouldn't leave her alone. She cleared her throat. "Like I said, I don't remember much about last night. Did you, um…that is…" She pinched the flannel nightgown between her thumb and forefinger and held it away from her body. "Are you responsible for this?"

"If you're asking, did I strip you and put the nightgown on you, then the answer is yes."

The reply was so blunt and matter-of-fact she didn't know how to respond. Before she could think of anything he went on.

"I thought you'd be more comfortable out of those clothes."

"Yes, I'm sure I was, but…well…"

Sam turned his head and pinned her with one of

his searing looks. "I've seen naked women before, Lauren."

She felt hot color surge up her neck and spread over her face. "I'm sure you have. Still..."

"You have a beautiful body," he said in a low voice that sent a shiver up her spine. "I'd have to be dead, blind or a eunuch not to have noticed that. But if you're worried that I ogled you or took advantage of you in any way, don't. That's not my style. I like my women responsive. Anyway, you were too exhausted to undress yourself, and since I wanted you to be comfortable and get the rest you needed, I did it for you. No big deal."

Maybe not for you, she thought, but the idea of him seeing her naked—or as good as—made her feel odd. Still, if he'd done it out of concern for her she could hardly complain.

But neither could she let it go. "You, uh...you slept in the bed with me last night, didn't you?"

"So?"

"Well...it's just that..." She glanced up at the loft and the beds that were clearly visible there.

"I thought it best. If I'd miscalculated, and those goons caught up with us here, I didn't want us to be separated."

Lauren's gaze flew to the front door. "Is there a chance—?"

"Relax." He turned his attention back to the skillet and started stirring the contents again. "It's blowing a blizzard out there. If they're smart, they're hunkered down somewhere, waiting for the storm to pass. If not, they're dead. Either way, they're no threat to us right now.''

Expelling a relieved breath, Lauren leaned back against the counter and took another sip of coffee. Then the delicious aroma filling the cabin drew her attention. ''I know it's impossible, but that looks and smells like ham and potatoes.''

''It is. With a little onion thrown in. Whoever owns this cabin keeps his larder well stocked. There's a root cellar and an old-fashioned icebox on the service porch out back, both brim full. Under the circumstances, I don't think they'll mind that we helped ourselves. I'll leave them a note and enough cash to cover the costs, but for as long as we're here we're going to have real food.''

''Mmm, that'll be nice.''

Lauren studied Sam. Not only had he shaved, he'd changed his clothes.

She became suddenly aware of how awful she must look. Her hair was mussed from sleep and two days without being brushed. She probably had circles under her eyes, she hadn't had a bath or a shampoo in...what?...four—or was it five days now? A fastidious little shudder rippled through her, and immediately her gaze wandered around the great room.

''If you're looking for the duffle bag, it's in the bathroom.''

Lauren's gaze whipped back to Sam. ''This cabin has a bathroom? An honest to goodness bathroom?''

"Uh-huh. Nothing fancy, mind you, but it has all the required fixtures. In fact, you're in for a real treat. This place is self-contained. There's a generator out back for electricity, though I won't bother to fire that up for no longer than we'll be here. There are plenty of candles and a couple of kerosene lamps that we can use for light. The gas for the cookstove is propane and the water is piped in from a hot spring out back. There's a shower and a big soaking tub in the bathroom."

Lauren's mug hit the counter with a *thunk*. "Why didn't you *tell* me?" She rushed out of the kitchen, but halfway across the living room she stopped and looked back at him. "Is it safe here? I mean...do I have time for a bath? What if the storm lets up and those men come?"

"Relax." Sam nodded toward the front window. "It's a complete whiteout out there, and according to the weather forecaster, this storm is going to be with us until midday tomorrow."

"The weather forecaster?"

Sam grinned and pointed toward the TV in the corner. "Yeah. The owner may enjoy the wilderness, but apparently he can't do without his TV. I picked up the *Weather Channel* on his satellite dish."

That startled a laugh from her. "A satellite dish? Way up here?"

"Yeah, well, some guys have withdrawal pain if they can't watch *Monday Night Football*."

"I'm just grateful he's civilized enough to have

installed a bathroom,'' Lauren said with a chuckle and headed for the bedroom.

The bathroom was rustic almost to the point of being crude. The shower, a prefab unit, was so small there was barely room to turn around, and the toilet and the clawfoot tub looked as though they had come out of a salvage yard, but Lauren didn't care. The water that flowed from the faucets was nice and hot.

In the shower she shampooed her hair and scrubbed herself until her skin was pink, all the while moaning in ecstasy. When done, she filled the deep tub and sank down into the hot water with another protracted moan. After all the hiking and climbing and snowshoeing she'd done over the past couple of days every muscle in her body ached and purple bruises splotched her skin. Leaning her head back against the rim, she sighed and closed her eyes. Heaven.

She was drifting somewhere between sleep and wakefulness when something thudded against the bathroom door. Lauren screeched and bolted upright, splashing water over the sides.

"Are you all right in there?'' Sam demanded.

She put her hand over her thudding heart and lowered her head, trying to breathe.

"Lauren? Dammit, if you don't answer in three seconds, I'm coming in.''

Her gaze flew to the door, which had no lock, and she hunched down beneath the water as far as she could. "No! Don't come in! I'm okay.''

"Thank God. You've been in there so long I

thought you'd drowned or hit your head or something. You sure you're okay? If you need help—''

"*No!* No, really, I'm fine. Just give me a minute."

"Well, hurry it up, will you? Breakfast is ready."

"I'll...I'll be right there."

She walked into the kitchen moments later with her wet hair combed back away from her face and wearing the smaller of the two white terry-cloth robes she'd found hanging on the back of the bathroom door. The garment was miles too big and dragged the floor, and she'd had to roll the sleeves up two turns, but it covered her from her chin to her toes and it had been the quickest thing at hand.

The small pine table was set with real dishes. A bowl of scrambled eggs and a platter piled high with the fried potato and ham concoction that Sam had put together, along with a basket of steaming biscuits, sat in the middle of the table.

"Sorry I took so long," she murmured, slipping into a chair next to Sam. "I couldn't resist having a hot soak in that tub after I'd showered."

Sam stopped in the act of picking up the platter. His dark eyes sizzled at her through the steam rising from the potatoes. The look in those ebony depths was so blatantly sexual and transparent that Lauren realized that he was picturing her naked, lounging in the steaming water.

Only then did she recall the stunning admission he'd made two days ago, and her heart gave a little flutter.

He'd claimed that he'd kissed her because he'd wanted to, that he'd been wanting to ever since he'd first seen her, but once she had recovered from her initial shock she'd dismissed the statement out of hand. She'd been so certain that he'd said those things merely to distract her from the danger they were in, which, of course, they had done.

After that the arduous two-day hike had taken all her concentration and so taxed her, physically and mentally, that she hadn't given the matter another thought. Until now.

The look in Sam's eyes told her that she had misread him.

Feeling her face grow hot, Lauren ducked her head and reached for the bowl of scrambled eggs.

"Those are from our supply of powdered eggs, I'm afraid, but the potatoes and ham are courtesy of our host," Sam said.

As she began to eat she glanced at him out of the corner of her eye and saw that his face wore its usual stern expression and that his attention had returned to the meal.

"It doesn't matter. Everything is delicious."

Neither spoke for several minutes, and as they ate Lauren recalled something else that Sam had told her.

"I think it's time you explained what's going on, don't you?" she said. "You said you would when you had the opportunity."

Sam looked up from spreading jam on a biscuit, his gaze direct and intense. To his credit, he didn't pretend to misunderstand. "You're talking about the dirty agent in our office, right?"

"Yes. If you knew that someone in the Denver office was working for Mr. Giovessi what on earth made you think you could protect me?"

"Like I told you before, besides myself, only five others knew about you when we left Denver. All five agents have excellent service records and they'd been handpicked by the SAC because he trusted them."

"The SAC?"

"The Senior Agent in Charge—in this case, of the Denver Office." Sam took a bite of biscuit and washed it down with a swig of coffee. "He figured if he kept you and your story contained to just the six of us we could hustle you out of town before it leaked out. It didn't work."

"Because one of the other five was your dirty agent."

"You catch on quick." Sam took a bite of potatoes and ham and watched her while he chewed. "At least one of those guys is Carlo's man. Hell, maybe all of them are, for all I know. That whole powwow in the SAC's office the morning of Frank's murder could have been set up to get rid of me at the same time as you."

"Why would they do that?"

"Because I'd been assigned the job of identifying the dirty agent, and I was getting close."

"Oh. I see."

"I think we can eliminate Dave as a suspect. He

hadn't been with the Bureau long enough to have been corrupted. Besides, he wouldn't have planted a bomb on the airplane, then climbed aboard."

"There was a *bomb* on the plane?"

"Had to have been. Bob Halloran was a fanatic about safety inspections and keeping his plane in tip-top shape. There was a bang that shook the plane an instant before the engines started sputtering. Whatever device they used was just enough to damage the engine and make us crash. They wanted it to look like an accident. Whoever rigged the bomb also planted a homing device on the plane so they could track us after we went down and verify the kill."

Lauren shuddered. She put down her fork and slipped her hands inside the sleeves of the robe to rub the goose bumps covering her forearms. "Who knew which plane you'd be taking?"

"No one. Not even Dave."

"Are you saying someone followed us to the airport and planted the bomb without you seeing them? That doesn't seem possible."

"It isn't. Bob was a close, personal friend of mine, but after he retired from the Bureau I used his charter service sparingly because I didn't want to establish a pattern. Someone who knew me and the way I operate must've figured on a case this important I'd hire Bob to transport us. While I was out gathering what we needed and making arrangements, he went to the airstrip and planted the bomb."

"Dear Lord. What if he'd been wrong? Innocent people would have been killed."

"Innocent people *were* killed," Sam reminded her.

Lauren looked at him with a stricken expression. She put down her fork and slumped against the chair back, her appetite suddenly gone. "I can't believe this is happening," she said forlornly.

"Believe it. And in case you haven't figured it out, we're on our own now. Since I don't know who I can trust, no way can I risk contacting anyone in the Bureau's Denver office."

"What are we going to do?"

"Don't worry. Things aren't as hopeless as they seem. There is someone higher up the chain of command who I think we can count on for help. Someone I trust."

"Someone in the FBI?"

"His name is Edward Stanhope. He was Assistant Deputy Director in Washington D.C. Even though he's retired, he still wields a lot of influence—within the Bureau and in the Federal Prosecutors Office. As soon as we get to a telephone, I'll give him a call."

He took a sip of coffee, watching her over the rim of the mug. Though rested, she still looked fragile. "In the meantime, eat up. You probably shed ten pounds over the last couple of days, and you can't spare them."

Lauren attempted a wan smile. "Are you calling me skinny?" The comment had been a lame attempt to lighten the mood, but his reaction was not at all what she had expected.

Sam gave her another one of those long looks, and she felt her heart go bumpity-bump. In a blink the taut somberness changed to tension of a different kind. Awareness crackled between them like heat lightning.

"I don't think you're skinny at all," he replied in a raspy murmur. "I think you're damned near perfect. But you're small, and you've got nothing in reserve and we still have a ways to go. So eat. Maybe we can fatten you up before we have to start out again."

Lauren experienced a flutter at the unexpected compliment, but the rest of his statement had been delivered in such a commanding tone that she cautiously resumed eating.

"I'm assuming, given this cabin's amenities, that we're fairly close to civilization," she said, as much to dispel the strange intimacy that had sprung up between them as anything.

"Not quite. As the crow flies, I figure we still have about three to five miles to go. Unfortunately, we have to walk over or around the mountains, so for us it's probably more like seven or eight miles to Purgatory."

Lauren nearly choked on her coffee. "To *where?*"

"Purgatory. Well, actually, new management has changed the name to Durango Mountain Resort," he corrected. "It's a ski resort thirty-seven miles north of Durango. Except for a few scattered ranches, it pretty much marks the beginning of human habitation to the south of here.''

''You mean we have to hike five more miles?'' she said with dismay.

''Actually we're in luck. There are four snowmobiles in the shed out back.''

''But we can't just take them. That's stealing.''

''The hell we can't. Not only are we going to take a couple, I'm going to empty the gas tanks on the other two so our friends can't follow us. Anyway, it's not stealing. I'm a federal law officer and this is an emergency situation. I'm commandeering the vehicles. All the owner has to do is file a claim and he'll be reimbursed.''

She looked at him doubtfully. ''Are you sure that's legal?''

Sam shrugged. ''Close enough.''

Damn, she's beautiful, he thought. Not a bit of makeup or artifice, her face scrubbed clean and shining and all bundled up to her chin in that too-big robe. Her damp hair was beginning to dry into wispy tendrils around her face, she looked so utterly fragile and vulnerable she took his breath away.

That exquisite delicacy, combined with an impressive inner strength and will was a potent combination, one he found damned near irresistible.

She was nervous, he realized. Skittish as a wild kitten. And not about the spot she was in or the men on their trail. No, she was nervous about being alone with him, something she hadn't been the whole time they'd been holed up in the old mining cabin together.

He could see it in her eyes, in the slight tremor in her hands and the wary glances she kept darting his way.

Good, he thought with satisfaction. At least he wasn't the only one experiencing this sizzling awareness. He felt as though a current of low-voltage electricity was humming through his entire nervous system.

Lauren ate the last bite of potatoes on her plate and washed it down with coffee. When done, she immediately stood. "Since you cooked, I'll do the dishes," she announced a shade too brightly.

Amused by her agitation, Sam watched her scurry to the kitchen with her plate and mug. She was trying to put distance between them, he realized. He also knew that it was probably a good idea, the wisest thing for both of them, but perversely, he was in no mood to allow her to retreat. If anything, her resistance only fired his male instinct to pursue.

"We'll do them together." Scraping back his chair, Sam calmly rose and gathered his own dishes.

"Oh, but that's not fair. You did the cooking."

"No big deal. Don't worry about it."

"But I thought while I did this you could...uh..." She waved her hand vaguely toward the rear of the cabin. "Do whatever it was you were going to do to the snowmobiles."

"That can wait. There's no hurry." He put his

dishes down on the counter, then turned and deliberately looked into her eyes and smiled slowly. "We're going to be here for a while."

"But—"

He placed two fingers across her lips. He felt them tremble beneath his touch. Desire streaked through him and settled in his loins, hot and heavy. Sam gritted his teeth to stop himself from snatching her into his arms. "No arguments, Lauren," he commanded.

Her eyes widened at his gravelly tone, but she nodded and turned away and began filling the sink with soapy water, focusing on the chore with a lot more concentration than it deserved.

Sam finished clearing the table then picked up a dish towel and moved to stand beside her at the counter.

She cast him another wary glance. "You don't have to dry them. They can drain."

"Give it up, Lauren. I'm doing this." He gave her a stern look, took the plate she had just washed, swished it through the rinse water and proceeded to dry it.

Damn, she smells wonderful, he thought, reaching around her to put the plate in the cabinet. Bath powder, soap and shampoo with a hint of flowers. And sweet, clean woman.

Sam dried another plate and eyed the top of her head. Her auburn hair was almost dry now and shining with fiery highlights. It draped around her shoulders like silk.

He itched to touch it, to bury his face in it, feel it slither across his skin.

For several minutes they worked in silence. They were almost finished when a glass she was giving to him started to slip out of her hand.

"Oh!"

"Easy."

Sam's hand clamped over hers, stopping the downward slide.

"Oh, that was clo—"

The words died on her tongue when her eyes met his. In their green depths he saw surprise and wariness. And something more.

Sam raised his free hand and ran his fingertips along her jaw. She quivered at the gentle touch but made no effort to pull away. "You're so damned beautiful," he murmured. His forefinger trailed across her cheek, touched the corner of her mouth, and the quiver became an uncontrollable shudder. Sam's gut clenched.

"So beautiful," he repeated in a barely audible whisper. With slow, deliberate movements he took the glass from her hand and placed it and the dish towel on the counter. Then he framed her face with his hands and stared down at her, devouring her with his eyes.

The lemony smell of dish soap teased his nostrils, and he felt dampness seep through the cuffs of his flannel shirt when Lauren grasped his wrists with her wet hands. He waited, but she made no effort to pull his hands away or step back from the gentle embrace.

She gazed back at him helplessly, her lips slightly parted. Her breath came out in shallow puffs. A host of conflicting emotions swam in her eyes—longing, uncertainty, need, a touch of fear, but most of all, the same burning desire that was tearing him apart.

His gaze dropped to her soft, unadorned mouth, and her lower lip trembled. It was more than he could take.

"Lauren." He breathed her name like a caress. His eyelids drifted shut as he lowered his head and settled his mouth on hers.

A small, agonized sound hummed from Lauren's throat—part despair, part surrender. Resistance was futile. From the first touch of his hand on hers she had been lost, her body weak with longing and need.

Why? She wailed silently, even as she melted into the kiss. Why did he have this effect on her? She should feel outrage, not this sizzling desire. He was hard and distant and he'd been rude and insulting to her from the moment they met. For two years she had rebuffed every man who had shown an interest in her. Handsome, wealthy, intelligent, charming, sophisticated—it hadn't mattered. She simply hadn't been interested. So why did this tough, taciturn man make her yearn?

The only thing that had kept Lauren from crumpling to the floor as she'd stared into those mesmerizing black eyes had been her grip on his wrists. Now, with his mouth on hers, her knees turned to liquid, and she moaned as she felt them buckle.

Sam wrapped his arms around her, pulling her tightly against him. Coiling her arms around his neck, Lauren held on, giving herself up to the kiss.

Her heart pounded and her body tingled as the searing heat in the core of her body built to a raging inferno and spread outward. The sensations pulsing through her were so lush, so voluptuous, she felt as though she was drowning in pleasure.

She needed this, she told herself as she kissed Sam back with all the seething emotions roiling inside her. For almost a week she'd been living with an icy knot in the pit of her stomach, operating on adrenaline and fear. In that period she had been terrorized and hunted, survived a plane crash, endured hardships she'd never imagined and had come close to losing her life more times than she cared to think about. She needed to feel desired, to feel pleasure again. To feel alive.

She felt Sam bend his knees, felt her feet leave the floor. Then he was moving through the cabin with her clamped against his chest, her feet dangling in air.

In the bedroom he fell with her onto the bed, twisting to take her weight, then rolling with her until she was on her back. Breaking off the kiss, he rose up on his elbows and looked down at her, and Lauren's breath caught at the raw desire in his eyes.

"If this isn't what you want, tell me now," he said

in a raspy voice that sent a delicious shiver down her spine.

"I...this...this is crazy."

"Hell, I know that. But do you want me to stop?"

"I..."

She caught her lower lip between her teeth, common sense and desire tugging her in opposite directions. She knew she should say yes. Getting involved with Sam was foolish and reckless. It would only complicate an already difficult situation. It wasn't like her to even contemplate taking such a rash and impulsive step. She would no doubt live to regret it.

Provided, of course, that she lived at all. Given the fix she was in, that was far from certain.

The thought brought with it a flutter of panic and urgency. Suddenly making love with Sam no longer seemed foolish but imperative. She desperately needed this, needed to be touched and held and caressed, needed to feel she mattered to someone, if only for a little while. Most of all, she needed to share this most intimate of acts with this man.

With nothing but uncertainty ahead of her, this was not the time for caution or common sense, or even propriety. This was the time to reach out with both hands and grab all she could from life, while she still had the chance.

"Yes." Her arms tightened around his neck. "Oh, yes. Make love to me, Sam."

The words had barely left her lips when his mouth covered hers again. He kissed her deeply, hungrily, as though he would devour her. Lauren responded with a frantic hunger of her own, driven by the twin demons of fear and need.

Sam broke off the kiss, and when Lauren tried to pull him back he splayed his hand over her chest and held her down. "Easy. Easy, little one," he soothed. "There's no need to rush. For days I've been tormenting myself, imagining this. I want to take my time and enjoy it to the fullest."

Lauren shifted restlessly and snatched at the buttons on his shirt. "No, Sam. Please, I want—"

"Shh. Shh. I know, babe. I know. Just trust me."

She whimpered and clutched at him when he rolled away and left the bed. He stripped off his clothes with rapid, jerky movements, his intense, dark gaze locked with hers all the while. Naked, he lay down beside her. Ignoring her efforts to pull him closer, he rose up on one elbow, grasped one end of the terry-cloth belt that secured her robe and pulled on it.

Lauren's restless movements halted, and she held her breath, watching his face. With agonizing slowness, the loose knot untwisted and collapsed. Taking his time about it, Sam separated the edges of the robe and spread them wide.

He stared down at her, his eyes glimmering like obsidian. His indulgent smile vanished as his face grew taut and darkened. "Beautiful," he whispered.

Slowly, almost reverently, he reached out to touch her, but at the last moment he turned his hand over and trailed the backs of his knuckles over her skin, from the base of her throat all the way to the nest of tight curls at the apex of her thighs.

The featherlight touch left a trail of fire on Lauren's skin and sent a delicious shiver rippling through her.

The tiny reaction seemed to inflame Sam's passion. His nostrils flared and his eyes blazed. Lauren moaned when he cupped her right breast. He lifted, squeezed, tested its weight in his palm, stroked his thumb across the velvety tip. When it swelled into a hard nub he stared at that rosy button like a starving man at a banquet.

Then he lowered his head and took her nipple into the warm wetness of his mouth.

Lauren moaned and clutched his head with both hands, her fingers burrowing deep into his ebony hair. His tongue circled her nipple, flicked, stroked. Teased.

Then he began to suckle, and she cried out, her back arching off the bed as he drew on her with a slow, hard suction that seemed to tug at her womb.

The delicious torment went on and on, driving her to the brink of delirium. Then he abandoned the wet, turgid nipple and treated the other one to the same lavish assault. Just when Lauren thought she would surely go mad, he released her.

"Do you like that?" he asked in a raspy whisper.

"Y-yes."

With the tip of his tongue, Sam drew a line down the silky valley between her breasts. "And that?"

"Yes." Eyes closed, she moved her head from side to side on the pillow. "Oh, yes."

Alternately nipping and kissing, he explored the undersides of her breasts, her ribs. All the while his hand explored the slight concave of her belly, the indent of her waist, skimmed down the long, curving sweep of her hip and thigh, then back again.

He dipped his head and circled her navel with the tip of his tongue, drew back and blew on her wet flesh, then delved into the tiny cavity with an evocative rhythm. "How about that? Do you like that, too?"

"Mmm. Yes."

"And this," he demanded. His head dipped lower still.

Lauren clutched handfuls of his hair as once again her body arced and quivered like a drawn bow.

"Yes! *Yes!* Oh! Oh! *Saaaam!*"

"Yes," Sam growled with hard satisfaction, and as her body seemed to explode in a starburst of unbearable pleasure, he quickly moved up into position between her legs and entered her in one swift stroke.

Sam groaned as he felt her sweet contractions squeeze him. Gritting his teeth, he began to move with slow, steady rhythm, pressing deep, drawing out the pleasure until it was almost pain.

He felt Lauren's muscles gradually go slack as her body's delicate pulsing faded away, and when he braced up on his forearms he saw that her eyes were closed and her face had that soft, dreamy look of a well-loved woman.

The corners of Sam's mouth tipped up in a smile of purely male arrogance, but he wasn't ready to let her rest.

"Wrap your legs around me, babe."

Lauren obeyed lazily and moved her palms in slow circles over his shoulders and back, absently stroking and kneading.

Sam increased his rhythm, stroking harder, deeper, and soon Lauren's breathing again grew rapid and labored, and small, desperate sounds issued from her. Instead of gently stroking, her hands began to knead and grip, her fingers digging into his flesh as her hips lifted to meet each powerful thrust.

"Tight. You're so tight," he growled in her ear.

"Sam...Sam, I..." Her head moved from side to side on the pillow. Her eyes flew open, and her neck arched back. "Oh. Oh, Sam!"

"Yes," he ground out through clenched teeth. "Go with it, baby. Let go."

Her body went taut and a long, keening sound tore from her throat. Sam placed his mouth against her neck, absorbing the erotic vibration even as he felt her body grip him. Before the sound faded he reached the end of his control. A hard shudder ripped through him and his own cry of completion blended with hers.

Fourteen

Lauren felt boneless. The awful tension that had dominated her every waking moment for days was gone—or at least, held at bay for the moment. Basking in the aftermath, she let her mind float like a leaf drifting with the current, aimless and free, disconnected.

Gradually, however, reality and awareness began to niggle at the edges of her pleasant lethargy. Slowly, as though weighted with lead, her eyelids lifted. She stared at the ceiling over Sam's bare shoulder. Dear God, what had she done?

Sam stirred and rolled off of her onto his back. "Jesus," he murmured.

Lauren turned away from him and scooted toward the side of the bed, but before she could escape, he looped his arm around her waist and hauled her back. "Hey, not so fast. Where're you going?"

"Let me go."

Ignoring the command, he rolled her onto her back and rose up on one elbow above her. He frowned when she quickly looked away and refused to meet his eyes. "What the hell is wrong with you?"

Her gaze snapped back to meet his. "What's wrong? What's *wrong?* Isn't it obvious?"

"Not to me. So why don't you explain it to me."

"This. Us," she said, gesturing between them.

He said nothing, merely continued to look at her, and Lauren groaned and covered her face with both hands. "I must be a complete idiot. How could I let this happen? How could I have made love with a man I barely know? And *you,* of all men."

Sam stiffened. "How could you let a half-breed touch you? Is that it?"

"What?" She took her hands away and gave him a blank look, which changed to exasperation a moment later when she realized what he meant. "Oh, don't be ridiculous. Of course not. You being half Native American has nothing to do with it."

"Then what's your problem?"

"You don't even like me. Which makes me an idiot to have slept with you. That's my problem."

"I like you."

"Oh, pul-leeze. You think I'm Carlo's mistress," she accused.

"Is that all that's bothering you? Hell, I stopped believing that days ago. After being around you for a while I realized that you're not mistress material."

"Oh, really?" Lauren huffed, absurdly offended. "And just why not?"

"You're too intelligent and hardworking. Too independent."

Disarmed, she blinked at him. "Really?"

"Really."

"Oh." He couldn't have said anything that would have pleased her more. She'd worked hard to achieve independence. Still...she couldn't quite believe that he thought she'd succeeded.

Turning her head on the pillow, she slanted him a doubtful look out of the corner of her eye. "If that's true, then why have you been so hateful to me?"

"To keep what just happened from happening."

"Oh, thank you very much. That makes me feel *sooo* much better. If that's how you feel then why—?"

"There are some things you just can't fight. God knows I tried. I tried to dislike you. I told myself you were a cheap whore and a parasite, but it didn't help. Even when I half believed it, I still wanted you."

"Wh-what?"

"The moment I first saw you, pacing that dingy little interrogation room in your shredded stockings and torn dress, I felt like I'd been run over with a steamroller. I think you felt the attraction, too, otherwise we wouldn't be here in this bed right now."

Surprise flickered through Lauren. Could he be right? She had felt something, she recalled. Something edgy and uncomfortable, but at the time she'd been too upset and frightened to analyze her reaction and had chalked it up to dislike. "That's...that's beside the point. I don't expect you to believe me, but I don't sleep around."

"I know that." Sam's mouth softened slightly

when she blinked at him again. He stroked his fore-finger along her jaw and his voice deepened to a husky murmur. "I could tell it's been a while for you. Hasn't it?"

Heat surged into Lauren's cheeks. She bit her lower lip and looked away again. "There's been no one since Collin," she replied in a subdued voice. Or before him, for that matter, she reminded herself.

"Why not?"

"After what he did? I'm surprised you have to ask."

"So the guy's a louse and a thief. That's no reason to avoid sex."

"I wasn't avoiding sex. I was avoiding being hurt. Now could we drop this please?"

"Not yet." He cupped her jaw in the V between his thumb and fingers and turned her face back, forcing her to look at him. "Look, Lauren, so we made love. So what? We're two healthy people under a lot of stress, stranded alone together. Add to that scenario a strong mutual physical attraction and what happened was probably inevitable. It's natural for two people caught in a dangerous situation to turn to one another."

Hurt, offended and relieved all at the same time, Lauren gazed up at him in silence, her chest aching. He couldn't have made it plainer that there was no real emotional attachment between them. Merely desire and the need for human contact.

Not that she expected anything like that from Sam.

Or wanted it. It was just that his explanation seemed so...so...casual and unfeeling.

"Well?" he said, lifting one eyebrow. "Do you agree?"

"I suppose so."

He studied her in silence. Lauren couldn't tell by his expression if her answer had pleased him, but after a few seconds he nodded. "Good."

He lowered his head and began to string kisses along her collarbone.

"Sam!" she squeaked. "What are you doing? Stop that."

"Why? I still want you and you still want me." The kisses traveled up the side of her neck, explored the tender underside on her chin. "You're unattached. I'm unattached. The future isn't all that certain for either of us," he murmured against her skin. "Why the hell shouldn't we take what pleasure we can from one another?"

With his warm mouth leaving a trail of fire on her skin, Lauren couldn't think of a single reason, logical or otherwise. Nor did it help when his hand slid up over her belly and midriff and cupped her breast.

He swept his thumb back and forth across her nipple, and she made an inarticulate sound deep in her throat. Struggling to hold on to her sanity, Lauren tried to resist the pleasure that spread through her like a shimmering hot flood. "S-Sam, I don't think—"

"Then don't. Don't think. Just feel." The low,

raspy command was so blatantly sensual it raised goose bumps on Lauren's skin and made her shiver.

As her body began to thrum with desire her heart rate speeded up and her breathing grew shallow and rapid, as though suddenly there was not enough oxygen in the air.

"We...we shouldn't...it's not..." With her last ounce of resistance, she groped for a sensible reason why they should stop, but when his hand slipped between her legs she was lost. "Oh, Sam."

An hour or so later, Sam surfaced from a light doze when Lauren shifted in his arms, but his eyes remained closed. With a contented sigh, she hooked her leg over his and snuggled closer, settling her face more comfortably against his chest.

Her soft breath fluttered his chest hairs, and a hint of a smile tugged at his mouth. For someone so cautious and reserved when awake, asleep she was one sexy cuddler.

Sam rubbed his chin against the top of Lauren's head, enjoying the scent of her hair and the sensual feel of the glossy strands slipping and sliding like silk against her scalp.

Strange, he mused, half asleep. He couldn't recall ever before truly wanting to snuggle with a woman after making love. The emotional intimacy that women seemed to need at those times had always seemed stifling to him. Sex was fine, but he just wasn't comfortable letting anyone get that close on an emotional level.

Most times he made the effort because he didn't want to hurt his partner's feelings, but he'd never been able to endure the intimacy for long, and the whole while he itched to escape.

With Lauren, though, it felt right, somehow. She fit so perfectly and felt so good in his arms that he didn't want to let her go.

Sam was not altogether comfortable with the admission. His smile faded, replaced by a pensive frown. What was it about this one, small woman that was different from all the others?

Awake now, he opened his eyes and stared across the room. Absently his gaze drifted to the window. He blinked once, twice. "Holy shit!"

Bolting upright in the bed, he tumbled Lauren onto her back.

"Wha—?"

Sam sprang off the bed, snatched up his briefs and stepped into them. "Get up! Get up! C'mon, we've got to get out of here. Now!"

He pulled on his long johns, cursing himself all the while he hopped from one foot to the other. "Of all the stupid... Dammit, Rawlins! What the hell were you thinking? Instead of rolling around in the sack all afternoon you should've been getting the snowmobiles ready in case something like this happened."

Lauren sat up, clasping the covers to her breasts with one hand and pushing her tumbled hair back with the other. Bleary-eyed, she watched Sam ram his legs into his wool trousers and drag on a flannel shirt.

"Sam, what's the matter with you?"

"It's stopped snowing."

"What?" Her head whipped toward the window. "But I thought the storm was supposed to last until midday tomorrow?"

"Could be this is just a break in the clouds, or it could be the system changed directions. Or the weatherman miscalculated. Whatever, we have to get moving. I don't know how long ago it quit snowing, but you can bet our friends were on their way before the last flake fell."

He checked his service pistol, shoved it back into the hip holster and strapped it on then scooped up the duffle bag from the floor and tossed it to her. "Grab some fresh clothes out of there and get dressed. While you're doing that I'll take this stuff out and load it onto a couple of the snowmobiles, and siphon the gas out of the other two."

"Uh, Sam." Lauren stopped pawing through the duffle bag long enough to send him a sheepish look. "I...I've never driven a snowmobile before. I've never even ridden on one."

He looked up sharply, his mouth flattening. Then he shook his head. "Okay, no problem. It's fairly simple. If you can drive a car you should be able to operate a snowmobile."

When he'd finished lacing his moccasins he put on his wool cap and parka, gathered up the backpack and duffle bag and slung the rifle over his shoulder. "As soon as you're dressed come out to the shed out back." At the door he stopped and pointed his forefinger at her. "And don't stop to straighten up this place, you hear? We don't have a minute to spare."

Leaving her scrambling into her clothes, he went out through the back door in the kitchen and the service porch, which jutted out from the rear of the cabin.

To make it easier on Lauren, Sam strapped the smaller backpack onto her vehicle. It was heavier than the duffle bag, but since she was so small he figured it would give her needed ballast. He then tied the duffle bag onto the machine he would drive.

Moments later, through the open door of the shed a movement caught his eye. Sam looked up from siphoning gas out of one of the other snowmobiles and saw three men carrying rifles emerge from the woods about fifty yards from the house.

With a curse, Sam ducked out of sight and snatched up the rifle. Holding the weapon in both hands, he stood with his back pressed against the shed wall just inside the doorway.

Cautiously he peered around the edge of the door and saw the leader of the trio signal to one of his cohorts. The man immediately split off from the other two and headed for the shed.

"Damn." Sam jerked back and flattened himself against the shed wall again, his mind racing. He had to get to Lauren. But first he had to take care of the goon heading his way. And he had to do it quietly. If he shot him, the other two would come running, and if he made a run for the cabin now they would all see him and open fire.

Gripping the rifle tighter, Sam held it at chest height with the butt end toward the door. Outside, he heard the crunch of approaching footsteps in the snow. His hands tightened on the gun's fore end and stock. C'mon. C'mon, you son of a bitch, he silently urged.

The footsteps halted just outside the door. Silence hung heavy in the air. Sam pressed back against the wall, waiting. C'mon, damn you. Just a couple more steps.

The man charged inside and spun to his left, the barrel of his gun pointed at Sam's midsection. Surprise registered in his eyes when he spotted Sam, but in that split second of time before he could pull the trigger the butt end of Sam's rifle smashed into his face.

He emitted a grunt and went down like a pole-axed steer, blood spurting from his nose and mouth.

Sam quickly grabbed the unconscious man by the collar of his parka and dragged him deeper into the shed, out of sight. He paused, then reached down and snatched the ski mask off the downed man, and found himself staring at a fellow FBI agent. Sam's mouth tightened. "Wayne Pickens, you sorry scumbag."

Tamping down his anger, he took up his position by the door again, and peered around the frame just as the other two men disappeared around the front of the house. Sam's gaze switched to the back porch, willing the door to open. Dammit, Lauren, where are you?

Left with no choice, he braced himself and charged outside.

Lauren headed for the kitchen and the back door, zipping up her parka on the way. Barely a step inside the cabin's main room, she stopped cold. "Oh, dear God."

Horrified, she stared through the glass in the front door at the two armed men stealthily climbing the front porch steps.

Lauren darted a panicked look toward the kitchen. She'd never make it to the back door before they were inside.

Quickly she stepped back inside the bedroom and closed the door. To her horror, she discovered that it didn't have a lock! Her stricken gaze darted around the room and when it landed on the wooden, ladder-back chair she snatched it up and wedged it under the knob, just as the front door of the cabin was kicked open.

Lauren jumped and gave a stifled cry. In a full-blown adrenaline panic, she spun around and raced to the window. She was operating on instinct now, the only coherent thought in her mind that she had to find Sam. Sam would protect her.

With no attempt at silence, she jerked up the window sash just as something thudded against the bedroom door. Whimpering, Lauren sat down on the sill, threw her legs over and jumped.

The window was only about six feet above the ground, but she sank up to her knees in snow and toppled forward. With single-minded purpose, sputtering and spitting snow, she scrambled to her feet and headed for the shed, plowing through the deep drifts like a woman possessed. Gasping every breath, she rounded the corner of the service porch and ran smack into a solid male chest.

"Lauren!"

A scream burst from her, but the sound was cut off almost at once by a gloved hand over her mouth. "Lauren, it's me! Sam."

"S-Sam?" She clutched his parka. "Oh, Sam. T-two men...they're inside!"

"I know. C'mon. Let's go!" With an arm around her waist, he turned and hauled her back the way he had come. Behind them, from inside the cabin, they heard a crash as the bedroom door gave way.

They charged inside the shed just seconds before one of the men stuck his head out the open bedroom window and shouted, "Pickens! You find anyone out there?"

"No! No one here!" Sam shouted back.

The instant the man drew his head back inside Sam pushed one of the snowmobiles out into the snow. "There's no time to teach you how to drive one of these things, so you're riding with me," he announced. Plucking Lauren up as if she was a sack of feathers, he tossed her onto the back of the seat, hopped aboard himself and fired up the engine.

"There they are!" The two men burst through the back door onto the service porch.

"Hold on!" Sam hollered. The rear treads dug in, slinging snow twenty feet into the air, and the snowmobile leaped forward on its skis and took off at full throttle.

Lauren locked her arms around Sam's middle, buried her face against his back and held on for dear life. They skidded around the corner of the shed just as a burst of automatic weapon fire erupted behind them. Lauren made a distressed sound, squeezed her eyes shut and clutched Sam tighter.

Sam drove like a madman. Going flat out, they bounced over bumps and swerved around rocks and trees and half covered deadfalls, went sailing over small drop-offs and drifts. Within seconds they were out of sight of the cabin and streaking down the valley.

After a minute or so, Lauren cautiously raised her head and looked around at the peaceful scenery whizzing by. She couldn't believe it! They were alive. They'd made it!

Just as her heart rate began to settle she heard the unmistakable *rat-tat-tat-tat-tat* of gunfire, and a shower of pockmarks dug up the snow to one side of the snowmobile.

She looked over her shoulder, and a fresh rush of

fear knifed through her. "They're coming after us!" she shouted over the roar of the engine. "Two of them on snowmobiles! I thought you emptied the gas tanks!"

"There wasn't time to do them all!" he shouted back. "I'd emptied one and about three quarters of another one when they showed up."

As they swerved around an aspen tree a spray of bullets splatted against the trunk, cutting off a small limb and sending chunks of wood and splinters flying. Lauren screamed and buried her face against Sam's back again.

She stayed that way until she felt the snowmobile tip upward. Opening her eyes, she looked around and saw that they had begun to climb a slope. Unable to resist, she glanced over her shoulder again, and caught her breath. "They're gaining on us!"

"Yeah! We're riding double! They're not!"

The slope became so steep the snowmobile's engine began to labor and slow down. Lauren feared they would topple over backward. Even more, she feared that at any second she would feel bullets ripping into her.

Then she realized that the men were no longer shooting at them, and she glanced back again.

Though the gunmen were still gaining, for the moment, they seemed to have their hands full coaxing their machines up the sharp incline.

The gap between them and their pursuers grew steadily smaller. Lauren pressed her forehead between

Sam's shoulder blades and moaned. "They're going to catch us!"

"Like hell they are!"

Sam urged the snowmobile up the last few feet of the incline, alternately cursing and cajoling. The engine whined and struggled, and several times Lauren was certain it was about to stall.

Miraculously they finally reached the summit and once they leveled off they began to pick up speed. Then they were flying down the slope on the other side, while behind them the other two snowmobiles still struggled.

Lauren and Sam descended into yet another valley and sped toward the opposite end, taking a wide, arcing route around the base slope of an enormous mountain.

"What are you doing? Why are you going around this way?" Lauren yelled. Even to her inexperienced eye it was obvious that the more direct, and certainly the quicker way, would have been to cut across the base slope. They had just climbed a pass far more difficult.

Sam ignored her and continued to skirt the gently undulating ground. Lauren glanced back, and had her worst fear confirmed. The two snowmobiles crested the summit and headed down after them. She and Sam had gained a little distance during the descent, but now the gap was rapidly closing again.

Partway down the mountain, one of the other snowmobiles began to slow down, and after a dozen or so yards it came to a stop.

"One of them stopped!"

"Out of gas! That's the one I was draining when they arrived."

The second man reached the bottom of the pass, and as Lauren had feared, he cut across the base slope to intercept them.

"Oh Lord, here he comes!" she cried. "And he's closing the distance fast!"

As though to underscore Lauren's statement, the other man opened fire again. Bullets pinged off the tail section of their machine and others kicked up the snow all around them. Lauren screamed and clutched Sam tighter.

Though she knew full well that he had the throttle wide open, she yelled at him to go faster. Instead, to her horror he brought the snowmobile to an abrupt stop, skidding around until they were almost broadside to the approaching machine. Like sitting ducks.

"What are you doing! Are you crazy?"

"Calm down," Sam ordered. Never taking his eyes from their pursuer, he lifted the rifle strap over his head and brought the butt of the Winchester to his shoulder and took aim at the assassin.

Steady as a rock, he waited.

"Shoot. Shoot!" Lauren screamed.

The man drove straight for them. Steering with one hand, he raised his assault weapon with the other. Lauren put her hand over her mouth to hold back a scream and braced herself for the bullets that would rip into her any second.

Suddenly Sam swung the rifle barrel away from the assassin, took aim on a cornice of snow near the top of the mountain and fired. The crack of the high-powered rifle echoed through the mountains.

Then came an ominous roar, and tons of snow, ice and rock came roiling down the mountainside.

Fifteen

"Oh, dear Lord!" Horrified, Lauren stared at the avalanche rumbling down toward them. "We're going to die!"

"The hell we are. Hang on!" Sam shouted and poured the gas to the snowmobile.

The machine took off like a horse out of the chute and flew across the snow at top speed, its engine revved up to a high-pitched whine. Eyes closed, Lauren clung to Sam, cringing against his back as the horrendous roar grew louder. At any second, she expected to be engulfed and crushed beneath a ton of snow.

Lauren did not want to look, but an irresistible morbid fascination drew her gaze upward. Her eyes widened, and she screamed again, but the sound was swallowed by the roar of tons of snow, ice, boulders and trees plunging down the steep slope in a giant white wave.

Lauren looked over her shoulder and saw that the other man was no longer following them. In that moment she realized that Sam had waited to set off the avalanche until the man was directly in the center of its path.

Now the pursuer was being pursued.

He had turned and was racing out in front of the roiling mass, trying frantically to outrun it.

He wasn't going to make it. As Lauren watched, the advanced tip of the avalanche gobbled up the gap behind the man like a ravenous monster and boiled over him.

On the edge of the slide area, Sam headed for the sideline and safety, racing ahead of the avalanche's curving left flank.

Fist-size pieces of snow and ice, shaken loose by the vibrating earth, raced out in front of the deadly white wall. Lauren screamed when the chunks pelted the left side of the snowmobile and knocked it slightly askew.

"Hang on!" Sam shouted. "We're almost clear!"

For the next hundred yards or so more chunks struck the side of the snowmobile and their legs before they finally began to outrun them.

Then suddenly, except for the snowmobile streaking away across the snow and the drone of its engine, all was quiet and still.

Twilight had fallen by the time they reached Durango Mountain Resort. Only a handful of diehard skiers glided down the slopes. Sam felt Lauren tense and clutch him tighter as he maneuvered the snowmobile down the ski slope toward the cluster of lighted buildings.

He could imagine the mixed emotions she must be experiencing. They'd been cut off from the rest of the world for almost a week, and though she was probably relieved to be out of the wilderness, she knew that contact with other people would increase her chances of being found.

"Don't worry. For the time being, getting lost in a crowd like this is the safest move," he said over his shoulder.

Sam drove slowly around the perimeter of the resort until he found the cluster of snowmobiles. He'd known they had to be there somewhere. Every ski resort used them for search and rescue.

He stopped in the shadows and scanned the area. When he was sure no one was around, as quietly as possible, he drove over to the fleet and parked between two identical machines bearing the Durango Mountain Resort logo.

"Remember. Just act casual," Sam said when he and Lauren dismounted. "As far as anyone knows, we're just a vacationing couple, here to enjoy a few days of skiing." He unhooked the duffle bag from the back of the machine and slung it over his shoulder and put his arm around Lauren's waist.

The resort resembled a European village, and when they reached the open courtyard area they merged in with the skiers returning from a day on the slopes and the others milling around.

"What now?" Lauren asked.

As they passed a restaurant, Sam noticed the longing look she cast through the plate-glass window at the diners inside. They hadn't eaten since breakfast, and the pack with their food supplies had been left behind on the snowmobile she was to have ridden.

"I need to make a couple of calls."

That brought her gaze snapping up to meet his. "Who are you going to call? You said we couldn't trust anyone."

"Easy. I'm not calling anyone inside the Denver office. I'm going to call Ed Stanhope. Remember, I told you about him? If anyone will know what's going on, he will."

"And you trust him?"

Sam could see the doubt in her eyes. He couldn't blame her, after all that had happened.

"Yeah, I do. Anyway, we don't have a choice. We need help."

Lauren gnawed at her lower lip and cast a nervous look around the courtyard. "I suppose you're right. Who else are you going to call?"

"A relative of mine. I'm going to ask him to come pick us up."

"Your father?"

Sam's jaw clenched. He met her hopeful look with a flat stare and an even flatter voice. "No. My aunt and uncle."

"Oh. I see. Do they live near here?"

"Not really. They live about ten miles outside of

Monticello, Utah. They own the ranch next to my father's. They'll come, though, if I ask them.''

He could tell by her expression that she wanted to ask why he wasn't going to call his father, but she didn't quite dare. It was just as well. He didn't want to argue with her, nor was he in the mood to discuss his strained relationship with his father.

Ahead a security guard walked toward them, checking inside the stores and scanning the street as he strolled. Turning his back, Sam stopped with Lauren in front of a shop window and pretended to look at the display until the man walked by.

''What was that about?'' Lauren whispered.

''Just a precaution. The fewer people who get a good look at us the better.'' He patted his parka pockets. ''Damn, I wish I had my cellphone. I don't suppose you have a prepaid telephone card on you?''

''No, I don't.''

''Great.'' He thought a minute, then grasped her elbow and steered her toward the entrance to the inn. ''We'll check in for the night, and I'll make my calls from the privacy of our room. I'll ask my aunt to pick us up early in the morning. Which will work out better. This way we can order room service and avoid other people while we're eating, plus get some rest.''

''But...what if those men catch up with us? What if they check and find out we're registered?''

''Relax. I'm going to register under the alias Roberto Montera and speak with an accent. With my coloring I can easily pass for Hispanic. I keep a credit card under that name which no one knows about. You never know when you'll need to use an alias. So remember, while we're here, you're Señora Montera.''

Inside the hotel lobby, Sam left Lauren standing with her back to the room pretending to check through a rack of brochures, and went to the front desk. On the surface she appeared calm, but he knew her nerves were eating her alive. He only hoped no one passing by noticed her hands. They were shaking so much she could barely hold the pamphlets.

He returned a few minutes later and touched her shoulder. Lauren jumped like a scalded cat.

"Easy," Sam murmured. "It's only me. C'mon, we're all set."

He grasped her elbow and led her toward the elevator, doing a quick study of her pale face on the way. "You okay?"

"Yes. I'm fine."

But she wasn't. Sam could feel the tremors vibrating through her.

Once they were inside their fourth-floor room with the door double bolted and chained she sagged against the entrance wall and closed her eyes. "Thank God. I felt as though I had a target painted on my back out there."

Sam tossed the duffle bag onto the luggage rack, shrugged out of his parka, peeled hers off and tossed both on top of the bag.

Without a word, he pulled her into his arms. He half expected her to resist, but Lauren melted against him. With a sigh, she rested her cheek against his chest and slipped her arms around his lean middle.

"Oh, Sam," she said in a small, plaintive voice.

"I know, babe." He held her close and rocked her from side to side. He rubbed his chin against the top of her head and inhaled the sweet smell of her hair. "It's been rough. But you're doing great. Just hang in there, and we'll get through this."

"I want my life back, Sam," she murmured in the same mournful tone. "Maybe it wasn't all that exciting or fulfilling anymore—or easy, for that matter—but at least no one was trying to kill me."

"Yeah, I know," Sam murmured. "I wish I could tell you it will get better soon, but I can't promise that. I won't lie to you, Lauren. The agent or agents who're working for Carlo aren't going to give up. They can't afford to."

A shiver rippled through her. "I know."

Sam cupped her chin and tilted her face up, and looked deep into her eyes, his own glittering with turbulent emotions. When he spoke his voice was a husky whisper.

"One thing I can promise you. I'll do whatever I have to do to protect you." His thumb brushed along her jaw, touched the corner of her mouth. Her lips trembled in response, and something clenched inside him.

The hand cupping her chin slid around to the back of her neck and his fingers speared through her hair. She gazed up at him, her eyes soft and trusting, her unadorned face so beautiful it made him ache. Through his palm Sam felt her shiver again, but this time he knew it wasn't from fear. His chest grew so tight it was almost painful, as though a giant hand were squeezing his heart.

Slowly, almost reverently, he lowered his head. The kiss was as soft as a butterfly's wing, a warm, whispery touch, a gentle rub of flesh on flesh, a mingling of breaths.

Even when his mouth settled fully on hers, the caress remained gentle and unhurried. The exquisite richness of the kiss inflamed Sam's desire, but he could not bear to hurry. He wanted to savor the sweet, sharp pleasure, draw it out as long as possible, absorb it deep into his soul.

Lauren responded to the soft seduction like a flower opening to the sun, kissing him back with the same trembling restraint.

As one, they sank down onto the bed together. Hands explored leisurely, boldly, while their lips caressed, their tongues twined and stroked, their teeth gently nipped.

Sam strung kisses down Lauren's neck, over her collarbone. "I want you," he murmured against her skin.

"Oh, Sam. I want you, too," she whispered back.

It was all the encouragement he needed. Buttons and zippers and clasps were dealt with and clothing stripped away and tossed aside. When they were naked Sam placed his palm flat against her chest and pressed her down onto the pillow, his intense gaze holding hers all the while.

He circled her breasts with his fingertips, trailed his hand over her collarbone, down the silky valley between her breasts, lower still over her rib cage, her belly. The silken texture of her skin fascinated him. So did the erotic contrast between its pale creaminess against the deep bronze of his hand.

"Sam?" Lauren smoothed her hands up over his chest and tugged on his shoulders, pulling him down to her. An instant later a long moan hummed from her throat as he took one pink nipple into his mouth and drew on her.

They explored each other's bodies, played and teased, tantalized, stretching the pleasure out. Finally, just when Sam thought he would surely go mad, Lauren moaned, "Please, Sam. Oh, please. Now."

He rose into position between her thighs and braced above her on his stiffened arms. "Look at me, Lauren," he ordered in a husky voice, and she complied. Holding her gaze, he sank into her in one smooth, powerful stroke that pulled a groan from each of them.

Neither spoke. Their passion was running too high for words. Sam made love to Lauren slowly, intently, telling her with his body, his eyes, his touch, what he could not put into words.

The only sounds in the room were soft sighs and moans, the rustle of sheet and the rhythmic squeak of the bedsprings as they made slow, sweet love to each other with an intensity that touched their souls.

Then there was only their hoarse cries of completion.

For several long, languorous minutes, while their heartbeats returned to normal and their breathing steadied, they lay sprawled together, unmoving. Then Sam startled her by abruptly rolling out of bed and scooping her up in his arms.

"Sam! What are you doing?" she squeaked.

"Time to head for the shower." He marched into the bathroom with her in his arms, plunked her down inside the glass-walled stall and stepped inside with her.

"Sam, this is positively indecent," she protested when he picked up the soap and began to wash her, but it was a halfhearted effort at best.

"So? Are you complaining?" Cupping her breasts with his soapy hands, he kneaded lightly.

Lauren's breath caught. She closed her eyes and tipped her head back. "I...no. No."

Working up great mounds of lather, they ran their hands over each other's body, massaging and caressing with long, sensual strokes. Inevitably the tantalizing bath rekindled their desire, and as the warm water rained down on them and steam rose all around, Lauren stood with her back pressed against the cool glass, one leg hooked over Sam's braced arm as he drove into her with a powerful, undulating rhythm.

* * *

"Mmm, that was good." Lauren leaned back in the chair and patted her lips with the linen napkin. "I didn't realize how hungry I was."

Sam fixed her with a steady stare. "That's what happens when you work up an appetite."

He watched her cheeks pinken, but she met his gaze squarely. Damn, she was really something, he thought. Sexy one minute and demure the next, but always full of that gutsy determination.

Rising, Lauren tightened the belt on the terry robe that the inn provided. "Yes, it has been a strenuous day. As soon as I push this room service cart into the hall I'm going to brush my teeth and go to bed. I feel as though I could sleep for a week."

"While you do that, I'll make my calls."

Sam fished Edward Stanhope's home number out of his wallet and picked up the telephone on the bedside table.

The other man answered on the second ring.

"Ed. It's Sam Rawlins."

"Sam. Thank God. I was hoping you'd call. Where the hell are you?"

Sam stiffened, instantly alert. "Why? What have you heard?"

"Enough to know you're in a heap of trouble."

"Yeah, you could say that. Look, Ed, I don't know what you've been told, but we have a witness who can put Giovessi away for good."

Quickly and succinctly Sam related Lauren's story

and the chain of events that had followed, ending with their wild escape that afternoon.

"Without knowing who's dirty and who's not, I don't dare contact anyone in the Denver office for help. It's even possible the corruption goes higher than that. That's why I'm calling you. I'm hoping you can get a message through to the top and get me some help."

"That may not be easy. Is there a television where you are?" Ed asked.

"Yeah. Why?"

"Turn it on to a news channel."

Frowning, Sam picked up the TV remote and clicked it toward the set across the room. The first thing he saw was a split screen, with his face on one side and Lauren's on the other. Lauren's photo was obviously a publicity shot from her concert days that someone had unearthed. Dressed in an elegant evening gown, she looked poised and sophisticated, even a bit aloof. And gut-wrenchingly beautiful.

"I repeat—a nationwide search has begun for Special Agent Sam Rawlins of the Federal Bureau of Investigation, and Ms. Lauren Brownley, a witness in the government's case against organized crime boss, Carlo Giovessi," the news anchor announced in his most serious voice.

"According to the FBI, they have evidence that Agent Rawlins has been taking bribe money from Carlo Giovessi for years in exchange for information on any evidence the Bureau had against the mob boss or any move planned against him.

"It is believed that Agent Rawlins has fled with Ms. Brownley, Mr. Giovessi's latest mistress, so that she can avoid testifying against him during his upcoming trial."

"What?" Lauren squawked around the toothbrush in her mouth, poking her head around the edge of the bathroom door. She stomped into the bedroom and stared at the television screen. Toothpaste foam still covered her lips.

"Agent Rawlins is believed to be armed and dangerous," the newsman continued. "If you see either of these people, please contact the FBI office nearest you or your local law enforcement agency."

Sam cursed roundly, then growled into the phone, "It's a setup, Ed. And the SAC knows it. I've been trying for months to flush out the rat—or rats—in the Denver office. At Harvey's insistence. He and everyone else in the office knew that I was getting close. Personally I think that's why he yanked me off that job and assigned me the job of protecting Lau...Ms. Brownley."

"Actually Harvey says he didn't want to believe you were dirty, but several of his agents convinced him otherwise."

"Yeah, right."

"The good news is, Giovessi has been arrested and charged with a laundry list of crimes," Ed went on. "He's being held without bond and a trial date has been set for March 20. The Federal Prosecutors are ready to go, but without Ms. Brownley's testimony they can't charge Giovessi with murder. Frank Pappano's body hasn't been found yet.''

"What about the drug trafficking?''

"Giovessi's slick lawyer has gotten him off on that several times before. Harvey and others are urging the Federal Prosecutor to drop all charges.''

"Damn.''

"They do have a point. The two charges are connected, and both hinge on Ms. Brownley's testimony. If Giovessi is found innocent, and they dig up more evidence later, he'll be protected under double jeopardy.''

"Look, Ms. Brownley *is* going to testify,'' Sam snapped. "My assignment is to keep her safe until the trial, and that's what I intend to do. Whatever it takes.''

There was a moment of silence on the other end of the line. "I have your word on that?'' Ed asked finally.

"Yes. You just make sure there is a trial and I'll have her there.''

Another silence followed. Sam could almost hear Ed thinking. "All right. You've got a deal. I still have some clout within the Bureau and the Federal Prosecutor's office. I'll make some calls. In the meantime, you keep your charge safe and show up at the Federal Courthouse in Denver on March 20 and we'll nail the old bastard.''

"You got it."

"And, Sam. Be careful. With your mug plastered all over the television someone is sure to spot you. If I were you, I'd find a safe hideaway and dig in for the next couple of months."

"Right."

The instant Sam hung up the telephone he sprang to his feet and started snatching up their belongings and stuffing them into the duffle bag. "Get dressed. We're getting out of here."

"What? Now?" Lauren wailed. "But we just got here a couple of hours ago."

"It isn't safe. Did you notice how nervous the room service waiter was when he brought our dinner? Or the strange looks he gave us?"

Her face paled. "You think he recognized us?"

"Maybe, maybe not, but it's not worth taking the risk."

Lauren agreed. She dressed and tossed her things back into the duffle bag in under three minutes. Out in the hall, she turned toward the elevators.

"No, this way." Sam grasped her arm and led her toward the fire stairs at the other end of the corridor. They clambered down the metal steps as quickly as they could, wincing at the racket they made. On the ground floor, Sam eased open the exit door and peered outside, looking up and down the narrow service alley that ran behind the inn. "Okay, all clear. Let's go."

They followed the alley for a ways, then cut be-

tween two buildings that faced onto the village courtyard. The crowd had dwindled but there were still a
few people milling around, moving from bar to bar
or window-shopping.

Staying in the shadows as much as possible, Sam
hustled Lauren through the courtyard and down the
terraced steps that led to the upper level parking area.
They had almost reached the bottom when two cars
turned off of the highway below and came racing up
the steep, winding entrance driveway.

"C'mon, hurry," Sam ordered, grabbing her hand.

They ran down the last few steps and ducked behind the first row of cars in the lot. Hunched down
behind a minivan, they watched through the vehicle's
tinted windows as the two patrol cars screeched to a
halt just a few feet away at the bottom of the stairs.
They had barely stopped when the doors were flung
open and two sheriff's deputies jumped out of each
car and dashed up the terrace steps.

"Looks like I was right about that waiter," Sam
murmured. "C'mon, we don't have much time. It
won't take them long to discover that we've flown
the coop."

He started down the line of cars, darting in and out,
trying the door handles. "Bingo," he murmured
when the fifth one opened.

He ran his hand under the floor mats, checked behind both visors and in the ashtray and console.
"Looks like I'm going to have to do this the hard
way. Stay here."

He walked away, searching the ground. Moments later he returned with a grapefruit-size rock and sat down in the driver's seat of the SUV.

"What're you going to do with th—! For heaven's sake! What're you *doing?*" Lauren squeaked when he smashed the rock against the steering column and shattered the outer sleeve.

"What does it look like? I'm hot-wiring this car."

"What! But that's stealing!"

The car started, and Lauren jumped and darted a guilty look around.

Sam jumped out of the vehicle and planted a hard kiss on her mouth. "Commandeering," he corrected. He grinned at her startled expression. "Don't worry, babe, it'll all come out in the wash eventually. Now get in. We gotta get outta here. Now."

"We're coming into Durango," Sam announced a half hour later. "Climb into the back and lie down out of sight. They'll be looking for a man and woman traveling together."

Lauren quickly complied, stepping over the console to squeeze between the two captain's chairs. "What about this car? Won't they be looking for it?" She found a wool throw tossed over the rear backrest. She curled up on her side on the bench seat and pulled the cover over her.

"I doubt the owner will miss it until morning. Maybe not even then if he's going to be at the resort for a few days."

Sam drove with panache, sitting slouched casually in the seat as though he hadn't a care in the world, but at the same time being careful to stay well within the speed limit and obey all traffic laws.

Durango was a long, narrow town built along the Animas River, and it seemed to Lauren that it took forever to go from the north end of town to the south end. She lay tense as a coiled spring beneath the blanket, jumping at every bump in the road or unexpected noise.

Finally the lighted areas grew farther apart as they reached the southern outskirts of town, but just when Lauren began to relax Sam pulled over and stopped.

"What is it? What's happening?" She peeked over the back of the front seat and saw that they were parked in a service station driveway.

"Take it easy. I'm just going to call my aunt from that pay telephone. I'll be right back."

Lauren huddled beneath the thin throw, expecting at any second to hear a police officer bark at her to put her hands up. She jumped when the driver's door opened and Sam slid back inside.

"All set. My uncle is going to pick us up in Cortez. We'll ditch this SUV there."

"Is it safe for me to sit up?" Lauren asked when they'd left the lights of Durango behind.

"As safe as it'll ever be. But why don't you just grab some shut-eye while you're back there? You said you were sleepy."

That was before they had become car thieves and

fugitives from the law. Lauren didn't think she could sleep a wink now. She was fairly comfortable, though, and most important, out of sight, so she decided to stay put.

The next thing she knew someone was shaking her shoulder.

"Wake up, Lauren."

"Wha—" She sat up with a start, her gaze darting all around. They were in the parking lot of an all-night grocery store, she realized vaguely.

"C'mon, let's go."

Responding automatically to the sharp command in Sam's voice, Lauren scrambled out of the vehicle. At once he ushered her into the battered pickup parked beside the SUV and ordered her to scoot over.

"Sorry," Lauren murmured, shooting the old man behind the wheel an apologetic look. He merely nodded.

They were driving out of the parking lot almost before Sam slammed the pickup's door.

"Lauren, this is Walter Price. He's married to my dad's sister, Eunice," Sam said. "Uncle Walt, this is Lauren Brownley, the woman you've been hearing about on the news."

Walter Price nodded and touched the brim of his battered Stetson with the tips of his first two fingers. "Miss."

"Has anyone been around looking for me?" Sam asked.

"Nope."

"Good.

"How about Dad's place? Anyone nosing around there?"

"Don't know. You'll have to ask him."

Sam snorted. "Not likely."

The taciturn old man kept his eyes on the road and said nothing, but he shook his head almost imperceptibly.

The steady hum and crackle of the tires on the snowpacked highway was the only sound for several minutes.

"I know you've seen the news on TV and read the papers," Sam said after a while. "Do you want to hear my side?"

"You do what those fellers said?"

"No."

"Then save the rest till we get home and your aunt can hear, too. No sense telling a story twice."

That was it? That's all it took for Sam to have this crusty old man's unquestioning trust? Lauren thought in amazement.

Apparently so. They drove for over an hour before reaching the Price spread, and throughout the trip both men seemed perfectly at ease and content with the silence that filled the cab.

Sam's aunt, on the other hand, could not have been more opposite of her quiet husband. The minute they stepped into the ranch house Eunice Price met her nephew with open arms and effusive greetings.

"So...this is Ms. Brownley," she said when she

finally released him from the choking bear hug. "My, my, child, if you aren't a pretty little thing. Even prettier than that picture they've been flashing all over the TV and papers."

Lauren felt her face grow hot. "I...um...thank you. And thank you both for helping us. I know this is a terrible imposition, and potentially dan—"

"Oh pooh. No need to thank us." Eunice dismissed Lauren's words with a wave of her hand. "Sam is family, and the closest thing Walt and I have to a son. Never had any young'uns of our own. After Augustus and his wife split up, me'n Walt helped raise this scamp. Of course we're going to help him. Why, it made me madder'n a wet hen when I heard that newsperson on television telling lies about our boy, here."

She looped her arm through Lauren's and urged her down the long central hall toward the back of the house. "Now come along to the kitchen. You can tell us over pie and coffee how the two of you got yourselves into this pickle."

"If you don't mind, I'd like to freshen up first," Lauren said.

"Why of course you would. What was I thinking?" Eunice directed her to the powder room with instructions to take her time and join them in the kitchen when she was done.

After using the facilities, Lauren looked at her reflection in the mirror and shook her head. Regardless of what Sam's aunt said, she thought she looked pale and washed-out. She hadn't put on so much as a speck of makeup in almost a week. Quickly she powdered her nose and applied lipstick and ran a comb through her hair. It wasn't much, but it was the best she could do for the moment.

She left the powder room and started toward the back of the house, but as she passed a wide, arched opening that led to an old-fashioned parlor she came to a halt. Against the wall, just inside the door, was an ancient upright piano.

Drawn like a moth to a flame, Lauren stepped inside the room for a closer look. She ran her hand over the mahogany surface, tracing the ornate carvings on the upper panel, the scroll-shaped music desk. The instrument was at least six and a half feet tall. Lauren knew it had probably been made in the mid-nineteenth century. She lifted the fallboard and trailed her fingertips lovingly over the keys. They were ivory and yellowed with age and a few were chipped, but she'd never seen anything so beautiful. It had been almost a week since she'd played a piano.

Unable to resist, Lauren picked out a few notes, and the sweetness of the sound tugged at her. Without quite realizing what she was doing, Lauren sank down onto the bench and placed both hands on the keyboard. She closed her eyes, and of their own volition, her fingers began to move, and the clear, opening notes of Mozart's Piano Concerto in A Major floated on the air.

As if from an opened floodgate, the music poured from her heart, from her soul. She drifted with it, lost to everything else. One piece led to another, then another. One moment her fingers danced over the keys, light as thistledown, filling the room with a haunting, sweet melody. The next her hands were grabbing great chunks of music, full of power and raw emotions.

At the end of one particularly moving piece the music trailed away on one sustained, high note. Moved almost to tears, Lauren hung her head as the sound faded, only to jump guiltily when applause broke the poignant hush.

She twisted around on the piano bench, chagrined to see Eunice and Walter sitting together on the sofa, and Sam standing in the arched doorway. All were watching her.

"Oh! I'm sorry. I'm so sorry. That was rude. I should have asked permission before playing your piano. I—"

"Lauren is a concert pianist," Sam explained, watching her in that unnerving way he had.

"Was," she corrected. "Was a concert pianist."

Sam walked to her and cupped her chin with his hand, forcing her to look up at him. "Honey, that was so beautiful it nearly broke my heart. If you played better than that before the accident, I'm not sure I could have survived it."

"Thank you, Sam." She gazed up at him, inordinately pleased, not just that he had enjoyed her playing, but that he believed her. He actually believed her.

For a moment, as she and Sam gazed into each other's eyes, she forgot about his aunt and uncle.

Then she noticed the older couple watching them, and she winced guiltily. "But I really do apologize. It was presumptuous of me."

"Nonsense, child. Why, that's the most beautiful music that's ever come out of that old piano. I'm honored you would play such an old relic."

"Oh, no. It's a beautiful instrument. I enjoy—"

She stopped abruptly, her gaze going beyond the older couple to the large window at the front of the house. Her heart began to pound.

"Someone's coming."

Sixteen

"Damn." Sam reached for his handgun, his gaze locking on the headlights approaching along the two-mile-long driveway.

"Simmer down," Walt advised. "That'll be Augustus. I called him."

Sam turned an accusing look on his uncle. "You called my father? Why?"

"Because the man's worried sick, that's why. Fact is, you shoulda called him yourself, instead of your aunt and me. Not that we object, mind you," he added before Sam could say anything. "Boy, you gotta know your aunt and I will do whatever we can to help you, and gladly, but Augustus is your pappy, and he deserves better from you than to be ignored."

"Uh…this is really none of my business," Lauren said uneasily. "Why don't I just go to the kitchen and give you some privacy." She started to rise, but Sam waved her back down.

"Sit. I don't want you out of my sight until I know for certain the driver of that vehicle really is my father. Anyway, you already know that we don't get

along. It's not like you'll hear any big family secrets.''

Turning back to his uncle, Sam countered, ''What
would be the point in asking for his help? He's never
trusted me or believed in me in the past. Why should
this be any different? He's probably swallowed those
news stories hook, line and sinker. Lauren and I will
be lucky if he hasn't already turned us in.''

''Oh, Sam,'' Eunice said sadly. ''Your father
would never do that. I know my brother was hard on
you, but don't you realize that was just because he
was afraid?''

Sam snorted. ''Afraid? Afraid of what? That old
man is tough as nails. I've never known him to be
afraid of anything in his life.''

''Except for one thing,'' his aunt insisted quietly.
''He's afraid of losing you.''

That caught Sam by surprise, drawing his gaze
away from the approaching headlights. He gave a
mirthless chuckle. ''Oh, sure. That's why he rode me
so hard, all those years. Why he found fault with everything I did. He did his duty by me because I was
his, but I was never the son he wanted. Never a son
he could be proud of. I finally figured out that it was
my Indian blood he couldn't stomach.''

''Sam!'' Eunice exclaimed. ''All these years?
That's what you thought? If only you'd told me. Oh,
dearest, you're so wrong.''

''I don't think so. If I so much as mentioned my
mother's people or spent any time on the reservation

he got furious." Sam looked back at the lights. They were much closer now. "Face it, he hates Indians, and he can't abide the fact that his only son has Indian blood."

"Don't be a danged fool," Walt barked. "Augustus doesn't hate Indians. He admires and respects them. Always has. And he adored your mama. Even after she went back to her people and divorced him, he never stopped loving her. It nearly killed him when she passed away. Hell, he still loves her. Why do you think he never remarried?"

Sam stared, at a loss for words. He'd never thought of that.

"Walt is right," Eunice put in. "Your dad loves you more than anything in the world, Sam. More even than he loves the Double R, and that's saying a lot. In the past, when you seemed drawn to your Indian relatives and their culture, it terrified him. He was sure he was losing you to that way of life…the same way he'd lost his wife.

"Over the years, the more Augustus's fear grew the more rigid and demanding he became. It was the only way he knew to keep you on the ranch. Ironically, the tighter he held on, the more he drove you away." Eunice shook her head sadly. "I think, deep down, he knew it, but he didn't know what else to do."

"That's right," Walt agreed. "He lived in fear that you would turn your back on him and the ranch.

When you left and joined the FBI all those years ago it was his worst nightmare come true."

"If all that's true, why didn't he just tell me how he felt?"

"Oh, please," Eunice scoffed. "You of all people should know the answer to that. You're just like him, after all. You Rawlins men are a stoic breed. You keep all your emotions locked up tight behind that tough exterior—like it would kill you for someone to see that you've got a tender side. Or to admit you're hurting."

Stunned, Sam didn't know what to say. He'd always assumed that he'd simply never measured up to his father's standards and expectations. It had never occurred to him that Augustus was afraid of losing him.

"He actually believed I'd leave the Double R forever? No way in hell. I joined the Bureau to give us both some space. Dad was still a vigorous man when I left here sixteen years ago. I haven't seen him in a couple of years, but from what you've told me, he still is. I wasn't about to knuckle under to his demands like some weak-kneed yes-man, but since all we did was butt heads over everything, I decided to do us both a favor and back off and let him run the ranch his way.

"I always figured I'd come back someday and take over for him when he began to slow down and needed my help. But I never had any intention of abandoning the ranch or him. I love the Double R." Sam's jaw clenched. "And all right, dammit, I admit it. I also love that crusty old bastard. God alone knows why.

"But just because I love my mother's people, too, that doesn't mean I'd ever abandon him. How could he even think that?"

"Easy, I imagine," Walt replied. "What you gotta remember, boy, is Augustus loved your mama to distraction, and she loved him. She truly did, and that's a fact. In the end, though, her longing for her people and their way of life was too strong, and Augustus lost her. Why would he think it'd be any different with you?"

Before Sam could absorb that the approaching pickup skidded to a halt in the U-shaped gravel driveway in front of the house and the truck door slammed. An instant later the front door burst open.

"Where is he? Where's my son? *Sam!*"

Even as the bellow left his lips, Augustus Rawlins's big frame filled the arched entrance to the parlor. The instant he spotted Sam, abject relief flickered across his weather-beaten face, followed quickly by anger and outrage. "Boy! What the devil is going on?"

Sam stiffened. The confusing tangle of emotions swirling inside him vanished and all the old resentment came flooding back. He met his father's demanding gaze with eyes like cold steel. "I'm not working for the mob," he ground out through clenched teeth.

"Hell, I know that," Augustus barked. "I want to

know who is feeding the news media that hogwash? And why?''

The reply surprised Sam. ''You believe me?''

''Dammit, boy, of course I believe you!'' the old man thundered. ''We may have had our differences, and maybe you don't want to have any part of me or the ranch anymore, but by God, you're still my son. You're a good man and an honest one. Anyone who says otherwise is either a damned liar or a fool.''

A queer sensation twisted inside Sam. His throat was suddenly so tight he could barely speak, but somehow he managed a husky, ''Thanks, Dad.''

Before he realized his father's intent, the old man stomped across the room and snatched him into a bear hug that sent Sam's breath whooshing out of his lungs like air escaping a balloon. Too shocked to respond, at first he stood as though turned to stone while his father thumped his back. Finally, tentatively, he returned the embrace and gave his father's back a couple of hesitant pats.

When at last Augustus released Sam he looked sheepish. Clearing his throat, he took a step back and shifted from one foot to the other. Then his gaze slid past Sam and zeroed in on Lauren, and his eyebrows jerked together in a frown. ''This must be that Ms. Brownley all the news men've been yammering about. She sure doesn't look like a mobster's mistress to me.''

Sam's jaw clenched. ''She isn't. Lauren is a concert pianist who just happened to be in the wrong place at the wrong time and witnessed a murder.''

''That's right, Gus,'' Eunice confirmed. ''Lauren just finished playing several beautiful pieces for us.''

Augustus barely heard his sister. With his head cocked to one side, he studied his son's angry expression. His gaze flickered to Lauren, then back to Sam. ''I see. I guess I should've known that if they were lying about you they'd be lying about her, as well.''

Whipping off his Stetson, he walked over to Lauren and stuck out his hand. ''I'm Augustus Rawlins, Sam's father. It's a pleasure to meet you, Ms. Brownley. And I hope you'll accept my apology for what I just said.''

''Certainly, sir. I understand. You had no way of knowing.''

Sam watched as Lauren's small, slender hand disappeared between both of Augustus's callused palms. He and his father were the same height and general build, although, with age, Augustus's shoulders were beginning to stoop a bit and his midsection had thickened. Even so, at sixty-four he was still a big man, rawhide tough and strong as an ox. He towered over Lauren, his great size and strength emphasizing her petiteness and delicate build.

Though Sam knew his father would never hurt Lauren, or any woman, he could barely restrain himself from going to her, putting his arm around her shoulders and pulling her close against his side.

What was it about Lauren that tugged at him? Sam wondered. He had protected witnesses before, and he'd done his job well, but he'd never felt this level of involvement nor intensity.

Of course, he'd never made love to any of the other witnesses, either.

But that wasn't it. He desired Lauren, certainly, and he couldn't deny that her beauty made him weak in the knees. But, hell, he'd desired other women in the past. Although...he had to admit he hadn't experienced this sort of randy passion since he was sixteen years old and trying to seduce their foreman's daughter in the hayloft.

No, there was definitely more to it than just sex.

Sam frowned, uneasy with the thought. Still...he knew it was true. There was something about Lauren that brought out a primitive protective streak in him he hadn't known he possessed.

Was it her dainty appearance? Or that air of refinement that was so much a part of her? Even when they'd been camping rough and tromping through the wilderness there had been a subtle elegance in every move she made.

Maybe it was her valiant spirit and keen intelligence that attracted him. Or that single-minded determination to stand on her own two feet.

Or was it simply the whole package?

"Would you mind telling me exactly what's going on?" Augustus demanded when he'd finished talking to Lauren. "Not an hour ago a whole caravan of FBI cars came roaring up to the house looking for you."

Sam tensed, instantly alert. "What did you tell them?"

"What do you think? The truth. That you weren't there and I hadn't heard from you. Didn't believe me, though. Those yahoos wanted to search every acre of the place, but I sent the whole lot of 'um packing. Told 'um without a warrant they could go suck eggs, and to get the hell off my land and stay off."

Sam's gaze darted to the window again. "You can bet they're still out there, waiting for Lauren and me to turn up. They've probably got every entrance to the ranch staked out."

"Guess it's a good thing you called Eunice and me, after all," Walt said. "We haven't seen hide nor hair of any federal agents."

That's because they don't know about this place, Sam thought. It was not his nature to confide the details of his life to anyone, but in this case his reticence had stemmed from something more. When he had applied to the Bureau he had found the routine, in-depth background check they ran on every potential candidate offensive. He had deliberately withheld the information that the adjacent ranch belonged to his aunt and uncle. Gut instinct had cautioned him to keep that secret—just in case he ever needed a haven.

"You still haven't told me how you got yourselves into this mess," Augustus said. "I thought the FBI was an honorable organization."

"It is. But once in a while you get a bad apple or two." For the third time that evening, Sam gave a succinct but thorough accounting of the events of the past five days. When he was done, his father gave a low whistle.

"What're you going to do, son? With no one to turn to at the Bureau, you're on your own."

"I know. I thought we'd rest here tonight and at first light I'd take Lauren up to our old hunting cabin."

"Is it safe to stay here now, with agents close by?" Lauren asked.

"For a time it should be."

"Uh-oh. Looks to me like that time's done run out," Walt pronounced, waving toward the window. "There's a string of cars coming fast up the driveway."

"Damn." Grabbing Lauren's arm, Sam dragged her away from the window and pressed back against the adjacent wall. He shot his father an annoyed look. "They must have followed you here."

"Don't see how. I'm not stupid, boy. I drove over on the ranch road that connects our two places. Not a soul saw me, I'd swear to it."

Sam's jaw clenched. That meant they'd found out about this place and his relationship to its owners. And there was only one way that could have happened.

Augustus stomped toward the gun case in the corner. "Let's break out your rifles, Walt. They're not taking my boy."

"No, Dad. No gunplay."

"Why not? We can take 'um, son. There's only fifteen or sixteen of 'um and five of us. Except for Lauren, we're all crack shots."

"Then what? Trust me, Dad, you shoot one of those guys and the Bureau will swoop down on this place with an army of agents. Lauren and I will be killed and you'll all spend the next twenty years in prison. The only chance we have is to get out of here."

"Okay, then, take my truck and go out the back road with the lights off before they get close enough to the house to spot you," Augustus ordered.

"Are you sure?"

"Just go, boy. Go on, get out of here. Now! Walt'n me'll deal with these yahoos."

With Lauren in tow, Sam headed for the door. After only two steps he hesitated, then swung back and snatched his father into a bear hug. "Thanks, Dad. I..."

"I know, son. I know," Augustus said gruffly. "Now go on with you. Git while you still can."

Father and son exchanged a long look, then Sam spun away, hauling Lauren with him.

In the front hall, he scooped up the duffle bag on the run and tore out the front door. Spanning Lauren's waist with his hands, he picked her up and tossed her into the cab of the truck and slung the duffle in after her. He eyed the line of approaching headlights as he raced around the pickup and climbed behind the wheel. They were almost halfway down the driveway and moving in fast.

The truck engine sprang to life at the first twist of the key, which, as always, was in the ignition. Sam didn't bother to back up and follow the driveway around back, but took off across the yard and his aunt's beloved flowerbeds and careered around the corner of the house. Out back, once they passed the barn and corrals they were in total darkness. Sam headed for the woods that butted up to the ranch yard on the east, and Lauren made a distressed sound.

"Oh Lord! We're going to crash into a tree!"

"Calm down, we're okay. I can see well enough in the moonlight. Besides, I know every inch of these woods. There's a dirt road right about...here." He jerked the steering wheel hard to the right. A low hanging branch scraped the side of the truck and Lauren shrieked as the pickup shot between two tall cottonwood trees.

"Hold on," Sam advised. "This road isn't used much and it's narrow and rough."

What little moonlight filtered down through the bare branches gave only patchy illumination. As they bumped along through the darkness Lauren sat forward and peered through the windshield, gripping the dash with one hand and the edge of the seat with the other and moaning at every scrape and thunk against the side of the pickup.

On the opposite side of the woods the dirt road continued through a clearing for about twenty feet to a gated entrance from a two-lane, paved back road. Sam brought the pickup to a slow stop at the edge of the woods and sat in the darkness with the engine idling, scanning the area.

"Damn."

"What? What is it?" Lauren's anxious gaze darted around.

"There's a car watching this road."

"Where? I don't see anything."

"About fifty yards to your right. Parked in the shade of that big spruce on the other side."

Leaning forward, Lauren peered through the darkness. "Are you sure? I still don't see it."

"I'm sure."

"What do we do now?"

"One thing is certain. We can't stay here. If they don't already have search warrants for this place and the Double R they will before long. Somebody is probably waking up a judge right now. It'll be tomorrow before Edward can get the manhunt called off. We have no choice but to make a run for it."

Sam turned his head and looked at Lauren. Even through the darkness he could see the fear in her eyes, but she met his gaze directly and didn't make a sound. Unable to resist, he reached out and hooked his hand around the back of her neck, pulling her to him as he leaned over and gave her a deep, passionate kiss. He felt her pulse leap, then take off with a mad thrumming that exactly matched his own thundering heart-beat.

When he was done he drew back just a few inches and looked deep into her eyes. "Ready?"

She stared back at him, her eyes wide and glittering like green glass in the darkness. Finally, sucking in a deep breath, she pressed her lips tightly together, squared her shoulders and nodded.

"That's my girl." Sam planted another quick kiss on her mouth, then straightened and gripped the steering wheel. "Hang on."

He gunned the engine, and they shot out of the trees. In seconds they bumped over the cattle guard, hooked a skidding left and blasted down the road. Only then did Sam turn on the lights.

"Brace yourself. Here they come."

Lauren twisted around in her seat and saw headlights where seconds before there had been only blackness. As she watched, they grew steadily larger. "Oh Lord, they're gaining on us, Sam!"

Sam made no reply. His profile looked as though it had been chiseled in stone. He pressed the accelerator harder and the truck picked up speed and for a moment the space between them and the car widened.

"They're catching up again!"

Grimly Sam pushed the accelerator pedal to the floor, and the pickup streaked down the deserted highway like a bullet.

Lauren looked over her shoulder again. "They're

not getting any closer but they're staying with us,'' she reported.

Sam looked into the rearview mirror just as a flash of fire appeared on the passenger's side of the pursuit car. At the same instant something *thunked* against the pickup's tailgate and Lauren shrieked.

''Oh my Lord! They're shooting at us!''

She barely got the words out when the back window shattered.

''Get down! Get down!'' Sam yelled. Steering with one hand, he reached over and shoved her down onto the floorboard as another bullet took out the side mirror on the passenger door.

Sam took what evasive measures he could, but going that fast he couldn't risk swerving much or he'd roll the truck.

Huddled in a ball on the floor with her hands over her ears, Lauren screamed and screamed as volley after volley of shots splatted against the pickup and whined past.

''Holy—!''

Thirty feet ahead a small herd of mule deer exploded up out of the bar ditch onto the road.

Sam jerked the wheel to avoid them. Veering onto the shoulder, the pickup lifted up on two wheels and hung suspended even as it continued to move forward. Cursing, Sam fought to bring it right again and Lauren screamed.

Finally, after what seemed like an eternity but in reality could have been no more than a few seconds, the truck's left tires slammed back down onto the pavement, bounced twice, then regain purchase.

From behind them came a prolonged screech of tires on paving, followed by a tremendous crash.

Lauren's head came up. "What was that?"

Sam's gaze flickered to the rearview mirror. "Our friends just got a close-up look at the local wildlife."

"What? Wait! Listen! They've stopped shooting." Cautiously she rose to her knees and peered through the shattered back window. "Oh, my goodness. I don't believe it! They've crashed! The car is in the bar ditch with its headlight pointing skyward. And there's something strewn across the highway. I think...it looks like dead animals. I don't see any sign of those men."

She turned to Sam, her face joyous. "We've done it. We've gotten away!"

"Yeah, well...don't get too excited. I'm sure they called in our position to the rest of the team. There'll be more agents coming along any second."

"But we have a head start. Surely they won't be able to catch us."

"Well...that...that depends."

"On what?"

"On whether or not...you can drive a...truck."

"Me? Why should I—Sam! What're you doing? Why are you slowing down?"

The pickup rolled to a stop in the center of the road. Feebly, Sam managed to shove the gearshift into Park an instant before he slumped over the wheel.

"*Sam!*" Lauren swept aside the pebbles of glass and scrambled up onto the seat next to him. "Sam? Sam, what's wrong?" She grabbed his shoulders and tried to pull him upright, but when Sam moaned she quickly stopped. "Oh Lord, Sam, talk to me."

His eyes flickered open and he grimaced at her. "S-sorry, babe...but I've...I've been...shot."

Seventeen

"Shot! No! *No!*" Lauren cried.

Terror clawed at her. Panic-stricken, she ran her hands over Sam's shoulders and upper arms, his back. "Where? Where are you hurt? Tell me, Sam!" she demanded. "Talk to me!"

His only reply was a moan. She wasn't even certain he was still conscious.

"Oh, Sam." Her fingers encountered something wet and sticky. Lauren drew her hand away and sucked in a sharp breath. Her palm was covered with blood. "Oh God. Oh God. Oh God."

She pressed her lips tightly together and fought to quell the bubble of hysteria rising in her throat. Glancing around, she saw that a mile or so behind them the lights of the wrecked car still shot skyward like a spotlight. Other than that, there was no sign of human life—or help—in sight.

She ground her teeth. No, don't think of it that way. Look on the bright side. At least there was no sign of those men's cohorts. Yet.

That thought brought a low moan from her throat, and she had to fight back another wave of panic. What was she going to do? Think, Lauren. *Think!* They had to get out of there. And fast. But first she had to tend to Sam. If she didn't stop the bleeding quickly he would surely die.

After fumbling around she located the switch for the overhead light and flipped it on. Kneeling on the seat beside Sam, she pulled him upright. He moaned again and his eyes flickered open. "Gotta...get outta...here," he mumbled.

"I know. I know. But let me do this first."

"You're...you're gonna ha...have to...drive."

"I know that, too. But I warn you, I've never driven a pickup before."

"N-nothin' to it. You'll...do fine, swe-sweetheart." Sam's words were slurred, and at the end his voice trailed off and he slumped back against the seat and went limp.

"Sam? *Sam!*"

He didn't reply. Lauren put her ear to his chest and sagged with relief when she heard his heart beating. Working quickly, straining and panting, she stripped off his parka and eased him forward until he was braced against the steering wheel. One look at his back made her stomach roil and sent her terror skyrocketing anew. Blood soaked his shirt all the way to the waistband on his wool pants.

Breathing hard and making unconscious, little distressed sounds, Lauren pawed through the duffle bag and pulled out a pair of long johns, then snatched Sam's shirt free of his pants and shoved it up to his shoulders. Bile rose in her throat at the sight of blood oozing from an obscene hole just above his shoulder blade.

Quickly she folded the body of the long johns into a thick pad and pressed it tightly against the wound. Struggling and straining to reach around Sam's inert body, she used the legs of the garment to tie the makeshift bandage in place.

When done, she sat back on her heels with a sigh of exhaustion and surveyed her handiwork. It wasn't the neatest bandage she'd ever seen, but it seemed to have stanched the flow of blood. Sam needed a clean shirt, but there was no time for that.

Lauren pulled the bloodied shirt back down and worked first one, then the other of his arms back into his parka and brought him upright again with his back propped against the seat back.

"Sam? Sam, can you hear me?" She gave his cheek a sharp tap, then another. "Wake up, Sam. You have to help if I'm going to scoot you over. I can't budge you on my own."

Sam's eyelids fluttered twice, then opened partway. His eyes were out of focus, and she could see that just remaining conscious required tremendous effort. "Ri-right."

Lauren put her arms around Sam's waist and pulled with all her might as he did his best to scoot sideways. It took a tremendous effort and caused him a lot of pain, but finally she maneuvered him to the other side.

"Are you okay?" she gasped.

"Y-yeah. Let's...go."

Lauren jumped out of the cab, ran around to the other side and climbed into the driver's seat. Gripping the steering wheel tightly, she darted Sam a nervous glance. "Here goes," she said and stomped on the gas.

Smoke and the smell of burning rubber rose as the tires squealed and spun on the asphalt paving. Then the truck leaped forward and shot down the road, going from zero to eighty-five miles an hour in ten seconds flat.

Lauren had little experience driving any vehicle, and compared to her car, the truck seemed enormous and awkward to handle. She held the wheel with a white-knuckled grip and concentrated fiercely on keeping the pickup between the faded center stripe and the bar ditch. Using the duffle bag to keep himself propped upright, Sam fought to stay conscious.

After a few miles the road intersected a main highway. "Turn right...here," Sam gasped. "And slow...down. We don't want to...get stopped for...speeding."

Lauren gritted her teeth and did as he ordered, but it was difficult. Instinct urged her to floorboard the gas pedal and put as many miles between them and their pursuers as possible. At that hour there were few vehicles on the road, and as she drove through the darkness Lauren had the eeriest feeling that she had somehow entered an alien world.

"Where are we going?" she asked when she could stand the silence no longer. She received no answer.

"Sam?" She glanced at him and saw that his eyes were closed and he lay slumped against the passenger door. Fear shot through her. "Sam? Are you still with me?"

Still no reply.

"Sam? Sam, wake up! Answer me!"

The only sounds were the engine's steady rumble and the rhythmic *thump-thump* of the tires on the highway. Another vehicle passed the truck, and Lauren jumped at the unexpected *whoosh* when it went by. She moaned and bit her lower lip. What in heaven's name was she supposed to do now?

She couldn't just drive around aimlessly, and she had no idea how to find that hunting cabin Sam had mentioned earlier. Besides, he needed medical attention.

Lauren choked back a hysterical sob. How she was going to manage that she had no idea. If she took him to a hospital or a doctor they would have to report the gunshot to the police, and if that happened she and Sam were as good as dead.

It was after midnight and she had no idea where she was, but the lights of a town glowed up ahead. Staring at twinkling lights, she came to a decision.

A highway sign identified the town as Monticello, Utah. Lauren stopped at the first motel she found and rented a room using Sam's bogus credit card, praying all the while she registered that the sleepy clerk wouldn't recognize her or ask too many questions.

She parked the pickup as close to the room as she could and somehow managed to rouse Sam enough to pull him from the cab. Holding his good arm looped around her shoulders she wrapped her other arm around his waist and staggered inside with him, nearly collapsing under his weight before falling with him, facedown, onto the bed.

Lauren scooted off the bed and dashed back out to the truck for the duffle bag, then dashed back inside and bolted and chained the door. After turning up the heat she noticed that Sam still hadn't moved or made a sound. She went to the bed and touched his shoulder. "Sam? Are you okay?"

He gave no response. She quickly checked his pulse and peeled back his eyelids and realized that he had passed out again. Just as well, she thought, considering what she had to do.

Fighting fatigue and fear, Lauren tried to think logically. The first and most important thing was to clean Sam's wound before infection set in. That would probably start the bleeding again, but she'd just have to deal with that.

It was almost one in the morning. Where was she going to get the bandages and medicine she needed? From the looks of things when she'd driven into town the sidewalks of Monticello had been rolled up hours ago. Looking at Sam's prone form, she gnawed her bottom lip. Did she dare risk leaving him alone long enough to drive around and look for an all-night drugstore? She pulled the keys from her parka pocket and fingered them, debating. Suddenly she snapped her fingers.

The truck! Why hadn't she thought of that before? Surely a rancher, or anyone who did physical outdoor work, would keep a first-aid kit handy.

Lauren unbolted the door and dashed back outside. Sure enough, behind the passenger seat in the extended cab section of the truck she found a large plastic box with a red cross on the top.

"Bless you, Augustus," she murmured fervently, and hurried back inside.

After considerable struggle she managed to strip Sam to the waist and remove his holster and gun. Slipping her hand beneath his chest, she felt for an exit wound but found none. Lauren groaned. The bullet was still inside.

Trying not to think about that, she washed his wound, then his entire back with warm, soapy water and a washcloth. When done, she leaned close and examined the hole and grimaced. The puckered edges were an angry red rimmed with gray and still oozed blood. She swabbed the area with the washcloth again and noticed that inside the hole there were tiny fragments of cloth and fiber from his clothing. Lauren frowned. That couldn't be good.

To her relief, in addition to the usual gauze pads, cotton balls and bandages, the first-aid kit contained a pair of tweezers, alcohol, iodine, a tube of antibiotic cream, a burn pack and even surgical needles and suture thread. The last items made Lauren shudder and marvel at the toughness of cowboys.

In the bathroom she poured alcohol over the tweezers then returned and knelt on the bed beside Sam. Biting her lower lip, she hesitated, her shaking hand poised over the ugly wound. "You can do this, Lauren. You *have* to do this." Closing her eyes, she said a quick prayer, then drew a deep breath and bent closer.

Sam moaned as she plucked out the first bit of cloth, and Lauren moaned right along with him. For the next ten minutes, in between swabbing away blood, she plucked and pulled and probed and tried not to gag. When she'd finally removed all the debris she swabbed away the blood once again and gently spread the edges of the hole a bit wider, drawing another groan from Sam.

Lauren peered into the wound, but she didn't see anything that looked like a bullet. She knew it should come out, but there was no way she was going to go digging around in there. She might do more harm than good.

"I'm sorry, Sam, but this is the best I can do," she murmured as she twisted the cap off the iodine bottle and poured a liberal amount of the brownish/orange antiseptic over the area.

Sam's head jerked up off the pillow. "Jesus! Wh-what're you...doing?"

"I'm sorry! I'm so sorry," Lauren cried. "I'm just

trying to doctor your wound. Lie still now, while I finish.''

The order was unnecessary. As she spread the edges of the hole once again and squeezed almost a half a tube of antibiotic cream inside he passed out. Lauren covered the wound with a thick wad of gauze pads and taped them in place.

Sighing, she sat back on her heels. Suddenly, in delayed reaction, she began to tremble from head to toe. She hugged her arms around her midriff and rocked back and forth on her knees. "Please don't let him die. Please, God, please," she murmured over and over. "I couldn't bear it.''

And not simply because she depended on him to protect her, Lauren realized, but because the idea of living without Sam Rawlins was too painful to contemplate. As unlikely as it seemed, as foolish as it undoubtedly was, she had fallen in love with this tough, taciturn, complicated man.

Lauren moaned and rocked harder and called herself all manner of uncomplimentary names, from weakling to imbecile to pathetic, but it made no difference. She loved him. Deeply, irrevocably.

When her shakes finally subsided and she had herself under control, she sighed again and wiped the sweat from her brow with her forearm and gazed at Sam and the awkward bandage on his back. It looked a stark white against his bronze skin. She climbed from the bed and tugged off Sam's moccasins, then pulled the covers up over him.

Well, she'd done all she could, she thought tiredly. Now she would just have to wait and hope that by morning he'd be feeling better.

Exhausted, Lauren stripped out of her clothes, took a quick shower and climbed into the room's other bed. The instant her head touched the pillow she fell into a deep sleep. A couple of hours later she jerked awake.

"What? Who—?" She sprang upright in the bed and looked around, disoriented. Then, in the sliver of moonlight slanting in through the gap in the motel draperies, she saw Sam, and everything came rushing back. In a flash she realized what had awakened her. Sam was groaning and thrashing around violently.

In an instant Lauren was on her feet. "Sam? Sam, be still. You're going to hurt yourself worse. You'll have your wound bleeding again if you don't stop that."

For all the attention he paid she might as well have talked to the wall. She reached out, intending to stroke his back, but at the first touch she sucked in her breath. "Oh Lord, Sam, you're burning up."

She brushed his hair away from his face, and blinked back tears. "Damn you, Sam Rawlins. Don't you dare die on me now. Not after all we've been through. You hear me!"

Sam rolled his head from side to side on the pillow. "Lau-ren," he croaked.

"Yes, I'm here. What is it, Sam?"

"Love...y-you."

Lauren sucked in a sharp breath and jerked back, her eyes widening. Her heart squeezed painfully. She wanted so much to believe him, and for an instant hope swelled inside her but she quickly battled it down. Don't be an idiot, she ordered. The man has a raging fever. He's delirious. He has no idea what he's saying.

Sam thrashed around and let out a loud groan, and Lauren gave herself a shake. For heaven's sake, quit acting like a lovesick teenager. He needs your help, she silently scolded. This was no time to indulge in hopeless daydreams.

As with almost everything else, Lauren had no nursing experience, but she'd picked up enough information to know that she had to get Sam's fever down. Fast.

She whirled around, ripped the top sheet off the other bed and took it into the bathroom. After soaking it in cold water under the bathtub spigot, she hurried back and wrapped the wet cloth around him.

Within minutes the sheet was warm. She had to resoak it a half dozen times before there was any discernible break in his fever. No sooner had that happened than he was seized with chills and began to shake uncontrollably. Lauren stripped off the clammy sheets and briskly toweled him dry, coaxed aspirin down his throat, covered him with the blankets from both beds and turned up the heat, but still he shivered. Finally she crawled into bed beside him and held him close.

After a while Sam quieted and dropped into a deep slumber—at least Lauren hoped that was what it was. Exhausted, she fell asleep snuggled against his side.

A couple of hours later, Sam's fever spiked again, and she hauled herself out of bed and repeated the entire procedure.

Throughout the remainder of the night and all the next day the pattern repeated itself over and over— Sam's fever yo-yoed up and down and, in between, chills racked his body so hard Lauren could almost hear his bones rattling.

The following morning, when the motel maid knocked on the door, Lauren told the woman her husband wasn't feeling well and took the clean sheets and towels from her and hung out the Do Not Disturb sign. By late afternoon, though she was too tired to be hungry, she was shaky from fatigue and lack of food, and she knew Sam needed nourishment as well. During one of his docile periods, she screwed up her courage and risked a trip to a restaurant and brought back a takeout order.

Coaxing the warm soup down Sam, a teaspoon at a time, was difficult and frustrating, and when she was done she barely had the energy to eat half the sandwich she'd gotten for herself.

Day turned into evening and Lauren grew more concerned. As the cycle of high fever and racking chills went on, Sam grew weaker, and she had no idea what else to do. Almost twenty-four hours after checking into the motel, holding him close as the latest bout of chills subsided, Lauren stared at the ceiling, sick with worry.

"N-number..."

She jerked her head back and stared at Sam's flushed face. She put her hand against his forehead and realized that his fever was rising again. "Sam? Are you awake? Did you say something?"

His eyelids fluttered.

"Oh, Sam! Sam, you *are* awake!" she cried. "Thank God!"

He frowned and tried to talk, but he couldn't manage more than a raspy whisper.

Lauren put her ear close to his mouth. "What?"

"In my...wa-wallet. My cousin La...Larry's... number. C-call...him."

She drew back, frowning. "Oh, Sam, are you sure? Can we trust him? Sam?" she prodded, but he had already slipped back into unconsciousness.

Lauren found his wallet in the inside zipper pocket of his parka. In it was a folded piece of paper, on which was a typed list of perhaps fifteen names and telephone numbers. The only Larry was a Larry Zah.

Lauren paced back and forth across the room with the list in her hand, agonizing over whether or not to make the call. Did Sam really trust this man? Enough to risk their lives? Or was he merely desperate? He could even have been delirious when he made the request.

She stopped and looked from the list to the telephone, and chewed on her thumbnail. Then her worried gaze went to Sam. He was beginning to flail around again. Lauren sighed. She had no choice. He needed more help than she could give him. She had to chance it.

The telephone rang five times before it was picked up and a sleepy voice mumbled, ''Hello.''

''Is this Larry Zah?''

''Yeah. Who is this?''

''I…you are Sam Rawlins's cousin, right?''

There was a short pause, and when the man spoke again his voice had changed from drowsy to alert. ''That's right. What about it?''

''Sam is with me, and he, uh…he needs your help. He's been shot.''

''Shot?''

''Yes, and he's in bad shape.''

He did not hesitate. ''Tell me where you are, and I'll come get you.''

Uneasily Lauren told him their location and the name of the motel and the room number.

''I'll be right there.''

During the hour and ten minutes it took for Sam's cousin to arrive, Lauren swung back and forth, sure one minute that she'd done the right thing and just as sure the next that she had made a grave error.

When she heard the pickup pull up outside the room she stood in the dark by the window, waiting, Sam's service automatic in her hand. If this Larry person had led Carlo Giovessi's assassins to them, she wouldn't be a lamb to the slaughter.

She twitched the curtain open a crack and saw a big, barrel-chested man get out of the battered pickup. He wore jeans, a plaid shirt, a leather, sheep-skin lined jacket and a domed-crown felt hat with a silver hatband. His straight black hair hung to his waist like an ebony waterfall. Lauren's gaze scanned the parking area. There appeared to be no one else around.

He tapped on the door.

"Who is it?" Lauren called in a low-pitched voice.

"Larry."

Holding the gun behind her back, she unlatched the chain and let him in. He barely spared Lauren a glance. Once at the bed, he picked up Sam's parka and put it on him, then scooped his cousin up in his arms. Sam was a big man, but Larry Zah carried him as though he weighed no more than a child. "Get your things. We're getting outta here."

While waiting for him, Lauren had put a fresh bandage and shirt on Sam and returned their belonging to the duffle bag. Surreptitiously she dropped the gun into her purse, grabbed the duffle bag, Sam's moccasins and the first-aid kit and scurried after him.

"That yours?" he said, nodding toward the pickup.

"No. We borrowed it from Sam's father."

"We'll leave it here. I'll call Augustus tomorrow and tell him where to pick it up."

The man was so terse, if it hadn't been for his appearance, Lauren would have thought he was a Rawlins instead of one of Sam's Navajo relatives.

Within seconds they were out of the parking lot

and speeding south. Sam lay slumped against Lauren, and she held him tight.

"My name is Lauren Brownley, by the way," she said into the silence.

"I figured." Larry Zah sent her an unreadable look. "We get TV on the reservation, too, you know."

"I...I see," Lauren said uneasily. She slipped her hand inside her purse and closed it around the gun. "Then you've heard the news reports."

"Yeah."

"They're not true."

"I figured. Sam's a straight-arrow."

She released the gun and put her arm back around Sam. "Where are you taking us?" she asked after another long stretch of silence.

"To the reservation. We have a doctor there."

"Oh, but—"

"Relax. He's Navajo, and we'll be on Navajo land. He won't report this."

Lauren closed her eyes and sagged with relief. "Thank you."

Larry grunted, but he seemed disinclined to talk, so Lauren settled Sam and herself into a more comfortable position and leaned her head back.

An hour later she was jostled awake and found they were creeping down a sharp incline on the roughest dirt road she'd ever seen. For miles the road wound through massive sandstone formations as tall as multistoried buildings, standing like eerie sentinels in the moonlight.

"This must be Monument Valley," Lauren said in an awed voice.

"Um. But not the part the tourists see. That's only a few acres. The rest of the reservation is for Navajos only."

Lauren started to ask, "What about me? I'm not Navajo," but she thought better of it.

They drove for miles across vast expanses, deep into the interior of the reservation. Dotted here and there were modest houses, all with dome-shaped hogans out back. Sam grew restless, and moaned at the constant jostling. Lauren felt his forehead, discovered that his fever was rising again.

Finally they arrived at a small cluster of dwellings, a small frame house and two mobile homes about a hundred feet apart. "This is my place," Larry said, pulling up in front of one of the mobile homes.

The door was opened by a Native American woman in her mid-thirties wearing a robe and slippers. Lauren assumed she was Larry's wife, though he didn't bother with introductions. As he carried Sam inside the woman clucked and fussed, her attention riveted on him to the exclusion of everything else. When she happened to notice Lauren, shock flashed across her face. She looked as though she was about to object, but her husband cut her off.

"Is a bed ready?"

"Yes. I thought it would be better if we put him in the boys' room, so I moved them out here," she replied, motioning toward the two teenage boys sleeping on the sofa bed in the living room. She bustled ahead of her husband, leading the way down a narrow hallway. Lauren followed at Larry's heels.

The small bedroom contained twin beds. Larry gently placed his cousin on the one closest to the door. An agonized sound came from Sam, and Lauren hurried to his side and placed her hand on his forehead. "His fever is worse," she said to Larry over her shoulder.

"I'll go call the doc."

The woman followed him, and though she tried to keep her voice low, Lauren heard her. "Larry, that woman cannot stay here," she insisted. "She is not one of us."

"She will be our guest."

"But others will not like having a white woman here. It is not allo—"

"Hush, Zeta. She is Sam's woman. She stays."

Sam's woman? A thrill shimmered through Lauren at the thought. She sat down on the side of the bed beside him and took his hand. If only that were true.

To Sam, she was an assignment. Oh sure, he desired her. He may even have developed a mild affection for her in the past few days, but no matter how she might wish otherwise, she was hardly "his woman."

Lauren knew full well that if they got out of this mess alive and she testified against Carlo, then she and Sam would part. He would return to his job, or perhaps to his father's ranch, and she would be given a new identity, a new life.

And she'd never see Sam again.

Tears threatened, and Lauren gave herself a shake. In the meantime, though, if his Native American relatives wanted to believe that she was his woman, she wasn't about to tell them otherwise.

The Zahs returned a short while later with a slender Navajo man in his thirties carrying a doctor's bag. With him was one of the loveliest young women Lauren had ever seen. In her early twenties, she had delicate features, magnificent big brown eyes and the shy demeanor of a wild doe.

The instant the girl spotted Sam she rushed to his side, opposite Lauren, and began to stroke the back of his neck. She gazed at him adoringly, oblivious to everyone else in the room. "Oh, Sam," she whispered. "Dearest Sam. What has happened to you?"

Lauren's heart sank. This beautiful Native American girl was in love with Sam!

Stunned and heartsick, she stepped back from the bed to give the doctor room. As he began removing Sam's shirt and bandage he spared her a glance. "You must be Lauren Brownley. I'm Dr. Sani, and this is my sister, Willow."

Lauren acknowledged the introduction with a nod. She didn't have to ask how the doctor knew who she was.

"How long ago did this happen?"

"About...twenty-seven hours ago," she told him

after glancing at the bedside clock. "I did what I could, but the bullet is still inside him."

"Mmm. It would have been better if I could have treated him immediately. However, you did an excellent job. The wound doesn't look infected.

"I'll have to remove the bullet. Ideally I should take him to the clinic and X ray his shoulder before I operate, but I don't think Sam would want to risk that. The clinic is in an unrestricted area of the reservation. The people looking for you would have access if they managed to track you this far."

"Do it here, doc," Larry urged.

The doctor probed the wound, and Sam bucked and cried out. Willow stroked his back and murmured soothing words, but he continued to thrash.

"Lau-Lauren? Where is…Lauren?"

Willow looked as though she'd been slapped. Her head came up and her hurt gaze sought Lauren, who was already moving. Quickly skirting the end of the bed, she elbowed the doctor's sister away and took Sam's hand in both of hers. "I'm here, Sam. I'm here."

"Sam? Can you hear me?" Dr. Sani asked.

His patient made an unintelligible sound, which could have been a yes, and the doctor went on. "I'm going to remove a bullet from your back. I'm going to inject a local anesthetic, but you'll feel some pain. I'm afraid that's the best I can do here. I want you to lie as still as you can, okay?"

"O…kay," Sam gasped.

The doctor looked around at the others. "I'm sorry, but I'm going to have to ask you all to leave—everyone but Willow. She'll assist me."

Sam's hand tightened on Lauren's. "S-stay. D-don't...go."

"I won't. I promise," she murmured. "I'll be here as long as you need me."

She looked at Dr. Sani. "I'm staying."

He studied her implacable stare for a moment, then nodded. "Very well."

At first Sam bore the probing stoically, gritting his teeth and squeezing Lauren's hand so tight her bones nearly snapped, but when the doctor began to dig deep it took the combined strength of Lauren and Willow to hold him down. Mercifully, after only a few seconds, he passed out again.

After removing the bullet and closing the wound, Dr. Sani gave Sam a massive injection of antibiotic and another of painkiller. After writing instructions and leaving orders to call him if Sam's condition worsened, the doctor left at dawn, promising to return later that afternoon.

Damn. His right shoulder hurt like hell. Emerging from the drug-induced sleep, Sam forced his heavy eyelids open. The first thing he saw was Lauren. She sat in a chair beside his bed, bent forward with her upper body resting on the mattress beside him, sound asleep.

As always, her beauty struck him like a runaway

freight train. She lay with her face turned toward him, her auburn hair spread out on the blanket, her eyelashes like tiny fans against her skin.

Gradually it occurred to him that she looked exhausted. Her flawless skin was paler than usual and there were circles under her eyes again. And what was she doing sleeping sitting in a chair?

Sam cast a quick glance around, and he knew at once that he was in the boys' room at his cousin Larry's house.

Then bits and pieces came back to him—the chase, being shot, Lauren driving the pickup like an Indy driver, staggering into a motel room. After that it was all pretty much a feverish blur of pain and disjointed images and sounds.

He looked at Lauren again, and his chest tightened with so much emotion it was painful. Somehow, she'd managed to get them here. And apparently she had watched over him during the night, as well.

Sam picked up a handful of Lauren's hair. He rubbed the silky strands between his thumb and fingers, let it slither between them and puddle on the blanket again. Without conscious thought, he trailed the backs of his knuckles over her cheek.

Lauren's eyes fluttered and opened. ''Sam.'' She blinked and smiled sleepily then jerked upright. ''Sam! You're awake!''

''Yeah,'' he replied in a husky voice.

''How do you feel? Are you in much pain? The

doctor left some pain relievers in case you needed them.''

"I'm okay."

"Can I get you something? A glass of water? Something to eat? You must be starving by now. I'll just go get—''

Lauren started to rise, but Sam manacled her wrist with his fingers and held her back, ignoring the stab of pain the movement brought to his shoulder. "Take it easy. I'm okay.''

She didn't look convinced, and before he could stop her she placed her palm against his forehead. "Your fever does seem to have broken.''

Sam reached up and removed her hand but he did not release it. "Will you relax? I told you, I'm okay.''

He studied her intently, his gaze running over her pale face, the sleep marks on her left cheek, the inviting softness of her mouth. Her hair framed her face in artful disarray.

Rubbing his thumb in a slow circle over the back of her hand, he looked into her eyes. "Every day, you amaze me more,'' he said quietly. "You have from the start.''

Lauren gave an uneasy chuckle. "Now I know you're still feverish.''

"I'm serious. All your life you were wrapped in cotton and insulated from life's day-to-day struggles. Yet, now that you're on your own, you stick out that delicate little chin and stand up to whatever life throws at you, tackle any problem, any obstacle. I've never known a woman with that kind of grit and determination.''

A rueful half smile twisted his mouth. ''Even when I thought you were Carlo's mistress I was amazed at your strength.''

A flush crept over her face, and she dropped her gaze to their joined hands. ''Don't give me too much credit. I didn't have much choice.''

''Sure you did. There are always choices. We all make them every day. Lauren, listen to me.'' Sam crooked his forefinger beneath her chin and tipped her head up until her gaze met his again. ''You're a special woman.'' His thumb caressed her jaw. ''A very special woman.''

''Sam, I—''

''And just who is this special woman you have brought onto our land?'' a strange voice snapped.

Lauren jumped up guiltily and twisted around, backing away from the bed. A plump, gray-haired Native American woman stood in the doorway, her brown, lined face as hard as the sandstone formations that dominated the arid landscape outside the window.

Sam turned his gaze on the old woman with remarkable calm. ''Hello, Grandma. It's nice to see you, too. This is Lauren Brownley. Lauren, this little whirlwind is my grandmother, Annie Zah.''

Lauren opened her mouth to greet the other woman but before she could utter a sound Annie Zah switched to the Navajo language and cut her off.

''Don't get smart with me, boy. You haven't come

to see your family in over a year, and now you show up in the middle of the night all shot up. That is bad enough, but you have offended our people by bringing this white woman with you. You know that only our people are allowed here.''

"I'm sorry, Grandma, but it was necessary," Sam replied, switching to his grandmother's native tongue as well. "Lauren is a witness in an important case, and I was assigned to protect her. There are men in the white man's world who are trying to kill us both. Last night, had it not been for Lauren, they would have succeeded. She saved my life."

Surprise flashed across Annie's wrinkled face. Previously she had barely spared Lauren a glance, but now her dark eyes zeroed in on her, assessing intently. When she turned back to Sam, however, she shook her head. "For that I am grateful, but it does not change things. She must go, before others know of her presence."

Confused and curious, Lauren looked back and forth between Sam and Annie, but they continued arguing in Navajo and paid no attention to her.

"If she goes, I go with her."

"Do not be foolish, my grandson. I have spoken to Dr. Sani. You are in no condition to go anywhere. You must stay here and rest and let your body heal."

Sam's unwavering gaze never left the old woman. "Not without Lauren."

"She cannot stay."

"If she becomes my wife she can."

Annie's eyes widened. She looked at Lauren with new interest. "She means that much to you, this woman?"

"Yes."

He expected an argument and braced for it, but to his surprise his grandmother nodded. "I will arrange it."

Sam's eyes narrowed. "That's it? You don't object?"

"Why should I object?"

"I thought you wanted me to marry a Navajo woman. Willow Sani, to be exact. You've been pushing her at me since she was about fourteen."

"I merely put her in your path so that you might notice her." Annie declared with the haughty dignity of a matriarch. She crossed the room and sat down on the side of the bed beside Sam and took his hand. "I admit, I would not object if you chose a wife from among our people, but more important to me is that you are happy.

"All of your life, I have watched you struggling to find your place, moving back and forth between your father's world and this one, never quite belonging to either. What? Did you think I did not know? That I am blind?" she demanded when she saw his startled look.

"You never said anything."

"It wasn't my place. You had to decide for yourself in which world your spirit truly belonged."

Annie sighed heavily. "It is past time that you took

a wife, my grandson, but I always knew that you would not do so until you found your place. I think Augustus knew that, too.'' She glanced at Lauren, and when her gaze met Sam's again, she smiled. ''I think now you have.''

Sam looked at Lauren, too, staring at her for so long that she began to fidget. ''I think you're right.''

He met his grandmother's gaze again and was surprised to see her wrinkled face stretched in a smile. ''You don't mind?''

''No, I do not mind.'' She patted his hand. ''It is probably for the best. The difference between our worlds are not so great now as they were when your parents met. Our people are picking up more and more of the white man's ways all the time. It saddens me, but what can an old woman do? Still there are differences. Important ones that will never change. In the end, those things destroyed your parents' marriage.

''Your father is a good man. He loved my daughter very much, and she loved him, but not even a love that strong was enough to overcome her need to be with her own people. I don't want that to happen to you. If your spirit belongs in the white man's world, that is where you should be.'' She patted his hand again and smiled. ''But no matter which you choose, you will always be my grandson, and as long as the sun rises you and your wife will be welcomed here.''

Sam stared at her, his chest tight, so tight he forgot about his aching shoulder. He knew that this conversation marked a momentous turning point, that what he said next would alter the course of his life and in some ways change forever his relationships with the people who lived here. A part of him wanted to take it back, to say he'd changed his mind and cling to the familiar. But in his heart, he knew his grandmother was right. He had to make a choice.

"You're a wise woman, Grandma," he said quietly.

She nodded, and if there was a hint of sadness in her eyes, it only made him love her more.

Bending forward, Annie kissed his cheek. "I will go now and make the arrangements."

"What was that about?" Lauren asked when she had gone. "Do I have to leave?"

"No."

"Oh, thank goodness." Lauren exhaled a long sigh and put her hand over her heart. "That's a relief. What did you say to change her mind? And what about the others? Won't they object?"

"No. In a few days, there won't be any reason. We're getting married."

Eighteen

"We're *what?*"

"I said we're getting married."

Lauren stared at Sam. He'd made the statement so matter-of-factly she thought surely she'd heard him wrong, but apparently not.

She couldn't breathe. Shock, excitement, hope and a host of other emotions careened through her, threatened to overwhelm her. "You...you're asking me to marry you?"

"It's the best solution. I'm in no shape to leave here right now and I doubt that Annie would let me if I tried. And I'm sure as hell not going to let you leave without me. If you're my wife, no one will complain. Nor will anyone be tempted to notify the authorities that we're here. Navajo people protect their own.

"Anyway, this is the safest place for us to hide out until the trial."

"I...I see. Then you, uh...you don't intend for this marriage to last?" She did her best to keep her expression neutral and her tone merely curious, but inside she felt as though a giant hand were squeezing her heart.

For several seconds Sam stared at her in that intent way he had. Finally he shrugged his uninjured shoulder. "It doesn't have to be."

What did that mean? Lauren wondered. That he was willing to give marriage a try if she was? Or that it didn't matter to him, one way or the other? She didn't know whether to be insulted or hopeful.

"What about Willow?"

"What about her?"

"She's in love with you."

"She may think she is, but that's only because she's been pointed in that direction by my grandmother. I've never encouraged her."

Lauren sighed. "It will still break her heart."

"I'm sorry for that, but she'll get over it. She's just a girl." He waited a beat, then asked, "So? Are we getting married or not?"

"I…"

"Look, the way I see it, we don't have much choice," he insisted in a voice edged with impatience. "Even if we could stay here a few days while I healed without anyone objecting, I guarantee you that as soon as we left the reservation those guys would be on us like a duck on a June bug."

"You think they know we're here?"

Sam hesitated. "Maybe. Maybe not. Not yet, anyway. They'll eventually put two and two together and get suspicious, but without a court order they won't force their way into this area."

"What makes you think that?"

"The Bureau has received a lot of bad press in recent years. The last thing they want is more. You need evidence, or at least strong probable cause, to get a search warrant. No judge is going to issue one on an agent's hunch.

"Actually I doubt they'd even try for one. They know that to search an area of this size would take an all-out army invasion, and that's not going to happen."

"How can you be so sure?" Lauren asked. "We've been the target of a full-scale manhunt for a week. Why would they back off now?"

"A couple of reasons. First of all, we're no longer in the wilderness with no witnesses around. I'd bet good money that every one of those guys who flew to the crash site were on the take from Carlo. That's why their ringleader picked them for the assignment.

"It should've been easy. They fly in and verify the kill. If we'd survived the crash they take us out however they can, and no one's the wiser. Now that we're back among people, they have to watch their step.

"Second, up until now the handful of agents on Giovessi's payroll have been agitating the brass and feeding them false information so that they could keep up a full-scale hunt for us, but I think my friend Edward has enough clout to put an end to that. He's given his personal guarantee to the brass that I'll have you at that courthouse for the trial.''

''I hope you're right,'' Lauren said, though she did not sound convinced.

''I won't lie to you, babe. Giovessi's guys will keep looking on their own. You can count on it. They have no choice. If they don't shut us up, they go to prison. But at least with Edward vouching for us they won't have the full might of the Bureau behind them anymore.

''So you see, if we get married we can just lay low here until you have to show up for the trial.''

Lauren twisted her hands together, and gazed at Sam, torn.

Though they hadn't known each other but a short while, the time she and Sam had shared had been packed with more intensity and horrendous experiences than most people go through in a lifetime together. Under such conditions, with all the polite veneer of civilization stripped away, you learned more about a person in one week than in a year of socializing.

Yes, Sam was tough and taciturn, a remote loner who guarded his heart by keeping his thoughts to himself and his emotions under wrap. She suspected that was the result of a lifetime of being torn between two cultures, of never feeling completely accepted by either, never sure of exactly who he was or where he belonged. In spite of all that, as Lauren had learned firsthand, he was a man of strength and character, dedicated, honest and absolutely reliable.

In the beginning she had bitterly resented being dependent on Sam, but during the past week he'd taught her the true meaning of self-reliance, and that some situations required cooperation and trust.

Gradually she had come to realize that behind that remote, sometimes forbidding face he presented to the world, Sam Rawlins was a man with a surprising capacity for tenderness and caring, a man of unshakable loyalty. Sam would never use a woman to gain social status and wealth, then abandon her when she was no longer of any use to him—the way Collin had. Lauren was sure of that.

She knew with absolute certainty that she loved this difficult, complicated man. Deeply and irrevocably. She would like nothing better than to marry him and spend the remainder of her life with him...but not this way.

Still, what choice did she have? She took a deep breath and let it out slowly. "All right, Sam. I'll marry you."

Lauren thought she saw something flash in Sam's eyes, but then he blinked, and it was gone, and she told herself that she had probably imagined it.

Sam nodded matter-of-factly, as though they had just decided something as mundane as what to order for dinner or what movie to see. "Good. Now, if you don't mind, I think I will take some breakfast."

"Oh. Yes, of course. You must be starving. I'll be right back."

She hurried from the room, but when she stepped out into the narrow hallway she came face-to-face with Willow Sani. The young woman's expression revealed that she had been eavesdropping and stopped Lauren in her tracks. Her heart clinched at the pain in the girl's eyes. "Oh, Willow, I'm so sorry."

"No, do not be." Willow met Lauren's gaze. "You are the one he wants."

"Oh, but you're wrong. You heard him. He's just trying to protect me. Really."

A small, sad smile curved Willow's mouth. "No, it is you who are wrong. Sam would never marry a woman he did not love. If all he wanted was to keep you safe, he would find another way."

Lauren's heart skipped a beat. Was it possible...? No, of course not. It couldn't be. Yet...he *had* told her that he loved her, but she had chalked that up to feverish delirium.

Willow turned to leave. "I must go now. I just stopped by to see how Sam was doing."

"Willow—"

"No, please. Do not concern yourself with me," she insisted. "I will be fine." With painful dignity, she walked back down the narrow hallway with her head held high.

Lauren and Sam were married at sunset the next day. Sam was still weak, and she worried that he was in no condition to be out of bed, but he brushed aside her concerns. Though unsteady on his feet, with the help of his cousin Larry, he walked the hundred feet or so to the spot beside a spectacular sandstone formation that his grandmother had chosen for the ceremony.

Twenty or so of Sam's Navajo family and friends had already gathered there by the time the wedding party arrived, including Willow Sani and her brother. Sam was shocked when his father emerged from the group, followed by Eunice and Walter.

"Dad! What are you doing here?"

"You're my son. Where else would I be?"

"That goes for your aunt and me, too," Walter said as Eunice hugged Lauren.

Augustus gave Sam a quick once-over, frowning as he took in his son's pallor and the sling that held his right arm immobile. "Anyway, I wanted to see for myself how you were doing. Larry telephoned and told me what happened, and assured me that you'd live, but ever since I picked up my truck, all shot to hell and gone, I've been worried sick."

"I'm sorry about the truck. I'll pay to have it repaired."

"To hell with the damned truck!" Augustus thundered. "It's you that I'm worried about. Dammit, son, don't you have any idea how much you mean to me?"

Sam's face remained immobile, but as he and his

father regarded each other Lauren saw his throat work, and she knew he was fighting to control his emotions.

Finally he muttered a "Thanks, Dad" and reached out with his good arm to initiate an embrace. Augustus reciprocated with alacrity, wrapping his son in a bear hug, his eyes squeezed shut.

When the two parted, Augustus gave Sam another once-over. "How are you really doing, son?"

"I'm fine. Give me a week, and I'll be good as new. But how did you know Lauren and I were getting married?"

"Your grandmother sent a message through mutual friends, bless her."

Sam, who seldom showed a reaction to anything, looked so shocked his expression was almost comical. "You're kidding. *Grandma Zah* invited you?"

"That's right. She knew we'd want to be here."

"But this area is off-limits to everyone but Navajos."

"Do not concern yourself. Your father and aunt and uncle are here as my guests."

Sam turned to find his grandmother standing behind him, dressed in her best, red-velvet gathered tiered skirt and hip-length blue overblouse, cinched at the waist with a belt made of silver discs. Around her shoulders was a brightly colored blanket.

He shook his head. "I didn't even know you were on speaking terms with Dad and his family."

"Our paths no longer cross, but your father and I

are not enemies. Why would we be? We both loved my daughter."

Sam cast a worried look around. "Look, I'm happy you came, Dad. I really am. But I'm not sure it was such a good idea. You may have led Carlo's men to us. I'm sure they've got both ranches staked out."

"Oh, they do indeed. But give me some credit, son. Those guys are watching the entrances to the ranches right now, sitting in their cars drinking bad coffee out of a thermos and freezing their arses off. There are more ways in and out of there than through the gates. We drove out through the back pastures onto federal land, then took a series of Forest Service roads to the highway. We'll go back the same way. Trust me, they'll never know we were gone.

"Now step aside and let me see my soon-to-be daughter-in-law."

Augustus took both of Lauren's hands in his and looked at her admiringly. "Welcome to the family, Lauren."

"Thank you, sir."

"No sir. Call me Dad."

He looked her up and down. Dressed much as Annie was, in a borrowed, swirly green velvet skirt, white, full-sleeved blouse with a colorful Navajo blanket wrapped around her shoulders, Lauren felt self-conscious and not in the least bridelike. However, when Augustus's gaze met hers once again his eyes were misty and his craggy face, so much like Sam's, had softened. "Ah, just look at you. Child, if you aren't a sight for these tired old eyes. You remind me of my own beautiful bride.''

Though touched by the compliment, his obvious delight made her feel incredibly guilty. ''That's very sweet of you, Mr. Rawlins, but I feel I should tell you—''

Sam clamped his hand around her elbow. ''Let's get this over with, shall we?''

The following few minutes seemed surreal to Lauren. Just a little over a week ago her life had been so predictable. Monday through Friday she taught music to bored college students, Wednesday nights she gave a private concert for her boss and Friday and Saturday evenings she played piano at Club Classico. It was ordinary and uneventful, and not at all the life for which, up until two years ago, she had seemed destined, but she had adapted.

Now, here she stood, feeling like an insignificant speck in this vast land of harsh, untamed beauty, surrounded by people she didn't know, whose culture was foreign to her, pledging her life to a man who hadn't even said he loved her. Not when he was awake and coherent, anyway.

A light snow had fallen the previous night, and it covered the desert in a veil of white and lay on the red sandstone formations like frosting on a cake, adding to the unreal feeling that enveloped her.

Lauren didn't understand a word of the Navajo ceremony, nor the significance of the rituals, but she muddled through with a bit of prodding from Annie and Sam. Before she knew it, everyone was crowding around, thumping her and Sam on their backs and congratulating them.

Then they all crowded into Annie Zah's small house to celebrate.

Out of consideration for Sam, the party was quiet and brief. One by one, after wishing Lauren and Sam health, happiness and long life, the guests departed, until there was only family left.

Sam and Augustus were still stiff and awkward with each other, but both were trying to mend fences. As Augustus and his sister and brother-in-law prepared to leave, he clamped his son's uninjured shoulder and muttered a gruff, "Take care of yourself, son. And if there's anything you need—anything at all— you just let me know."

"Actually, Dad, I could use a cellphone. But not one registered to me."

"You got it. I'll bring you one in a couple of days."

Eunice and Walter added their well wishes and each gave Lauren a kiss and a hug and welcomed her to the family. When it came Augustus's turn, his eyes were suspiciously moist as he cupped her cheek in his callused palm. "I've always wanted a daughter, and I have a hunch you're just what that boy of mine needs. I'm glad he found you, little one," he said, and leaned down and kissed her cheek.

When he straightened he glanced at Sam, who was watching them intently. "When all this is over, I hope you can talk him into coming home to the ranch where he belongs.''

Lauren answered with a wan smile. She could hardly explain to this hopeful father that she had no influence over his son, that within a year this marriage would probably be dissolved. She felt like a complete fraud.

After another flurry of hugs, Augustus and his sister and brother-in-law departed. No sooner had Lauren closed the door behind them than Annie stepped out of the bedroom carrying two shopping bags stuffed with clothing and toilet articles.

Sam cocked one eyebrow. "Going somewhere?"

"Yes. I'm moving into the hogan. While you are with us, you and Lauren will stay here in this house. Your bag is already in the bedroom.''

"Oh, no, please. We couldn't possibly put you out of your home,'' Lauren objected.

"C'mon, Grandma, be reasonable. You can't live in the hogan.''

"Why not? I was born in a hogan and lived most of my life in one. I prefer them. It was your grandfather who insisted on building this house for me. I moved into it merely to please him.''

"For Pete's sake, the only source of heat in that place is a woodstove. Look, Lauren and I can stay at Larry's.''

"That arrangement was fine for a few days, but not for months. Your cousin's place is too small, and it would be a strain on his family. Besides, newlyweds need privacy.''

''Okay, then, Lauren and I will move into the hogan.''

''Does your wife know how to cook on a wood-stove?'' The pained look that flashed across Sam's face told her all she needed to know. Annie folded her arms and smiled smugly. ''There, you see. I will move into the hogan.''

''Lauren is good at adapting. We'll manage just fi—''

''No. It will be best if you stay here. It will be easier for her to take care of you and nurse you back to health that way.''

''Dammit—''

''Give up, cousin,'' Larry said from the kitchen doorway. ''I have talked to her, Zeta has talked to her, but it makes no difference. She's been looking for an excuse to move back into the hogan ever since our grandfather died. Now that she has one, there is no stopping her.'' He looked at Annie and shook his head with affectionate exasperation. ''You're a stubborn old woman, Annie Zah. Hold on a minute and let me help Sam to the bedroom and Zeta and I will take you to the hogan.''

''Go ahead,'' Sam said. ''I can make it that far on my own.''

''Okay, if you're sure.''

''Well, apparently we're going to be living here for a while,'' Lauren said uneasily when they had gone.

"Looks like it," Sam agreed. He sat slouched on the sofa with his head resting against the back, watching her.

Twisting her hands together, Lauren shifted under that intent stare. "You really should be in bed, Sam. You look exhausted."

"You'll get no argument from me." Wincing, he struggled to stand, and instantly Lauren leaped forward.

He accepted her help getting to his feet, but when she tried to slip her arm around his waist and support him as he walked, he brushed her aside. "That's all right. I can manage. There's nothing wrong with my legs."

Accepting the rejection, Lauren hovered anxiously at his heels as he slowly made his way into Annie's bedroom.

By the time he sat down on the edge of the bed he was pale and breathing hard, and when Lauren knelt before him to remove his moccasins he did not object.

"Now, let's get you out of these clothes and into bed," she said when done and went to work unbuttoning his shirt.

"You know, usually it's the groom who takes the bride's clothes off," Sam murmured.

Lauren glanced up and was startled to find that he was watching her, his dark eyes heated and intent beneath heavy eyelids. Though helpless to prevent the blush that spread upward from her chest all the way to her hairline, she ducked her head and finished unfastening buttons. When she stripped away his shirt the sight of his broad shoulders and all that bronze skin made her mouth go dry. Desire coursed through her in a hot tide, but she managed to reply with credible insouciance, ''I suppose so. But then, most grooms aren't recovering from a gunshot wound, are they?''

What is the matter with you? Lauren silently admonished. Has making love with Sam turned you into a sex maniac? For heaven's sake! The man was shot and in critical shape just two nights ago. And you'd do well to remember that this is not a true marriage.

''Now your trousers,'' Lauren said briskly, doing her best to act unconcerned and not to stare at his body. To make it easier for her to unfasten his pants, Sam lay back on the bed and continued watching her through slitted eyes.

With as much dignity as she could muster, she lowered the zipper and he lifted his hips to allow her to tug his wool trousers down to his ankles then slip them off, leaving him in only a pair of snug navy briefs. Quickly averting her eyes, Lauren made a production of neatly folding his shirt and trousers and placing them on a chair.

Her nerves were twanging, and when she turned and saw Sam lying there, spread-eagle, wearing only that scrap of blue cotton knit a trembling began deep inside her.

Gritting her teeth, she marched back to the bed. ''Okay, now, sit up.'' She grasped his hand, pulled him to a sitting position and used her other hand to throw back the bedspread and covers.

It was difficult, but finally Sam was settled in bed with the covers tucked up to his armpits. "There. All set," Lauren declared with profound relief. "If there's nothing else you need, I'll just go lock up for the night and get ready for bed myself."

"Go ahead. I'm good," Sam replied. His face wore his usual stern, impassive expression, but those dark eyes still watched her with unnerving intensity.

Annie's home was tiny—a living room, kitchen with eating area and one bedroom with an attached bathroom. It didn't take long for Lauren to lock both doors and turn out the lights in the other part of the house. Sam was still awake when she returned. Doing her best not to look at him, she took the duffle bag into the bathroom and shut the door.

Lauren took her time in the shower, shampooing her hair and shaving her legs. Afterward she applied lotion onto her lower legs and feet and dusted her body with the scented talc she found on Annie's counter. She had to towel-dry her hair, as Annie didn't appear to have a blow-dryer, nor had Sam thought to purchase one for her before they left Denver. When her hair was merely damp she combed through it, then donned the flannel nightgown that until now had remained folded in the duffle bag.

The garment covered her from neck to toe, the only adornment a modest lace yoke trimmed in pale blue ribbon and a two-inch ruffle of matching lace at each wrist.

After dawdling so long, Lauren expected Sam to be asleep, but when she stepped from the bathroom his dark eyes were trained on the door, as though he'd been waiting for her.

"Sam, why aren't you asleep?"

As she sat down on the edge of the bed beside him the smell of clean sheets that had been dried in the sunshine rose to tease her nose, and she realized that Annie must have put fresh linens on the bed before she left.

Trying not to think of the implications of that, Lauren gave Sam an assessing look. "Is something wrong? How do you feel?"

"I'm okay."

"How's your shoulder. Any pain?"

"Some, but nothing I can't live with."

"Would you like for me to get you one of the painkillers Dr. Sani left for you?"

"No."

"Do you have a fever?" She felt his forehead. "Mmm, you feel normal. That's good."

"I told you, I'm fine." Sam removed her hand from his head. "Stop mothering me, Lauren," he warned in a low voice that sent a trickle of goose bumps down her spine.

"Sorry," she said contritely. "Would you like a drink of water before you go to sleep?"

"No."

"Isn't there anything you want?"

Something flickered in Sam's eyes, something dangerous, and unbearably exciting. His gaze skimmed over her face, drifted downward over her neck and shoulders, then settled on her breasts. When he looked up again his eyes were dark and blazing with fire. "Yes," he said in a husky voice. "I want you."

A startled laugh burst from Lauren's throat. "Sam! You know we can't."

"Wanna bet?"

"But...but I thought...that is..."

"What?"

"Well...I didn't think this was going to be a real marriage. I was going to sleep on the sofa."

"To hell with that." Sliding his hand beneath her damp hair, he cupped the back of her neck and tried to tug her down on top of him, but she resisted.

"Wait, Sam...your shoulder."

"Let me worry about my shoulder."

His gaze skimmed over the high-necked night-gown, and a ghost of a smile hovered around his mouth. "I bought this thing because I thought it would be a turnoff, but damned if it isn't sexy as hell." His hand slid from her neck over her shoulder, then with his forefinger he traced the lower edge of the lace yoke down over the tops of her breasts and up to the other shoulder.

Lauren closed her eyes partway and trembled. Even through the lace his touch left a trail of fire on her flesh. Smiling that slow, devastating smile, Sam fingered the row of tiny buttons that ran down the center of the lace yoke from the neck down the blue ribbon threaded through the lower edge. Watching Lauren's face, he worked the top button open, then the second, the third.

When the last one popped free he hooked his forefinger into the opening and tugged her closer.

Mesmerized by his touch and the intent look in those dark eyes, Lauren could not find the will to resist. "S-Sam this isn't a good idea."

"Shh. We'll do this slow and careful," he murmured.

He slid the garment off one of her shoulders, then the other. At his urging Lauren slipped her arms out of the sleeves, and the soft flannel and lace puddled around her hips. Sam cupped one breast in his palm, lifted it, squeezed. His thumb swept across the velvety nipple, and she moaned as it pebbled.

He treated the other breast to the same gentle abrasion, then braced up on one elbow and circled each turgid nub with his tongue.

Lauren threw her head back and gasped. "Oh, Sam."

He drew a nipple into his mouth, and she cried out and arched her back. He drew on her deeply, and she clasped his head between her palms to pull him closer, wanting—needing—more.

After lavishing the same attention to her other breast Sam eased back a bit and urged, "Lift up a second, sweetheart. There, that's it," he whispered, and shoved the nightgown downward over her hips. As it slid to the floor he hooked his hand around her neck again, gave a sharp tug, and Lauren found herself sprawled on top of him. He felt warm and firm, and so sexy she couldn't think. Before she could respond, he rolled to his side with her. With a little cry, she clutched at his shoulders, but when her fingers encountered the edge of the bandage on his back she stiffened. "Sam, I don't think—"

"Then don't. Don't think. Just feel. Feel how much I want you." He took her hand and guided it downward, and as her fingers wrapped around him, Sam grimaced with exquisite pleasure.

"Are you okay? Did I hurt you?"

Lauren jerked her hand away and tried to scoot back, but he held her fast and growled, "God, no. Relax, babe. Everything will be fine."

Looking deep into her eyes, he rocked his hips against her, and smiled when she gasped with pleasure. "Now. I want you to do exactly as I say." He kissed his way up her neck and nibbled her earlobe, and in a voice gone gravelly with passion, he whispered instructions in her ear that made Lauren's face flame.

"Sam!"

He leaned back and chuckled as her shocked expression turned to curiosity. "Can we really *do* that?"

"Why don't you try it and find out?"

Gnawing at her lower lip, shyly at first, then with growing confidence and boldness, she did as he asked.

"Yes. Yes, that's the way," Sam grated between clenched teeth. "That's it. Oh, God, yes! *Yes!*"

"Ahhhh, babe."

Nineteen

The weeks and months that followed were the happiest of Lauren's life. She recognized the irony of that, given her situation, but it was true nevertheless.

Though Sam would always be the strong, silent type, he was gradually loosening up. In his own masterful way, he was affectionate and attentive and a wonderful lover. He made love to her frequently and with a depth of passion that never failed to rock her right down to her toes and leave her so limp she felt boneless.

If their lovemaking had hurt him or inhibited his recovery in any way, it wasn't apparent. As Sam had promised his father, he recovered quickly from his wound and was up and around within a week of their wedding. After only a month, he was as strong and agile as ever. Except for the puckered scar on his shoulder, you'd never know he had been shot.

Five days after the wedding Augustus returned to the reservation. Following along behind as he eased his pickup over the bumpy road was a large delivery van, and in the cab were three men.

Sam, Lauren, Annie and Larry were sitting in

lounge chairs on the front porch when the two trucks rolled to a stop in front of Annie's house.

"What the devil is this?" Sam demanded.

"Don't get your shorts in a wad, son. I brought you that cellphone you wanted."

"Cellphone? Hell, it looks to me like you brought a whole microwave tower."

"What, this? Naw, this is for Lauren."

"Me?" Lauren said, surprised.

"Yeah. Just a little wedding gift. C'mon, I'll show you. Open 'er up, men," Augustus yelled.

Lauren rose, and the others did the same and followed Augustus around to the back of the truck. When the workmen threw the double doors open Augustus beamed and Lauren's jaw dropped.

"A piano?" Tears stung her eyes when she swung to face Sam's father. "You bought me a *piano?*"

"Yeah. My sister and Walter kept carrying on about how talented you are, so I thought you might like to have one to play while you're staying here."

"But…but they're so expensive! This is really too much, Mr. Rawlins. I can't let you do this."

"Can't stop me," he declared. "And Mr. Rawlins won't do, little girl. I'm your father-in-law now. You can call me Dad or Pappy or Pops—whatever suits you. Anything but that Mr. Rawlins stuff. As to the other, why, this is just a little bitty ol' piano. Probably not what you're used to playing at all, but I figured this little spinet was all Annie's place could hold. 'Course, if you don't like it…"

"I *love* it! Truly, I do. It's just that—"

"Now none of that. The piano is yours. I'm not taking it back. Besides, the world's in a sorry state if a man can't give a simple gift to his brand-new daughter.

"If it'll make you feel any better, when all this mess is over, you can leave it with Annie. That way, her other grandchildren can have the use of it and it'll be here for you when you come to visit. You won't be needing it back at the Double R anyway. There's a big, brand-new grand piano waiting for you in the parlor there."

"A grand..." Lauren gaped at him, at a loss for words.

"Okay, you men. Take 'er inside," Augustus barked. "Annie, you mind showing 'um where you want this thing?"

"Damn, Dad, you got a little carried away, didn't you?" Sam muttered.

"Nonsense. I've been waiting for years for you to get married and give me a daughter. I intend to spoil her rotten, so just you be warned."

Sam looked at Lauren. "You'll get no argument from me. If there was ever a woman who deserved to be indulged, it's my wife."

Lauren heard the remark and it filled her heart with joy, but she was too excited and too busy supervising the men to comment. She danced from one foot to the other, barely able to contain herself.

As they followed the movers into the house, Sam

shook his head. "How the hell did you get this thing here without it splintering to pieces? That road has more craters than the moon."

"We inched it in, that's how," his father replied. "Took us four hours to get from the visitor's center to here. I was determined that little gal was going to have a piano."

One of the three men who came with Augustus was a piano tuner. He went to work on the instrument as soon as it was in place in Annie's living room, while Lauren paced impatiently.

The instant he pronounced the job done, she slid onto the bench and spread her fingers over the keyboard. After she'd played only a few notes, every person in the room stood stock-still and listened with awe as the beautiful music flowed from her fingertips and filled the room.

Soon, Larry's wife and two sons wandered over from their house next door. A few minutes later, a car full of people who had heard the music as they were driving by eased into the crowded living room. When Sam noticed more people outside, he opened the windows so they could hear better. Over an hour later, when Lauren finally took a break, the porch and area in front of the house were full of people.

After that, word spread. Whenever passersby heard the music coming from Annie's house, they parked their pickups out front and sat and listened. Sometimes close family and friends slipped inside and sat quietly, absorbing the soul-stirring music, then slipped out again when it ended.

The Navajos began referring to Lauren as the woman who makes music for the gods, a name that touched her deeply.

It was a halcyon time for Lauren. She was in love, and though Sam hadn't said the words, as the days passed she began to suspect—to hope—that he loved her, too. His actions certainly said he did. Every touch, every kiss spoke of a depth of feeling that sent her dreams soaring.

There were times when Lauren caught Sam watching her in that intense way he had, and the proprietary gleam in his eyes always made her heart give a little bump.

She had Sam, she had her music, she had the love of his family and the admiration of his mother's people. Zeta and Annie were teaching her how to cook, and Sam's grandmother told her endless Navajo stories and legends and instructed her on their customs and culture.

There were problems on the reservation, to be sure. There was poverty, unemployment, a lack of many services and amenities that were taken for granted on the outside. And there was alcoholism among some, which often led to abuse and hostilities. Yet, on the whole, life on the reservation was pleasant—slow and simple and undemanding, and after that first frenetic week on the run with Sam, Lauren took to the tranquility like a duck to water.

Carlo Giovessi's slick lawyers had gotten the trial postponed twice—no doubt to give his henchmen more time to locate her. It was now scheduled for the end of May.

Every time the trial was pushed back it seemed a little less real to Lauren. So much so that she could sometimes go for hours, even whole days, without remembering what had brought her to the reservation.

She felt safe among Sam's relatives. As winter gave way to spring she thought less and less about the trial or what would happen when it came time to leave. She was content and happy with life as it was.

Only a handful of people had Sam's new cellphone number—his father, his aunt and uncle, and Edward Stanhope. When the telephone chirped one afternoon in late May, Sam instinctively knew who it was.

He had been helping Larry tune the engine on his pickup and had just come inside to fetch them both something to drink when the call came through. Sam put the cans of soft drink he had just pulled from the refrigerator on the counter, fished the phone out of his shirt pocket and flipped it open.

It wasn't unusual for Edward to call. He and Sam talked four or five times a week, but even before Sam pressed the power button, a premonition told him what was coming.

"Yeah?" Sam said without preamble.

"The trial is still set for Monday morning."

Wincing, Sam cupped the back of his neck and

rubbed the tense muscles there. He glanced toward the living room. Lauren was playing a dreamy piece that floated on the air like elegant notes of purest gold. "You said just yesterday that the defense was trying for another postponement," Sam growled.

"The judge has had it with the constant postponements. All systems are go. You need to have Lauren in Denver by eight Monday morning."

"Yeah, I know."

Sam turned off the telephone and slipped it back into his pocket, but for several moments after that he just stood there, his expression thoughtful. Finally he ambled over to the door that led into the living room. Leaning his shoulder against the frame, he watched Lauren play.

She was never more beautiful than when she was playing the piano. The music seemed to give her an inner glow, as though it lit up her very soul. She was totally absorbed, her nimble fingers dancing over the keys, her eyes closed.

Damn, he hated to break the news to her.

The truth was, he was in love with her, and he had no idea what to do about it.

Sam studied her elegant profile. He didn't want to lose her. Maybe...maybe he just wouldn't tell her about Edward's call. Maybe they just wouldn't show up for the trial. Why should they risk their lives?

Why not stay? he asked himself. For the first time in his life, he was at peace. Finally, he and his father were coming to understand each other and were developing a relationship. Lauren felt safe and she seemed happy. As for him, he would prefer to return to the ranch, but he could adapt to this life.

Sam was even certain that his father would understand, given the circumstances. If they stayed put, no one would find them. They could just disappear.

Lauren's piece ended. She opened her eyes, then jumped when she saw Sam standing in the doorway, watching her. "Sam. I didn't know you were there." Then she took a good look at his expression, and her smile faded. "What? What is it?"

"I just received a call from Edward. We have to be in Denver by Monday morning for the trial. It's time to work out a plan."

The group of twenty or so Native Americans approaching the Federal Courthouse in their native dress drew only curious looks from others as they passed on the street. The citizens of Denver were too sophisticated to gape.

"There are Federal Marshals on either side of the main entrance. Stay calm and ignore them," Sam murmured under his breath from the center of the group. He kept one arm around Lauren and the other hand near the revolver in his hip holster, hidden beneath his shirt. His hair had grown long during the last four months while they were on the reservation. It now hung below his shoulders, and his skin was several shades darker from the sun. He wore his moccasins and a felt hat with a silver-and-turquoise hatband and the brim turned down all around. He doubted any of his old colleagues would recognize him.

Lauren wore one of Zeta's velvet skirts, this one in royal blue, and a print overblouse cinched in at the waist with a belt. Her auburn hair was pinned up and covered with a dark scarf, and over that she wore a broad-brimmed straw hat and kept her head down.

"When we reach the fourth floor there will be more lawmen, probably FBI agents," Sam prompted again. "Just remember what I told you. As soon as we get within earshot of those guards and I give the signal, everyone start complaining. And keep it up until I tell you to stop."

"Hey, no problem, cousin," Larry replied. "Who knows? We may even get something done while we're here."

The ploy worked. The men stationed outside the door barely spared them a glance and the ones inside directed them to Judge Holloway's chambers when they asked and warned them to keep it down.

Sam had been testifying in this courthouse for years and didn't need any help finding Judge Holloway. His courtroom was directly across the hall from Judge Bruno's, where the Giovessi case was being heard.

As Sam expected, two more Federal Marshals stood outside Judge Bruno's doors, scanning the hall in both directions and eyeing every person who stepped off the elevators or climbed the ornate stairs. Standing with them were two FBI agents. One was

Sam's old friend Todd Berringer; the other was John Scudder, known around the bureau office as Scud.

Sam coughed twice, and on cue his companions began to grouse about their water rights being stolen, and muttering that the judge had better come up with a solution fast, or they were going to file suit against the government.

It was the acid test, and Sam held his breath, but neither Todd's nor Scud's eyes showed the slightest flicker of recognition when they trailed over Sam and Lauren. They merely shook their heads and looked away, not interested in a bunch of ragtag Native Americans.

The elevator doors opened and Augustus and Walter stepped into the hall. As per the plan they'd worked out, Sam's father and uncle walked right past him and the others without making eye contact. They were stopped and questioned briefly by Todd, but a moment later were allowed to enter Judge Bruno's courtroom.

Sam and his friends filed into the courtroom on the opposite side of the hall. Court was in session but everyone was so absorbed in the proceedings that they barely drew a glance as they slipped into the last two rows of seats at the back of the spectators gallery. They were careful at all times to keep Lauren in the middle of the group.

"Now what?" she whispered to Sam when they were seated.

"Now we wait until Dad comes and tells us they're ready for you."

They didn't have long to wait. Barely fifteen minutes later Augustus poked his head in the door and nodded to them.

Sam saw the panic in Lauren's eyes and felt the shudder that rippled through her. He pried her hands apart and gave one a squeeze, then hauled her to her feet. He bent and kissed her, then looked deep into her frightened eyes. "C'mon, babe, let's go. It's time to kick ass and take names."

The others surrounded Lauren and Sam, and as one they walked across the hall past the stern faced Federal Marshals. Todd and Scud had moved inside Judge Bruno's courtroom and stationed themselves on either side of the door.

Sam and his friends created a commotion when they entered. Immediately, the agents standing around the perimeter walls moved to block them.

"Here now! What is this!" Judge Bruno thundered, banging his gavel. "Order. Order in the court!"

Sitting in the front row, Augustus leaned forward and whispered something to the prosecutor, who promptly jumped to his feet.

"Your Honor, these people are merely escorting the witness into the courtroom for her protection."

"I strenuously object, your Honor!" a member of the defense team shouted. "This is nothing but theatrics, staged to prejudice the jury."

"Not true, your Honor," the prosecutor fired back.

"There have already been several attempts on Ms. Brownley's life."

The judge pondered for a moment. "Objection overruled. Which one of you is Lauren Brownley?"

Lauren glanced up at Sam. Her eyes swam with terror. "You'll do fine," he whispered, and gave her hand one last squeeze before releasing it.

She swallowed hard, then nodded and squared her shoulders. "Here I am, your Honor," she said, stepping forward.

Sam and the others took their seats at the back of the room, but he covertly kept an eye on the agents standing around the perimeter of the room. He also noted that Harvey Weiss sat in the front row, two seats down from Augustus and Walter.

Though Lauren's voice was not quite steady, she gave a clear and detailed accounting of the events of that January night at the Club Classico. When the defense tried to poke holes in her story she remained composed and resolute.

Through it all, Carlo fumed. Even from behind, Sam could see the angry color that rose in his neck and ears. When the judge excused Lauren and she started to step down, the old mobster jumped to his feet and exploded in rage.

"You bitch! I helped you when you had nobody! And this is how you repay me! You're dead! Do you hear me? Dead!"

Two guards rushed over to restrain Carlo, but he

somehow managed to shake them off and grab a gun from one of the men's holsters.

"Shit!" Sam sprang to his feet and bolted for Lauren.

Several agents rushed to join the fray and all around pandemonium erupted as shouts and screams went up and people dove for cover.

"I'll kill you myself, bitch!"

From several feet away, Sam made a dive for Lauren. They went down together just as Carlo got off a shot. At the same instant another agent managed to knock the old man's arm up, and the bullet went wild and embedded in the ceiling.

The lawmen finally gained the upper hand and wrestled Carlos to the floor.

"Are you okay? Are you hurt?" Sam demanded, anxiously running his hands over Lauren.

"I'm okay. Just…shaken up is all."

Sam rose and helped her to her feet, but his worried gaze continued the examination. During the tackle her hat and scarf had been knocked off and now her auburn hair hung around her face and shoulders, its vibrant color accentuating her pallor.

"Are you sure you're okay?"

"Yes, Sam. Really."

He was about to say more when he glanced toward the back of the courtroom and spotted Todd, sidling out the door. Sam grabbed Lauren's arm and hauled her down the aisle to where Larry and the others were getting to their feet. "Larry, look after her, will you?" To Lauren he said, "Stay here. I'll be right back."

In the hall outside the courtroom people were scurrying this way and that. Sam craned his neck and searched through the crowd for Todd but he didn't see him anywhere. Then he noticed the door to the fire stairs at the end of the corridor was slowly closing.

Sam sprinted down the hall and jerked the door open again.

Startled, Todd paused on the landing a few steps down and looked up.

"Hello, Todd. Going somewhere?"

"Sam? Damn, is that you? You look like— Hey! What's with the gun, ol' buddy?"

Sam eased down the stairs, his revolver pointed squarely at Todd's chest. "It's over, Todd. I know you're Giovessi's man. One of them, anyway."

Todd started to argue, then thought better of it and sighed. "How did you figure it out?"

"You were the only one I ever told about my aunt and uncle. I knew the moment those agents came up their driveway."

Todd rolled his eyes and grimaced. "Damn. You always were quick."

Disappointment rose like bitter gall inside Sam. Though he'd known better, deep down he'd hoped his friend would turn indignant and deny the accusation, that he would somehow explain everything away and prove him wrong. He wouldn't even have minded if Todd had exploded in righteous anger and taken a swing at him. Anything would be better than this.

"Those guys in Utah? Were they on Carlo's payroll, too?"

"Naw, they were just agents out of a local office following orders."

"You want to tell me who else is in Carlo's pocket?"

Todd grinned. "I think I'll wait until my lawyer is present to do any more talking."

"Dammit, Todd. Why?" Sam ground out. "You were always a by-the-book guy. How could you sell out to scum like Giovessi?"

"Ol' buddy, you'd be surprised how easy it is to turn off your conscience when the money's right. Hell, I got tired of working my butt off for peanuts. And for what? So our judicial system can turn the bad guys loose again? I figured if I couldn't beat 'em, why not join 'em and rake in my share of the dough. I woulda cut you in on the action, except I knew a straight-arrow like you would just slap the cuffs on me and start reading me my Miranda rights."

"You got it." Reaching the landing, Sam motioned with the gun for Todd to turn around. "You know the drill. Hands above your head, against the wall, and spread 'em."

Todd was about to comply when the door to the landing above them burst open and banged back against the adjacent wall. Sam's head swiveled toward the sound, and his heart leaped right up into his throat as Lauren rushed into the stairwell and came clattering down the metal steps.

"Sam! What is going on? I was so worried when you ran out like th—"

"Lauren, get back!" Sam shouted, but he was too late.

Taking advantage of the distraction, Todd shoulder-butted Sam out of the way and grabbed Lauren. Before Sam could recover, Todd had her in a choke hold and his revolver in his other hand, the barrel pressed against her temple.

"Drop it, Sam."

"No! Don't do it, Sam!"

"Shut up, woman!" As punishment, Todd squeezed Lauren's neck tighter, making her gag.

"Let go of my wife, Berringer."

"Your wife!" Todd shot Sam an astonished look then laughed. "I don't believe it. You married our *witness?* Man, she must really be something in bed."

Rage ripped through Sam. He took a half step forward but jerked back when Todd pressed the gun tighter against Lauren's temple.

"Back off, or she gets it right now!" he snarled.

"Hurt her and you're a dead man, Berringer. That's a promise."

"Very touching, Sam. But if you don't want her hurt, all you have to do is drop your gun and back off. *Now,* dammit! Or so help me, I'll kill her right here, right now."

"I suggest you do as he says, Sam."

Startled, Sam looked over his shoulder, and saw his boss, Charley Potter, standing on the landing above them, his gun pointed at Sam's back.

"You? You're in on this, too?" The heavy weight of disillusion pressed down on Sam like wet cement. Charley was the last man in the Denver office he would have suspected of being on the take. He would have no problem believing it of Harvey Weiss, but not Charley. Sam had always believed his long-time friend and boss was incorruptible. He would have staked his life on it.

"Drop the gun, Sam. It's over."

"Noooo!"

Lauren's outraged cry as she grabbed the barrel of Todd's gun and knocked it skyward startled all three men, but Sam recovered quickest. Before the echo died away, he spun around and fired. Charley slammed back against the wall behind him, then slowly slid to the floor, a red stain blossoming on the front of his white shirt.

Sam spun back just in time to see Lauren gouge Todd in the eye. Howling, he dropped the gun and grabbed his face as the weapon clattered down the next flight of stairs.

"Why you—" With an enraged growl, Todd made a lunge for her, but in a move so fast even Sam didn't see it coming, she hauled off and kicked him as hard as she could in the groin.

Todd dropped like a stone and curled into a fetal position, screaming and writhing.

"God, sweetheart." Sam snatched Lauren into his arms and held her tight against his thundering heart. "Are you all right?"

"I—I think so."

"Oh, God, Lauren, don't ever scare me like that again. I thought I was going to lose you." He began to rain frantic kisses over her forehead, her eyelids, her cheeks, the side of her neck. "I couldn't bear that," he declared fiercely. "I love you. I love you. Ah, little one, you're everything to me. Everything."

"Oh, Sam." Joy gushed up inside Lauren. "Sam, I—"

The door on the upper landing burst open again and a half-dozen armed men, led by Harvey Weiss, rushed inside. "What the hell is going on in here?"

It took the better part of an hour for Lauren and Sam to explain all that had happened since he had spirited her out of Denver the previous January and to convince Harvey and the local police and the Federal Prosecutor that Todd and Charley had tried to kill them. They were helped on that score when another agent stuck his head inside the room they were using to tell them that Carlo had suffered a heart attack on the way back to his cell.

"He's in the hospital now, under guard. The docs say his heart is so bad they doubt he'll make it." The agent chuckled. "He was so pissed that the agents he paid to protect him didn't keep him out of prison that he squealed his head off all the way to the hospital. Gave us the names of seven agents he'd bought.'' The man tore a page out of his notepad and handed it to Harvey. "You're not gonna believe whose names are on that list.''

Finally, everything was sorted out. After promising to come into the Bureau office the next day and make a formal statement, Sam and Lauren left and joined Augustus and Walter and the rest of their group, who were waiting outside in the hallway.

"How'd it go, son?'' his father asked the instant they emerged.

"Good. Especially considering that I just blew away my boss and I've been hiding a federal witness without official sanction for over four months.''

Lauren watched Sam shift from one foot to the other, and she knew something was bothering him. Sometime during the session with Agent Weiss and the other lawmen, he had retreated back behind his stone-mask expression. She'd also noticed that he wouldn't look directly at her.

The joy she had begun to feel earlier had seeped away. Replacing it was a growing knot of uneasiness.

"C'mon, let's get out of here,'' Sam said. Without waiting for anyone to agree, he headed for the stairs and loped down them at a fast clip, as though he couldn't stand still another moment.

Lauren and Augustus exchanged a puzzled look and followed more slowly with the others. When they stepped outside, Sam was waiting, impatiently pacing back and forth at the top of the courthouse steps.

He swung around, and Lauren's heart contracted when she saw his grim expression. "We have to talk."

"All right," she replied calmly, but inside she was shaking. His expression and tone told her that she wasn't going to like what he had to say. She clasped her hands together to stop them from shaking and waited. The others stood by quietly, looking back and forth between them.

Sam paced away rubbing the back of his neck, then swung back. "Look, things have changed for you. It looks like Carlos is going to cash in. If that happens, you won't have to start your life over. Not in witness protection or with me."

Each word he spoke struck her like a fist. The awful knot just beneath Lauren's breastbone tightened painfully.

Her chin came up a notch. "What are you trying to tell me, Sam?"

"Look, I know I coerced you into this marriage. Now that the danger to you is gone, if you decide you want out I won't hold you to it. Hell, I'm not even sure the Navajo ceremony would be binding for a non-Native American. If you want to test it, you can probably have it set aside."

"*What?*" Augustus thundered. "What is this nonsense?"

"Stay out of this, Dad," Sam ordered, but his gaze never left Lauren's.

"I see," she said quietly. Her chest was so tight she could barely breathe.

Hurt coursed through her, but she fought against it. Not an hour ago this man had told her he loved her, had kissed her passionately and held her as though he'd never let her go. She refused to believe all that was a lie.

Knowing she was about to take the biggest chance of her life, she walked up to Sam and put her arms around his neck. He stiffened and watched her uncertainly.

Doing her best to ignore his less-than-encouraging response, she smiled up at him. "In that case, we'd better go back inside and have the judge marry us again. Because, like it or not, you're stuck with me. You see, I love you, Sam."

His dark eyes blazed. "Lauren...you've been through a lot. If you're not absolutely sure—"

"I'm sure. I've never been more sure of anything in my life."

He stared down at her, his fierce warrior's face taut with emotion. Then he threw his head back and laughed, a rich, full-body sound that did strange things to her insides. "Oh, I like it, babe," he said when he recovered his voice. "I like it a lot. But are you sure this is what you want? Really sure? Because if you stay, there's no turning back. This is for life."

She smiled slowly. "I'm counting on it."

He cupped her face with his hand and gazed at her tenderly. "I love you, Lauren," he murmured, and there on the courthouse steps, as his family looked on, hooting and cheering, he kissed her.

When at last their lips parted, Lauren's head was spinning and she sagged against him. She looked up and wrinkled her nose at him. "What about you? Are you sure about this? I'll probably make you a terrible wife, you know. Other than music, I have no skills, no training, no experience. I can barely cook enough to stave off hunger, as you've already discovered, and my other domestic skills are still rudimentary. The only jobs I could get would be in music, and those are scarce. I'll just be a millstone around your neck."

Sam laughed again and hugged her close. "Trust me, babe, you're no helpless powder puff. You just proved that by whipping Todd's sorry ass. You also kept your head when you witnessed a murder. You survived a plane crash and a trek through the wilderness in the dead of winter, took charge when I got shot and saved my life. Not exactly the acts of a helpless female. You're a strong, competent woman, sweetheart, and I haven't a doubt in the world that you can do whatever you set your mind to."

He ran his hands over her back and hips, and a slow, sensual smile curved his lips. "Believe me, babe, being married to you won't be a hardship.

"Although, before you make up your mind, I should warn you. I intend to quit the Bureau and go home to the ranch. So if you have any objections..."

"Why on earth would I object? Oh, Sam, I think that's wonderful."

The relief she saw in his eyes told her how much her answer had meant to him, and her heart contracted with love.

Sam bent and planted a hard kiss on her mouth. When he straightened, he kept one arm hooked around her waist and turned back toward the courthouse doors. Smiling, he looked deep into her eyes. "C'mon, sweetheart, let's go find that judge."

New York Times **Bestselling Author**

HEATHER GRAHAM

Moira Kelly returns home to Boston to the family pub
and discovers that it is at the center of a political
conspiracy. Torn between two men, her trust for
them pushed to the brink, she becomes a pawn
in a game with deadly consequences.

NIGHT OF THE BLACKBIRD

Available October 2001 wherever paperbacks are sold!

New York Times Bestselling Author

DEBBIE MACOMBER

It's a season of change for the small prairie town of Buffalo Valley, North Dakota. When plans are made to bring in a retail conglomerate, the townsfolk are concerned that the small local businesses, along with the town itself, will be lost forever.

It's a season of change for a man named Vaughn Kyle, who discovers he's at an impasse. Just out of the army, he's looking for a place to live, a *life* to live. As Christmas draws near, he decides to visit his family in Grand Forks, North Dakota—while he waits for his reluctant fiancée to make up her mind.

Vaughn decides to visit Buffalo Valley, and as he learns more about the town and the people who live there, he begins to question his feelings about the woman he *thought* he loved. He knows now that he wants to stay in Buffalo Valley and fight for its way of life, a life that's all about friends and family— not just at Christmas, but every day of the year.

Will the season bring peace and joy—to Vaughn and to the town?

Buffalo Valley

Available October 2001 wherever hardcovers are sold!

GINNA GRAY

66603   THE PRODIGAL
                DAUGHTER   ___ $5.99 U.S. ___ $6.99 CAN.

(limited quantities available)

TOTAL AMOUNT $_____
POSTAGE & HANDLING $_____
($1.00 for 1 book, 50¢ for each additional)
APPLICABLE TAXES* $_____
TOTAL PAYABLE $_____
(check or money order—please do not send cash)

To order, complete this form and send it, along with a check or
money order for the total above, payable to MIRA Books®, to:
In the U.S.: 3010 Walden Avenue, P.O. Box 9077, Buffalo,
NY 14269-9077; **In Canada**: P.O. Box 636, Fort Erie, Ontario,
L2A 5X3.

Name:_____
Address:_____ City:_____
State/Prov.:_____ Zip/Postal Code:_____
Account Number (if applicable):_____
075 CSAS

*New York residents remit applicable sales taxes.
  Canadian residents remit applicable GST and provincial taxes.

MIRA®